BETWEEN A ROCK AND A DARK PLACE

Between a Rock and a Dark Place

SUZANNE SCHIFFMAN

© 2018 Suzanne Schiffman

ISBN (softcover) 978-1-7320189-3-8
ISBN (EPUB) 978-1-7320189-4-5
ISBN (MOBI) 978-1-7320189-5-2

Printed in the United States

Design: Magdalene Carson / New Leaf Publication Design

This book is a work of fiction. Names, characters, places, businesses and events are products of the author's imagination. Certain events in the book may be very loosely based on actual events in the past. For the purposes of the story, these events have been condensed, modified and portrayed through the author's imagination or used fictitiously. Names, locales, businesses and other identifying details have been changed to protect the privacy of individuals.

First Edition

Typeset in 10.5/14 Sabon.

BETWEEN A ROCK AND A DARK PLACE

CHAPTER ONE

AT FIRST, SHERIFF STRYKER thought it was a bear roadside. It was well after 2 a.m. and he'd just finished defusing a domestic dispute at the Plunketts, the second one this fall. Hester hadn't wanted to press charges even after her desperate call to the department that Otis was brandishing his granddaddy's Remington, yelling that she was unfit to be his wife. He had warned Otis: One more call like this and he would have to arrest him. Otis had gotten all sheepish, hung his head and mumbled that he didn't know what got into his head sometimes.

"She just frustrates me sometimes, Spike. I mean I want a good meal in front of me, a cleaned up house, maybe a little poke now and then. Is that too much?" Otis was red in the face, watery-eyed, and Spike knew he'd been drinking. He was this close to taking him in, but he knew Otis was basically a good man, hardworking. Work was scarce for the semi-skilled, uneducated folks who lived up in the hollows. Otis was a part-timer with the Highway Department, cut back from full-time last spring, and made ends meet by picking up the odd paving job, hoping for snow removal work in the coming winter. Hester took care of their two young grandchildren while their daughter, Sissy, worked at Belks', thirty miles away.

Some of these folks have it pretty rough, he thought. Their roots were in the Welsh and Irish clans that had come to work the mines in the 1800s, stayed, turned to farming (some) or the trades, and intermarried (many). They were a stubborn, fiercely proud lot, loyal to kin and friends, quick to temper and suspicious of perceived outsiders. Their insular pockets in the county were the most run-down; not poor exactly, just untidy. Sheriff Stryker had shaken his head at the vehicles and parts of vehicles strewn across the Plunketts' front yard as his patrol car headlights illuminated the scene when he finally turned into their place after the long ride up the gravel road to their ridge-top house. He could have ticketed Otis for that too, but decided it wasn't worth the ordeal of having Otis vent his anger at him for all eternity. His sort never forgets a thing, especially an affront.

"Otis, look, get to bed, it's late. Tomorrow you and Hester have a nice talk over coffee. Everything will look better in the morning." He pushed himself up heavily from the lumpy gap in the sofa into which he had sunk, and gave Otis a pat on the shoulder, Hester a wink. "I'll check in with you later this week, but I don't want to have to come out here again in the middle of the night. You got that?" He flipped his notepad closed and stuck his pen into his breast pocket. He'd have to go back to the station to write this up instead of going straight home. With a tired puff of air, he picked up his hat and positioned it carefully on his head.

"Thank you, Spike," Hester whispered, her eyes filling with tears. "I'm sorry about this."

"Don't be sorry, just work this out, 'kay? I'm countin' on you two acting like adults here." He forced a final half-smile and made his way out the door to his car. He squeezed into the driver's seat — *Jesus, gotta lose some weight* — and nosed the car back down the mountain, out of the hollow and onto the main two-lane highway that cut through the whole county. He was tired and still had a couple of hours of patrol left though he longed for bed. He sped up as though that would make time pass faster then eased off the accelerator. Deputy Talon had hit a deer a couple of weeks ago around this time and it almost totaled the vehicle — $10,000 worth of damage and a month in the shop. Deer, raccoon, fox, and weird rodents scurried across the roads at all hours of the night. Someone's horse had even gotten out of its paddock one night and stood right in the middle of the highway. It had scared one of the weekenders coming out late on a Friday night near to death. That had been fun, trying to corner it in a neighboring field, tie it up and figure out where it belonged.

Sheriff Stryker listened to the soft crackle of police communications on his two-way radio. It was standard stuff tonight, speeders and DUI's, mostly from the state police band the next county over. He radioed his location to dispatch and noted the time. Two more hours until he could call it a night. He actually didn't mind being out in the wee hours. He'd minded when he'd been a small-town cop, but out here in the countryside where crimes, really, were few and far between, he often relished cruising the empty roads alone, late. Now, in the early fall, leaves scuttled across the highway as periodic gusts swirled through the wayside thickets of goldenrod, thistle, and black-eyed Susans. The sound of the leaves blowing across the asphalt made the sheriff think of that Bruce Springsteen song, — *what was it?* — "Lonely Valentine" or something, where the guy's out late, alone and driving, missing his girl. He sighed, wishing he was younger, fifty pounds lighter, had more hair. He and Pearl were happy together, but he had to admit desire was pretty much a thing of the past. Pearl was a good woman, he couldn't complain; she'd been a real knock-out once. But first her back went, then her shoulder blade hurt and she'd gotten a little doughy in the arms — "my cafeteria lady arms," she'd laugh. And then her neck had filled out just like her mother's. Well, nothing to be done about it, it's just the way things roll on. But still, it'd be nice for once to feel that old rush, that...

What the...? The sheriff slowed his patrol car and strained his eyes to see what his headlights illuminated at the base of a string of mailboxes affixed to wooden poles: a mound, bunched-up and blackish. Bear? A contractor's giant-size garbage bag that took wing out of the back of a pickup? Puzzled, he rolled to a stop several feet behind the strange heap and flipped on his flashers and side light beam. It looked like something was covered up or inside some kind of dark canvas.

If this is a bear, why would someone cover it up? Illegally hunted maybe, or hit and killed, an act of empathy? It wasn't big enough to be fully grown. Killing a bear cub wouldn't be something you'd want everyone to know you'd done.

Spike checked his rearview, but the ribbon of road behind him disappeared in complete obscurity, threading back into the darkness of the mountains and its hollows. No one on the road at this hour. He hesitated, thinking he might call for backup. If it was just a pile of construction garbage, though, he'd look silly, wouldn't he? If it was a bear, it was more than likely dead so there wouldn't be any use getting a deputy over here at this time of night. Once he got back to the station to write up his visit to the Plunketts, he'd leave a note for

Ronnie Swiggert, one of the deputies pulling the early morning shift today, in case he missed him. He'd ask him to call MDOT right away and they'd pick it up, hopefully before the school buses came by.

He checked his gun but left it in its holster, felt for the flashlight attached to his waistband and left the patrol car running.

"God, I hate to see this," he muttered as he pushed open his door and slid his legs around to get out. It took two heave-hos, but he stood and clicked the door shut quietly. After all, it *might* not be dead yet. If it was a bear.

Poor guy could have been heading up the right-of-way to Ed Marconi's farm to attack his hives and gotten hit or killed somehow. Marconi'd been complaining all summer that the bears were getting into his honey and ruining his hives. Since the feds had put a stop to bear poaching in the county and the adjoining park over the past few years, the population had increased dramatically pushing them down from the mountains in search of food. Now, in the fall, they were boosting their intake for winter and getting into peoples' vegetable patches and garbage cans.

Spike shook his head. He'd never been a hunter, believed in live and let live. He knew bears could cause lots of trouble; his neighbor's cherry orchard had been devastated this year by bears. But part of him figured they were here first so what right had he to disparage the animal? 'Coons did a lot more damage anyway, digging up Pearl's bulbs, and rabbits managed to get into his garden and eat his lettuce until he spent a small fortune on fencing.

He clicked on the flashlight and took a few steps towards the dark shape a few yards away, the shoulder gravel crunching beneath his boots. He began to make out the contours of what looked like a sleeping bag. It was not a canvas or tarp but a forest-green sleeping bag, laid out there with something exposed at the top and on one side. Spike edged closer as quietly as he was able. *That definitely don't look like fur*, he thought as he moved a little closer. *Holy shit!* Spike sucked in his breath in surprise and stopped short, his pulse quickening. His eyes were now accustomed to the dark and the contrast with the brightness of the flashlight and spotlight. Protruding from a rip or tear in side of the bag was a human foot, shod in a bright yellow flip-flop. At the far end, the top of a human head was exposed. There was no sign of movement and Spike feared whoever was inside was probably not alive.

Spike's heart was pounding as he backed away, retracing his steps, setting the flashlight on the hood of the patrol car all while not taking his eyes off the dark mass. The headlights were trained on the area and his flashers were on, but Spike felt swallowed up in the dark, black all around him, black like the inside of a burnt skillet, despite the clear, starry night and waxing moon.

He pushed his bulk headlong into his patrol car and grabbed at the dashboard for the radio. The new guy, Frank, was on dispatch duty at the station, pulling the all-night shift. *Gotta get him to get me an all-hands-on-deck over here right away, get backup rounded up and block the highway.* Spike had seen dead bodies before in the line of duty, three to be exact, but he'd never been first on the scene. Two had been at Bristow National Bank in a botched robbery. The teller and robber were shot dead, the latter by the SWAT team. The other had been a hit-and-run, a Hispanic man crossing a dark highway at 3 a.m., later found to have been intoxicated.

Wedging himself into the driver's seat, he brought the radio to his lips, not letting the dark mound out of his sight.

"Hey, Frank, come in, it's Sheriff Stryker, over on Highway 622 at Marconi's right-of-way. Got a suspicious package, roadside, do you read?" Spike waited. Nothing but white noise. *Stupid kid, what the fuck's he doing? He's supposed to be right near the dispatch desk.* "Frank, calling for backup, possible 10-54..." The radio scratched to life.

"Yeah, I read you, Spike. Go ahead."

"I need all hands on deck, whoever's scheduled for duty, Highway 622 at Marconi right-of-way, suspicious package, a possible 10-54. Frank, get me Detective Judd Koons and Chief Deputy Bodie Talon. Radio this in for two units, backup, need to block off this area both ways. Who ya got there and who's due in?"

"I'll get a hold of Cody and Mabel, due in for the early shift; 'course you know Buck's got his kids this week, his ex-wife's got night duty over at the hospital and..."

"Yeah, yeah, who else can get here?"

"I think that's it; Deputy Swiggert called in sick a little while ago, said thinks he's coming down with the flu or something. Department's kinda thin tonight."

"Okay, okay, get Detective Koons first 'cause he's gotta drive all the way out here from Chester. And I need any of his forensic investigators he can get a hold of."

"Gotcha, I'm on it."

Spike thought maybe he should have called in on the cell, as whoever might be involved with this could have a scanner and listen in, but he was more comfortable with radioing; it seemed more efficient, urgent. "Okay, get 'em all up here and ASAP!" Spike sat back in his seat and unwrapped a stick of gum from his shirt pocket. Popping it in his mouth and savoring the sweet mintiness, he listened to Frank's dispatch and the deputies' responses. Then he eased himself out of the patrol car with his hand on his holster and reached for the flashlight on the hood. There'd been no change, just a few wayward leaves blowing lightly across the bag and disappearing into the dark grasses behind the mailboxes.

He edged around to his patrol car's trunk. Popping it open, he pulled surgical gloves from a box inside and unclipped a small camera from his belt. He'd need some good shots of the entire area, but first he thought he might as well feel for a pulse, just in case. Training his light on the area of the bag right up against the mailboxes, he noted a shock of light-colored hair sticking out. He shone the flashlight across the mound, from one end to the other. *How'd this get here?* He set the flashlight down on the gravel and pulled on the surgical gloves thinking the camera's flash was probably good enough, but he wanted to keep some extra light on the situation.

This was a first. Whatever happened, this bag, with someone in it, had been dumped here, no question. He felt bristling on the back of his neck tickle under his shirt collar, and, despite the cool evening, perspiration broke out under his arms and down his forehead.

"Get a grip on yourself," he hissed through clenched teeth. First things first. He leaned cautiously over the bag and without touching it or the zipper placed his thumb against the exposed foot to feel the ankle for a pulse. Nothing, as he feared. It was stone cold. Circling to where the head protruded, he carefully placed two fingers to the carotid artery at the neck without touching the bag. Again, no sign of a pulse. He detected the odor of blood as he bent forward to get a closer look. Plenty of blood caked what he could see of the head, mostly on the back.

He shot pictures of the gravel shoulder all around the area and the road from four directions, then cautiously moved around the site to take photos of the mysterious mound inside the sleeping bag from all angles keeping a good distance so as not to compromise any evidence. He unspooled his crime scene tape, tied it to the post holding a string of mailboxes, unfurled it all the way to the closest roadside scrub tree he could find and, for lack of anything else, looped it around his passenger side mirror.

Finally, he re-clipped the camera to his belt, retrieved the flashlight and stood hesitantly beside the tape. He checked his watch: 2:28 a.m. Damn, all this had happened inside of twenty minutes.

He'd have to resist the temptation to touch anything further. For the moment, he walked a wide berth around the body, nosing the flashlight here and there to see if there was a weapon, blood, tire marks, anything that he'd be able to point out to the detectives when they got here. He'd have to wait for Koons before the sleeping bag with the body could be opened and it could start to tell its story. He shifted the flashlight to his left hand and stooped at the knees, acutely aware of the painful cracking, to get a closer view of the ground around the sleeping bag. Nothing that he could see.

Jeez, where's my units? Any minute, a car'll come by, gotta get this area cordoned off. Spike rolled his shoulders to relax and took a deep breath. Who'd be lying here inside a sleeping bag presumably brought here and left somehow? The deceased didn't walk here like this, collapse then tuck himself into this thing. What happened? This kind of thing doesn't happen in our quiet little rural county. Spike thought of the Plunketts, whose minor domestic altercation seemed like a situation comedy next to this. Mostly boredom was the problem around here, leading to drunk driving or drugs, but murder? Not your everyday event out here, that's for sure.

Just then, three patrol cars with lights flashing and sirens off, careened from all directions, screeching to a halt behind and in front of Sheriff Stryker's vehicle.

"'Bout time." Spike pushed himself up from a squatting position with difficulty and brushed the gravel from his hand. "I don't much take to being out here all alone with a body. Cody, Mabel, get the highway blocked at both ends where folks can turn around. Lucky no one's come along yet this time of night, good for us."

"Whatcha got going here, Spike?" Deputy Talon asked, striding over from his patrol car with a new addition to the force, Rudy Jenks.

"Thinkin' this must be a dump, Bodie, but whoever did this wanted to make sure this body was found pretty damn quick. Let's get more pictures. Hey, Rudy, can you get the medical examiner over in Castle Hill on your cell?" Spike felt comfortable now, in charge, with his men here. Spike's cell beeped.

"Detective? Great, how long 'til you're here? Okay, scene is secure, we're waitin' on you. You got Pete with you? Good, good." Spike clicked off and looked at Deputy Talon. "He'll be here in five."

"Okay," Deputy Talon responded, moving his flashlight along the bag. "Looking at the foot, seems clean, taken care of, flip-flop thong still in between toes. Appears to be a male foot."

"Yeah, I assumed so, too. I'm waiting on Koons to open these mail boxes, see if there's anything in there might be connected. At least get all the names down. We gotta walk the entire stretch along here, see what evidence his friends may have left behind. Rudy, is that the medical examiner's office on the phone?"

Rudy nodded and gave a thumbs up.

"Tell 'em they gotta get a transport out here for a body. And we're gonna need an autopsy done on a possible homicide victim." Spike looked off to where the patrol cars, lights flashing, blocked the road at either end about half a football field away. He got a warm feeling of brotherly love for his men (and Mabel too, of course) as they went about the business of securing whatever had happened here. Everyone on the force worked in tandem, one of the best teams in the region.

Deputies Mabel Crone and Cody Crawford were already approaching from opposite directions, scanning the road and shoulders with their flashlights. Mabel took a picture of a skid mark about thirty yards from the body and traced the trajectory to see if there were tire marks on the shoulder. "Tough to tell if this is new or not," she indicated to Spike, "but it's the best I could get. Pretty sure Detective Koons can better analyze this for what it's worth."

Detective Koons pulled up a few minutes later in his unmarked SUV, with Pete Karnes, the forensic expert from up Chester way. Both men quickly emerged from the vehicle, acknowledged Spike and his deputies and drew their crime scene kits from the back of the suv.

"Well, good Lord, Spike," Detective Koons drawled, "this sure was a surprise phone call." He shook his head. "Our peaceful, little hamlet getting what looks like a body dump. We've got a bit of work ahead of us. What did ya see, exactly? And when?"

Spike described his evening's chain of events and when he'd come across the mysterious heap. "Checked the time when I pulled over, 2:07 a.m."

Koon's checked his watch, 3:19 a.m. "Didn't touch anything, did you?" Koons and Carnes both snapped on surgical gloves.

"Nope, of course not, Judd. Just felt for a pulse on the exposed ankle and at the neck, gloved. We've been looking for tire marks, any type of possible weapon and secured the area but haven't touched a thing. There's no clear disturbance of gravel around the bag, appears to have somehow been carried here from some vehicle or other and laid down like some kind of offering. I don't get it." Spike swept his flashlight around the area again to show no unusual lines or skid marks from the road to the resting place of the sleeping bag against the row of mailboxes. "And Bodie here walked up towards Marconi's just to see if there was anything unusual up that way."

"Good. Let's get started." Judd and Pete walked around as Spike and his deputies had done, examining the gravel and grass, snapping pictures. Finally, both knelt next to the body and Detective Koons carefully tugged at the zipper with his gloved hand to fully open the bag, but it snagged and wouldn't budge. He gave up, retrieved a boxcutter from his evidence box and proceeded to slit the bag open along the zippered side. He carefully folded it back and the body, released from its cocoon, was revealed at last. Pete took pictures.

"Jesus," Spike breathed. It was, as he'd already determined, a man. He was on his stomach wearing only gray sweat pants and one yellow flip-flop. Spike focused his flashlight on one side of his face. The neck seemed twisted unnaturally and a small puddle of blood stained the inside of the sleeping bag. Spike flinched in spite of himself. Deputy Talon squatted next to the body, aiming his flashlight onto the man's back and legs to assist.

"Hmm, looks like he's got one nasty wound on the back of his head." Judd closely inspected the wound caked with blood and the exposed side of the face then scanned along from neck to toe. "Appears to be from some blunt object, club or stick maybe. Someone took time to tuck him into the sleeping bag, though, you're right Spike. I see a few lacerations on his bare foot, no rips in his sweat pants. He's got some scrapes and bruising on his back, dirt particles on his skin and pants. Let's roll him."

"Bag seems in good shape, not that old," Pete noted. He took a picture. The upper body had bits of dried blood on the neck and shoulders in addition to the face. Spike peered intently at the face where a large, angry bruise covered the upper right cheekbone. The right eye, too, looked swollen, black and blue. His worst fear was that the victim would prove to be a local and he searched the features to see if he recognized him, his heart racing.

"Yep, looks like he took a blow to the right side of his face and something appears to have struck him from behind on the lower left of his skull," Judd continued, "and..." he turned the chin, "looks like someone tried to stop the blood flow from the head wound. See the smearing along the back of the neck? Pete, make a note for the medical examiner to determine which occurred first, the face or head wound."

"Medical examiner will see if there are indications he tried to defend himself, scrapes or abrasions on arms or hands. Hard to tell in this light," Pete suggested as he snapped numerous pictures, zeroing in on the head wound at the last.

"Is his neck broke too?" Spike asked. "His head's twisted in a funny way."

"Hmmm. Not thinking it is. He's suffered a bad wound to the base of his skull and whoever carried him here could have caused further bleeding, twisted it unnaturally maybe, but broke, I don't think so, Spike," Judd replied. Continuing his examination, Judd noted no wedding ring or watch. "Damage unique to the right side of face may indicate a left-handed assailant. Make a note of that too, Pete."

"Victim was healthy and fit, muscular, weighing approximately 165, clean shaven. Blood splatters on the back of the neck. In my humble opinion, a shirt he may have been wearing was removed and used to try and staunch the blood at the back of his head. See here, another line of dried blood smeared around the front of the neck." Detective Koons zeroed in on the neck with the flashlight. "The medical examiner would have to confirm this. Time of death is important, obviously." Pete leaned in closer with his own flashlight and nodded in agreement.

Pete photographed the entire body several times, especially the face, neck and head. "Got to have been attacked elsewhere, not here, then carefully toted here to our main road to be found ASAP."

"There'd have been evidence of some kinda struggle around here," Spike said. "And the gravel looks completely undisturbed recently."

"Agreed," Judd nodded absently. "We're gonna have to assume he was killed in a car and brought here or attacked somewhere and driven here. There must be some tire marks somewhere connected to this. Unusual situation, seems to me. Whoever did this to this man wanted his body to be found pretty quick, we agree. Whole thing is uncommon and kinda bold given this is our main road. Doesn't make sense — if you're gonna get rid of a body, why practically in plain sight of the whole county? Why'd they want him found so quick? Is it possible our killer or killers might be remorseful? Or maybe just plain stupid, but don't quote me. Wonder if it's a local or stranger to these parts. Pete?"

"I'll get some pictures of the road and any tire marks or footprints we may have missed around here," Pete said, "and some preliminary samples from the feet and fingernails." He searched his kit for sterile vials.

"We'll have to keep the area closed off until daylight, though. No sign of the other flip-flop, Spike?"

"Nope. This is gonna be one complicated investigation, with a dumped body, possible homicide, could have happened anywhere," Spike said. "Bodie, I need you and Rudy to keep the road cordoned off until Pete here is done examining the area. Go through the mail boxes, too; might be something useful to know. We'll have to talk to the folks who own them, see if they know anything. Maybe our killer's making a statement to someone who lives up this hollow."

"'Til first light is fine," Pete said, "then we'll probably have all we'll be able to get from the scene, if there's anything around here that can help us."

"Sure, Spike," Deputy Talon said. "Open the road at dawn?"

"Judd? That okay? It'll start to get busy by then and people are gonna get curious." Spike studied the deceased's face again.

"Yeah, we'll wrap it up here quick," Judd agreed. "By the way, do you recognize him at all, Spike? Any possibility he's from around here?" Bodie raised his eyebrows in anticipation.

"Can't say I do but that don't mean he's not a local. We gotta get an ID soon's possible. See if there's a missing persons report come in here or another jurisdiction. Jesus, this is one helluva puzzle."

Judd turned to his forensic expert. "Pete, tag the sleeping bag, transport should be here any minute. Spike, I'll get the medical examiner to call you soon as she's got something to report. In the meantime, you look tuckered out. See if you can get one of your deputies to help write up the report on this back at the station, then get a little sleep. This is gonna be a pretty intense investigation for your team."

Pete took a few more pictures and pocketed his notes. While he waited, Koons nudged his flashlight along the lining of the sleeping bag down into the innermost corner at the bottom. "Well, lookie here," he said. He focused the light on a thin leather wallet wedged in the bag's interior lining which had frayed or been cut. "Pete, let's get this photographed *in situ*." He then lifted it out while Pete took more pictures and opened it. "Our victim is a Daniel Perrault. Two credit cards and a driver's license, no cash. Huh, weird, this looks like a lock of hair tied with a small ribbon. Pete, make sure you get a good, clear shot of this."

"Whoa, did you say Daniel Perrault?" Spike widened his eyes and strained to read the license card Judd held up. "That name's familiar, lemme think."

"You think it's someone from here? Foreign sounding name. Couldn't be from here originally."

Spike snapped his fingers and peered again at the body. "I know who this is. He's the French guy who owned the restaurant over in Nickel, "Perigo" or something like that was the name as I recall, the one just closed end of August."

"Huh. Know who might want him dead?"

"All's I know is he had plenty of money 'cause he renovated that old apple packing plant and turned it into a restaurant, must've cost a fortune. Had that farm store in Nickel too. And those art studios on the art tour last year? He built them from scratch I heared. Had some messy problems with his chef. I think Deputy Swiggert went up there at least once, last Christmas as I recall. Can't imagine who'd want him dead, though."

"Hmmm. Well, have someone at the department get a list of people he was close to out here, contacts, written up," Judd stood. "We'll get the medical examiner to get us a timeline for the wound, time of death and how long he may have been out here. Wife?"

Spike nodded, "I think so, least that's what I seem to remember."

"That'll be tough."

"Yeah. I'll have to call in and find out where his residence might be. For some reason, Madison Ridge comes to mind. Mabel, I'll radio you and Cody soon's I get that info, and you two get on up to the house at first light and see what's going on. If he has a wife and she's there, we got to find out what she knows or doesn't know, first and foremost. Bodie, you get up there and join them soon's you can. And, let's be clear — before we know anything further, we're gonna classify this as a possible, and I mean *possible,* homicide." Mabel signaled her understanding and headed for her patrol car after giving Spike a small salute. Cody peeled off to his own patrol car.

"At least we can confirm identity," Spike said. "But how, and why and in this manner? One for the textbooks, if you ask me."

Spike undid the yellow police tape from his patrol car mirror and turned it over to Deputy Talon to stake. "Bodie, we gotta get the whole department briefed ASAP, soon's we can get everyone in, so an investigation can get underway. For now, once our detectives here are done, have Deputy Jenks get the area back to normal. Did you check and get the names off the mailboxes?"

"Yep, Rudy here and I got the info and I'll get him on it to see what those folks might know about this first thing. Have Mabel and Cody radio in what they find up at the deceased's house and I'll get up there quick's I can. Back by Madison Ridge, you say?"

"Yeah," Spike said, "I think I remember it being up that way. Lord, I'm not liking this turn of events one bit."

The transportation van contracted by the medical examiner's office arrived and Daniel Perrault was placed in a body bag. Sheriff Stryker told the driver he would get one of his deputies over to the morgue later in the morning to be present at the autopsy.

Spike cruised slowly back to headquarters alone. It was nearly 5 a.m. *This is big*, he told himself. *This is a huge story for our little county. He was French as I recall, maybe a French citizen, owned a fancy restaurant and more. It'll be all over the papers around here and maybe beyond. I'm not turnin' this investigation over to anybody. I'm handlin' this as my case; it's in my jurisdiction and I'm gonna see it through, wherever it leads.* He pulled into his space and cracked the patrol car door open. He hesitated before stepping out and with the dome light on, checking that nobody was around, he looked at himself in the rearview mirror.

He removed his hat and looked at the star affixed to it with his name and the county embossed on it: Sheriff Spencer Stryker, Wayne County. He'd never liked "Spencer" but maybe the gravity of the case warranted using his given name instead of Spike. He'd think about it. The mirror showed his thinning hair and he ran his fingers across his scalp. *My picture will be out there, people'll know who I am all over the place. I'm gonna have to lose some weight, get in shape. Wait'll I tell Pearl about this!*

He popped a fresh stick of gum in his mouth. *Who kills a guy out here like that? Then places him roadside in the middle of the night? And smack dab in the middle of the county so it wouldn't be no secret. With his wallet intact, no less. It don't make any sense. Someone — but who? — really wanted this guy dead. And they wanted him found and identified quickly, why?*

Inside the station, he barked at Frank the dispatcher to come to his office. "We gotta get everyone on board and brought up to speed on this. I don't care what they got goin' on! Send out word everyone meets here with me and Chief Deputy Talon nine a.m. sharp!"

"Yes, sir. I'll get on it. Don't know if I can get Buck or Ronnie in this morning, though."

"Okay. I'm countin' on this department pulling together with this, but if we're short two men, so be it." Spike exhaled noisily, loosened his tie then tossed his hat on his desk. "All right, Frank," he growled. "Get yourself a cup of coffee and help me get this report wrote."

CHAPTER TWO

Three and a half years earlier

DANIEL PERRAULT AND his new bride, Beth, raced down Route 39 in their hunter green Aston Martin, a wedding gift from Daniel's wealthy parents. Beth was worried about Daniel's burgeoning homesickness for his beloved Périgord region of France, more intense now in the weeks since they had returned from their honeymoon there. She had loved Daniel from the first time he'd said her name at a conference they'd both attended in Geneva. "Bet," he'd said with a slight lisp, unable to manage the combination of "th." "Do you have plans for lunch?"

Their romance spanned France and the U.S. for a year until Beth lost her job and spent all her time looking for work, finally landing a good but lower-paying job with the state energy department. Transatlantic travel days over, she pressed Daniel to join her in the States. He'd sold his interest in Zephyre, a French wind turbine company he'd help create with his father and a tech-savvy pal, and was now flush with money.

"What prevents you," she asked every time they spoke, "from starting a similar company in the U.S.? I could help. I have contacts."

Beth disliked Daniel's seemingly idle lifestyle far from her and feared their love affair would peter out if she didn't pester him. No invitation to join him in Périgord seemed forthcoming and the thought of losing him gnawed at her constantly. She challenged him to duplicate his success stateside either with or without his father's help.

"This country is ripe for more wind energy projects. You'd be a smash hit with investors here. They'd stumble over each other to get in on the ground floor with a tried-and-true clean energy expert."

Daniel wavered. On the one hand, he liked how his affair with a beautiful American woman, a couple of years his senior with a successful career to boot, made him look exotic to his circle of friends. He often boasted how desperately Beth loved him, about the pressure he was under to join her in America and maybe even marry her.

"I feel like she'll do something crazy if I don't go, so go I must," he would say stoically, and then laugh as though he'd made a joke.

On the other hand, the money from the business made for a comfortable lifestyle. He spent freely on his friends and traveled all over Europe when he wasn't visiting Beth. Women were easily seduced by his engaging manner and comely looks and he could rarely resist them, if they were beautiful. But where were the challenges for him in France going forward? The playboy lifestyle was losing its glitter. Maybe Beth was right that the American energy sector was primed for a European approach to wind. Making a splash in America was just the ticket in a way. If he could launch another successful business *there*, imagine how impressed his friends, his father, would be. He had to admit, the idea enticed him.

Ultimately, he backed himself into a corner as everyone, including his parents, assumed after all his blustering that he wanted to pull up stakes, start a fresh life with Beth and launch a new company on his own. Neither of his parents liked to see him fritter away his days, and money.

"What are you waiting for, Daniel?" his mother asked almost daily. "You can't keep running back and forth across the ocean to see Beth or stay out all hours with your friends. She's a nice girl, you love her, don't you? I see us visiting, you'll be back often. You've got an apartment here, after all. Your father likes her too and wants you to settle down."

He surrendered albeit with more than a little hesitancy and joined Beth in her three-story townhouse on a busy street in a "transitional" part of the city. Almost immediately he regretted what he'd done, initiating a sour frame of mind he couldn't shake off. Time dragged on and months of effort to engage investors in the Zephyre concept, using more than a little of his own money, failed.

"The big boys are already in," he complained. "They've bought up most of the smaller companies. I don't see any room for another start-up right now."

He wouldn't admit complete defeat but griped that he was stuck with not much to do other than follow his stocks.

Beth fretted and sympathized but was more concerned about the months ticking by without a commitment from him to *her*. After all, they still had plenty of money and here she was closing in on the other side of her mid-thirties.

"Daniel, what are your plans, really? You were never pessimistic before. If you're unhappy here, we can change things around. You know I'd give up my job and follow you back to France, if that's what you want. Just tell me how to make us work. Please." Beth's eyes filled with tears and Daniel turned away in embarrassment. He liked Beth strong and supportive, as she'd always been, and found the sniveling over commitment and, by implication, marriage vexing and unbecoming.

"Returning to France is unthinkable right now, Beth. I have to do *something* here, leave a mark somewhere." Daniel winced at the thought of his father making sport of his fruitless endeavor, probably insinuating he couldn't make a go of things on his own without papa's backing. No, admitting the whole thing was a mistake would be too difficult for his pride to absorb and he resolved to find another way to make an impact.

But the winter weeks crawled along with little to show for Daniel's somewhat impractical ventures. In his frustration, he began to complain about the insularity of his and Beth's daily life.

"All we talk about is work and whether we should commit to each other. It's really quite *pénible,* chérie."

"I thought you came here because you loved me, and we had a future. That's usually how relationships evolve. I really don't know what you want anymore." Beth began to wonder if Daniel had come for her or to prove something to his father. In her worst moods, she accused him of using her.

Yet, Daniel really did care for Beth; he'd never met a woman quite like her, glamorous and sexy as well as his intellectual equal. Perhaps he should bite the bullet, make some serious decisions, marry her. In any case, he refused to return to France without anything short of indisputable success in the U.S. Even if he had to obtain some kind of notoriety to get it.

He proposed.

Though slight of build and not much taller than Beth, Daniel had a handsome, patrician face resembling his flamboyant father who had made a fortune in timber in Périgord. His lips were full, his nose a bit crooked as though it had once been broken, and he had intense, cobalt-blue eyes. His neatly parted, white- blonde hair, slicked back with gel, gave him a Nordic look. Beth was the polar opposite: sturdy, a tad overweight with a flawless olive complexion and a lush head of auburn hair that made heads turn wherever she went.

They married in May and honeymooned, of course, in Périgord.

Seeking to extend that nuptial bliss, Beth booked a country inn online an hour or so from the city for a summer weekend hoping to ease Daniel's painful nostalgia for home. As they hummed down the highway, she could see this respite from their usual city weekends spent running errands and socializing with, in Daniel's opinion, dull government bureaucrats, was already doing wonders for Daniel's melancholic mood.

With the top down on a sun-kissed June morning and The Police on the radio, they laughed and sang, feeling happy, carefree and energized. The countryside was lovely, smelling deliciously of honeysuckle and fresh-cut grass. There was nothing to see but rolling hills and farms with fields of hay blowing gently like ocean waves in the breeze, small clusters of grazing cows and, in the distance, the azure blue of the mountains. They had the strip of highway all to themselves, and Daniel pressed the accelerator with a Gallic whoop as Beth protested in mock alarm and tied a billowing scarf around her wildly blowing hair.

The flashing blue lights behind them were an unwelcome surprise. Daniel swore and pulled over.

"Leave it to the *flics* to ruin a good time," he groused.

"Be on your best behavior, Daniel. Your Aston Martin says 'city people' all over it. We don't want to start off on the wrong foot here." If they liked the area, Beth wanted to come back as often as they could, maybe buy something if they could figure things out. Daniel would be so much happier. The rural region where he'd grown up in near the Dordogne River with its thousands of kilometers of woods and valleys to explore was in his blood, of course. From what Beth had read, this little county was similar in topography even if it lacked medieval castles, Lascaux cave paintings and truffles!

Sherriff Stryker lumbered up to Daniel's side of the car and peered at him through aviator glasses.

"You in a hurry, mister? I clocked you doing eighty and this is a fifty-five-mile zone."

"Sorry, officer. I think I got carried away with the beauty of your county here…"

"Sure you did," the sheriff interrupted. "License and registration, please." He took the cards and walked around to the rear of the Austin, looking it over, noting the Obama/Biden bumper sticker and that stupid "COEXIST" sticker he hated made out of religious symbols. He went back to his cruiser and wrote up a warning. *She's too pretty to ruin her day though I'd probably not lose much sleep if I slapped him with a $75 speeding ticket. Guy's clearly loaded with a car like that.*

"Here's a warning to slow down. If you like it here, you'll want to take your time to see it."

Daniel took the paper and thanked the officer.

"Nice of him not to give me a ticket but a bit pompous, don't you think?" Daniel steered back onto the highway and drove at a granny pace the rest of the way.

"Oh, let's forget about it. Look, here's our turn. The inn should be only a couple more miles up this way."

They pulled into Scarcity, population 163, at the confluence of the Catawba and Spendthrift rivers, two narrow but crystal-clear rivers, the former named after a little-known Indian tribe while the latter's origin was unclear, according to the guidebook. Ample spring rains had swelled the streams and rivers flowing down from the mountains and the water bubbled over stones and rocks like the curls in a woman's hair. The sound of rushing water was mesmerizing, and Daniel slowed further to take in the scenery.

"What a find, Beth. I can't believe this little gem is so close to the city. We really need to get out and explore."

Beth was happy Daniel seemed enthusiastic. "It's a shame we've never been out this way, always heading for the shore or Europe when this was at our doorstep. The town was established in 1769," she read from the guidebook, "and is famous for a skirmish between the French, an offshoot tribe of the Shawnee and the British during the French and Indian wars."

"Aha — the French knew a good spot to defend when they saw it!"

"Of course, you know they lost, darling. It says George Washington marched right through here on the way to his first battle in the Ohio Valley, on the British side at that point."

"Well, he soon learned who his friends were, didn't he?" Daniel sniffed. "Who saved these young revolutionaries anyway? Lafayette to the rescue!"

"I know, sweetie." Beth continued to leaf through the guidebook. "Ooh, it says four miles from here during a skirmish in 1755, 54 French troops were surprised and massacred on a ridge where they were camped..."

"Yes, yes, history isn't on our side before the Revolutionary War, so what? Now we rule the world anyway with our *produits de luxe* and *savoir faire*. Everyone loves French cooking and design, the French, *quoi*! You of all people know that. Enough of history, ha, ha! — that's all in the past so to speak."

Daniel slowed as they pulled into the small parking area of the inn, built in 1788. Their room turned out to be charming and beautifully furnished with a view across open meadows to the majestic, rolling mountains beyond.

Standing at the open window surveying the landscape, Daniel sighed in contentment. "It isn't Périgord, but I will say it is very close in its beauty." Beth paraded happily around the room organizing their things, elated her idea for a getaway and the inn she had chosen made Daniel so happy. When he was happy, Beth felt the tightness in her chest vanish, a tightness, she realized, that gripped her almost daily as Daniel complained about the city, the townhouse, his lack of purpose, the country, Americans in general. She often felt she could be on the brink of losing him, that Périgord would reclaim him.

When he stretched out on the bed clasping his hands behind his head, she lay beside him and snuggled against his ear.

"It's so good to see you like this, Daniel. The countryside does you good, I think."

"Yes, it's nice to see something other than buildings and other people. I miss the greenery, I must admit."

He turned towards her, grasping her hips, pulling her closer and nuzzled her jaw line with his lips.

"I'm feeling something here, about this place. It's so close to the city, maybe we could look into buying a little house to use on the weekends. Tomorrow, let's explore! See what's really out here, what do you think?'

"I think that would be wonderful, Daniel. Let's do it before anything changes our minds." Beth melted under his soft kisses and sat up to kneel beside him. She pulled off one then the other of his shoes, undid his belt and slowly undid his shirt buttons one by one.

"Now? Really? I mean, what are the acoustics here?" Daniel protested.

"You mean soundproofing, I think," Beth laughed.

"Whatever."

"It's an inn, for Christ's sake, Daniel. They'd think you were weird if you didn't, you know, have fun."

Beth loved Daniel, every part of him. For all his annoying, daily complaints and personal flaws, he was hugely seductive. She'd been under his spell since their first encounter and would do nearly anything to help him find satisfaction in their new life, as challenging as that could sometimes be.

She stood and disrobed letting her summer shift shimmy down her legs into a feathery heap as though swept off by a puff of air while Daniel pretended to close his eyes. For his part, Beth's luscious curves and thick dark hair never failed to bewitch him even as, deep down, he held a part of himself back from her. He never thought he would actually marry Beth. He often wrestled with himself as to why he took that step; they could have remained lovers and he could have simply traveled to see her. He could easily have retreated from his, admittedly, arrogant pronouncements about conquering both Beth and the U.S. and used his charm to pretend that it was all a ruse to see his friends' and family's reactions. He was good at playing two sides of the same coin. He rationalized that he didn't fall into this situation by accident; he always knew what he was going to do, even if it was his oldest friend expressing envy that pushed his decision in the end.

"Oh, so now you leave us, go where we're all dying to go, marrying who we'd all like to marry," his friend Gilles had lamented. "To L'Amérique! *Toi, t'es un conquistador!*"

Since their return from the wedding celebration and a month in

Périgord, the shock of what he'd done began to soak in even more. Now instead of marriage, Beth talked about how they needed to start a family. Daniel felt like he was looking down a black hole of wife, baby, some boring work, home, work, home, work. He needed something to provide the zest he felt in his home town among his old friends and colleagues. He missed the thrill of uncertainty, of the unknown, the smoldering feline glance from the corner of a smoky bar. Sex with Beth was very good, no doubt about that, but he'd always had exciting sex with women. There wasn't anything otherworldly about that. He was a sensual, attentive lover. He needed more, though, much more.

Beth's clean, silky body slid over his and he drank in her scents and feasted on her creamy breasts, enjoying how his tongue, circling her nipples, hardened the tips that he then bit gently with his lips. She groaned and pushed his pants down, guiding him in while she sat up and began rhythmically moving in circles until Daniel pulled her under him. She was on the pill as Daniel insisted he didn't want children yet, so they always made love with abandon.

Something about the charming room with the window open to the soft lowing of cattle in the distance energized their love-making to a level they hadn't felt since their honeymoon. When Daniel finally rolled aside he exhaled deeply in contentment.

"This place does something to me, Beth. The scenery, the history — as I see it of course," he added with a grin. "Even the smells bring back something of my childhood somehow. It's very strange, — I feel like I'm connected here, and I haven't even been out the door."

"We must explore, but tomorrow. Tonight, dinner's down the road at a well-known place, — it's in the guidebook anyway. French-inspired of course! Hope it'll be good." Beth kissed Daniel one more time on the side of his nose and rose to dress.

"Can I see the guidebook, chérie?" Daniel skimmed the history and flipped past the one page on Scarcity looking for anything else in town, but the inn where they were staying, and the restaurant they were going to, were the only things listed. There wasn't much else in the county either — one casual dining establishment at the county line and a general store in Nickel, Farrin's, that had a small eating area inside. Most of the attractions listed were vineyards, orchards and farms.

"There's not much going on here, is there?" he mused. "Hard to believe so close to the city. Where is the life, the cafés, street life? If this were France so close to a big city, this place, charming as it is, would be sprinkled with dozens of little businesses, don't you think?"

"I guess there's a reason for the name 'Scarcity' but I agree it's surprising there're so few eating places. Lots of hungry people are scattered around this county, plus city people like us would come out more often for a weekend if there were more attractions."

Their young waiter at dinner confirmed the backwater nature of the county.

"Oh, yeah, it's very quiet out here and that's the way folks like it, I guess. There's a bunch of old-timers who keep to themselves, you know, the people back in the hollows, farmers, 'been heres,' they like to call themselves. Then the big landowners who've moved out here, the 'come heres.' We have a few artist types, originals or descendants of a big hippie commune that used to be out here somewhere — wild times, those years, I hear." The waiter grinned and blushed. "Then there're a few entrepreneurial sorts starting shops or something. And, of course, the weekenders."

"And your chef? Where does he fit in?"

"Oh, he grew up here, went somewhere for cooking school and came back to start this place. Locals are proud of his success with the restaurant but, by and large, they take poorly to big changes out here. Get a little frisky when they think newcomers are trying to take things over and make us into something we don't want to be."

"How did you end up here? A young guy like you?"

"Grew up here, too, love it, but jobs are few. I'm gonna have to figure things out eventually, whether I'll ever be able to leave or not. I've only got a high school degree, never done anything 'cept waitering." He gave a slight bow. "Well, enjoy your meal," he said, and scurried off.

Daniel glanced around the dining room where most tables were occupied. The décor was charming in a rustic kind of way.

"Incredible. One restaurant, one inn. A gold mine like this and completely untapped." Daniel cut into his *cote d'agneau*, cooked to a perfect pale pink.

"Succulent," he proclaimed, "and the *asperges* equally cooked to perfection. Clearly, Beth, this little county has at least some people with a sophisticated palate but hardly anywhere to indulge it."

"You're right," Beth agreed. "All these people here tonight would probably love to try different places out here, if only they existed."

Daniel spent the meal mulling over potential opportunities in Wayne County. The place needs shaking up a bit, someone to jazz up the scene, and he could be the one to do just that. He knew food by virtue of being French, he had European flair and sophistication. God, he had money and time — this was it! He would bring life to this sleepy, culture-starved region.

The next morning, Daniel rose early after a night of energetic lovemaking and wandered the main street and back lanes of Scarcity, peering over garden walls and into the windows of the handful of small shops — a yarn store offering knitting classes, a gift shop that looked like it hadn't changed its window since the 1940s, and a cute art studio with two or three excellent oils displayed in the tiny bow window made of what looked to be the original eighteenth-century glass. From the scraps of information he'd gotten at the restaurant last night, Scarcity was becoming a new mecca for artists from the city who wanted to work in the quiet splendor of the region. With no central venue to show their works, most displayed the fruits of their labors in their own studios or, if they lived here full time, at home, opened once a year for a fund-raising art tour.

"I've got a fantastic idea, Beth. It will put this place on the map," he'd told her last night as they savored cognac after dinner.

"I'm all ears."

"It will take some time, but there's no way it wouldn't work. We find some building for sale out here, outfit it as a restaurant and bring in a really good chef. Along with that, we build a sort of atelier with access from the restaurant where local artists can rent studio space. They can work and display in the same place. There'd be an unending source of browsers from the restaurant and an equally large bunch of people meandering over to eat from the gallery space. No one's thought of this, I can't believe it! It makes so much crazy sense for a place like this."

"But how would you, we, go about this without living out here at least part-time?"

"That's part one, of course. We'll have to buy somewhere to live, yes, part-time at first and then more than likely full-time. Are you game for this?" Daniel gently tucked a wisp of hair behind her ear and ran his fingers along her jaw line. "It's the chance of a lifetime, chérie. You know nothing's going to become of the wind turbine idea, at least not now. This place is too good to be true: charming, historic, close to the city, people probably itching for more to do and next to nothing going on. It's begging for me — us — to work some magic here, some hocus-pocus, I think you call it." He rolled his napkin into a cylinder, waved it around his head and tapped Beth tenderly on the nose. "And you, my beauty, will be the gracious goddess who will run the show."

Beth, in high spirits from the food and wine, could only smile and nod, unable to keep her eyes from welling with tears. God, she loved him and whatever put that happy sparkle in his eyes was what she wanted too.

"Daniel, I'm with you no matter what." She put her hand on his and drew it to her lips. "Let's take our time, though, and do this right, not rush. One step at a time, presumably look and see if there is indeed anything out here to buy we could call home, right?"

"Of course, ma chérie. Nothing happens without your approval. But let's start looking tomorrow. If we can pick something up to use on the weekends, that would help me start doing research on all this."

"And I can keep my job for the time being. If this really happens though..." she took a deep breath and glanced up at the ceiling, "we'll give this lovely place a run for its money, yes?" She laughed, and Daniel squeezed her knee under the table with relish.

Daniel strode back to the room after his survey of the town with a realtor's card in his pocket and an appointment to meet at a cabin two miles out of town after lunch. First, he wanted to drive around with Beth to get a sense of the surrounding nooks and crannies.

"There wasn't a soul out this morning, can you believe it, on this beautiful day? I saw two pickup trucks and a BMW, — ha! This place is for me — it's got a split personality, no doubt about it."

Daniel and Beth first drove to Nickel, the closest neighboring town to Scarcity. "What could this mean, naming a town after a coin with the closest town to it meaning something's missing?" Beth wondered aloud. They stopped at a roadside marker just before entering the town and read it had been mined for nickel as late as 1910, but the mines were worked out after only a few years and closed before the Great Depression.

While lacking the historic charm of Scarcity's pre-Revolutionary stone and brick buildings, its main street was a jumble of colorful nineteenth century wooden houses, most empty. There was a now-closed general store occupying one corner and, at the opposite end of town, a general store with a few tables where you could order and eat breakfast or lunch, Farrin's.

"Both these towns have treasures to exploit, Beth. Artsy types scattered around, only one stylish restaurant, everything else basically run-of-the-mill — in this glorious place with mountains out the door and a city an hour's drive off — who knew? It's unbelievable no one has gotten here first with my idea."

"But nary a true grocery store in sight. Which reminds me, how will you run a restaurant with nowhere to buy anything in an emergency?"

"That will be the chef's problem. We are the visionaries, chérie. We will create the setting, the ambiance if you will, and the rest will fall into place with people we will direct. I've done it before with Zephyre, very successfully if you recall. Compared to that venture, this is a 'pièce de gâteau,' a cake walk, as you would say." Daniel patted Beth's knee. "Don't you worry. Of course, we will weigh the situation and proceed with caution. It's not for tomorrow, it will take time. But I think this is what I've been looking for. It's creative, needs some business insight and — mon Dieu! — it could be a money maker and damn good fun at the same time."

They met the realtor at the log cabin. While it hugged the bank of the Spendthrift River, the same one skirting Scarcity, the cabin itself was in a dark glen. Beth immediately raised her eyebrows in a "get me out of here" look toward Daniel.

"This isn't what we had in mind, honestly," Beth said. "With the wonderful mountain views here, we would really like something looking out on them."

"I wasn't sure of your price range when Mr. Perrault stopped at our office. We can look at something more along those lines, but prices will be higher." The realtor glanced at Daniel. "Significantly higher."

"This place is charming and rustic and is probably a good buy but it's too claustrophobic for us," Daniel replied. "There isn't any land with it, is there?" The realtor shook his head. "We're quite taken with your wide-open vistas. Prices don't matter to us at all. Perhaps I should have made that clear."

The realtor slipped the information on the cabin back in his brief-case and snapped the clasp shut. "Well then, I'll just stop at the office for some more information and we can make the rounds. I can think of a few places that might appeal."

"I don't think this guy gets it," Beth complained after they'd had to leave the Aston Martin at the bottom of a steep, rocky road that climbed to a mountain top rambler. "What a waste of time to look at that ugly thing, view or no view." They were following the realtor down yet another long right-of-way wondering if anything would click.

"It's true, what he's shown us so far is either completely inaccessible or truly horrible. What do you think? Give up for now?"

"Let's look at this last place and then call a day. We could try to come out later in the summer and look. Maybe more would be on the market." Beth saw Daniel set his jaw in disappointment. "I'm sorry, darling."

"*Non, non*, don't worry. Nothing will stop me from getting on with the rest. Did you see that building we passed, turning out of Nickel? I don't know if it's for sale, but it would be worth checking into for the restaurant."

Beth smiled wanly and turned to look out at the mountains as they zigzagged to avoid potholes on the gravel road. She was tired from the driving, the car wasn't really right for these back roads, her hair was a mess, and Daniel throwing himself into something out here was starting to seem like a bad idea to her. Was he going to be out here flitting from one place to the next while she worked all week? She wanted him to have purpose again, of course, but not if it meant spending all their time apart. Would he be able to get things done here on the weekends so she could be with him? If he was successful launching something out here, that would be different. But in the meantime?

The gravel road meandered across several rolling fields, three cow guards, and two creeks. Twice, they glimpsed structures in the distance until at last they pulled up behind the realtor at a white house with pale gray trim. It had clean-looking lines in a style somewhere between a bungalow and American Craftsman. Intrigued, they stepped from the car to explore further.

"Now I'll be honest with you," the realtor said as he exited his car, "it's been empty awhile and before that a family of eight or so lived in it. It'll need some work, no doubt about it. Built in 1889, though, so it's good and solid. They're asking a very reasonable price, $335,000. That building over there," he pointed to a smaller structure about fifty feet away, "was where they kept their farm tools, their dogs in the winter, I don't know what all. Before that, it may have been lived in. Has a fireplace and all."

Daniel wasn't listening. He'd turned to look around at the setting. The house and its 'annex,' as well as another smaller structure further on, had been dropped like sugar cubes in a vast, green bowl of billowing hay fields with a three-hundred-and-sixty degree view of indigo-blue mountains beyond. There was no other structure to be seen except an old barn they'd passed and bits and pieces of old fencing.

"And, of course, quite a bit of acreage comes with it," the realtor continued. "Well now, let's see." He flipped through his papers. "Parcel's never been subdivided, says here it's 235 acres, about 35 of it woods, and there's a pond just over that hill." He turned to the east and pointed.

Daniel put his arm around Beth's waist. "Let's have a look at the inside; the setting and views are fantastic, aren't they, chérie?" Beth telegraphed her agreement with a slight nod and smile. They strolled together from the drive to the dirt pathway leading to the house, inspecting the few scruffy shrubs bordering it and the contours of the property around the house itself. Wooden steps leading up to the front door were rotting; on closer inspection, paint was peeling from the trim and there were several cracked window panes.

"I know it doesn't look like a great beauty, mostly 'cause it's been empty so long. But I've seen the inside and it's really a diamond in the rough, you'll see," the realtor said, trailing them as he continued to study his sheaf of papers. "Says here it's three floors with a lower level and with the other building factored in, you've got yourselves almost 4,000 square feet. That last building could be for storage, maybe, or your car." He looked appreciatively towards the Aston Martin parked behind his pickup truck.

Inside, the air was musty, the windows pimpled with dead bugs, the ceiling mottled with smudges of mildew. But the oak floors were in good condition, random-width planks, still showing a pleasing luster. Daniel pointed out the oak beams traversing the ceiling then moved to the west window.

"This is an amazing view. Was this the kitchen?"

"Yep. Of course, as you can see, all the appliances are gone but it's got a propane line into the house, so you could get yourself a gas stove."

Daniel walked to the stone fireplace and ran his hand across the surface. "Does the fireplace work?"

"Yes, sir." Referring to his notes, the realtor continued. "There's a furnace in the crawl space under the house that was put in about fifteen years ago, but before that the fireplace would have been the main source of heat. I think the ductwork runs to the second structure over there, not sure about the smallest building. But this is an old and historic place, so the fireplaces were once the sole source for heat."

"I know that, thank you," Daniel responded sharply. He gave Beth a slight nudge in the back and they headed into the next rooms and then upstairs. The top floor consisted of four small rooms in a chopped up configuration with one small 1950s-style bathroom.

"We could make this the master suite, Beth, take down the walls, create a huge bath and walk-in closet. Look at these views!" Daniel flitted around the room from one window to the next, windows on all sides that brought in ample views even as Daniel calculated raising the roof for skylights. "Imagine lying in bed and staring at stars, creating a state-of-the-art bathroom."

"I know, I agree, but we're a long way from the main road, not to mention civilization generally," Beth said. "I mean, will we even find someone to do this kind of work out here?"

"Beth." Daniel placed his hands on her shoulders. "Anything is possible with money, chérie. You of all people know that." He dropped his arms. "Let's look at the lower level and then the annex and other building. We can easily connect the two houses with a bridge of some sort, maybe even all three buildings together. It could be exotic and modern. Come on, you love projects like this, get some enthusiasm going." He frowned at her impassive face and marched downstairs.

"This will be the office, perfect. It's not even below ground. We'll put a beautiful garden outside and sliding doors. And 235 acres, there's no end to what we could do out here. I see plenty of room for a swimming pool even. Done, I'm buying this!"

Beth laughed. "Well, am I along for the ride?" She *was* happy and excited. It would be a fun project and she knew Daniel would throw himself completely into it. But there were so many tangents to this, not least, what her role would be? What about her job, their life in the city? She hated to admit she'd gotten the ball rolling by bringing them here and encouraging Daniel, but now the thought of what might lie ahead left her feeling unmoored, uneasy. They walked back to the main room and stood together with their backs to the realtor who started to speak but was silenced by a pointed glance from Daniel.

"Of course, you'll design the whole thing, Beth, while I work to bring some life to this wasteland." Daniel took both her hands and gave them a little shake. "Beth, this is the challenge I've been looking for. We've got to do this. I know it will be crazy for a while, but the end will be fantastic, you will see. We'll be the toast of the county for what we'll accomplish here, trust me on this."

"So, Mr. Perrault, would you like to come back to the office for some paperwork?" The realtor studied his watch and flashed Daniel a yellow-toothed smile.

"Give us a moment, please." Daniel released Beth's hands and guided her to the front door and out to the landing.

"Beth?" Daniel searched her face with doleful eyes and an expression not unlike a small child asking for an ice cream from its mother. "This will be our project together. Nothing needs to change for now. I can oversee renovating this place from afar while we continue our lives in the city. Then we'll see, no need to rush."

"I know, Daniel. I just want to be sure we won't be separated too much while you" — she wanted to say '*play*' — "develop out here. It's a lot to swallow all at once, is all. But if you promise we'll go slow and see how we like it, the house first, of course, then I'll be okay with it. I mean, I still have a job you know, so I don't think I'll be able to be out here as much as you probably plan to be."

"Agreed, I understand completely. You will call the shots, my darling. Now let's see how much I can get this little jewel for." He gave her a wink and squeezed her around her waist. "Then I'll have to bring a contractor from the city, your buddy Marcus no doubt. No way a local crew would be able to do what I have in mind for this wonderful site."

"That might offend some people out here but you're probably right. Knowing you the way I do," she said with a coquettish smile, "you'll be insufferable, peering over shoulders and interrupting work with millions of questions. I trust Marcus, though. He'll be able to handle it, at least I hope so." Beth took a deep breath. "Okay, let's put in an offer."

CHAPTER THREE

SHERIFF STRIKER PULLED into the weed-choked parking lot of the Rooster building which had once been a small rubber factory in the county employing fifty-odd local people making balloons, latex gloves and condoms. Everyone in the county wondered whether the name of the building or the product associated with it came first, and chuckled at whoever's sense of humor was to blame. It shut down when jobs like that went south or to Asia. It was empty for years until a local entrepreneur bought it and a few small businesses undertook a modest renovation and moved in. One of these was MMG Enterprises.

After Spike had written up a brief report on Daniel Perrault's apparent homicide and gone home that morning to get a couple hours sleep, he'd taken a long hot shower even as Pearl hovered around the bathroom door with the coffee pot and mug.

"Don't want any of that right now, sweetheart. I'm 'bout dead to the bone and gonna try and catch an hour or two of shuteye before bringin' the department up to speed and everything starts ringin' off the hook." He toweled off, wiped the condensation from the medicine cabinet mirror, and peered with concern at his flabby jowls and yellowed teeth. "I'm short two of my best deputies, Buck Topping — you know him, had that pretty little wife, ran off with the football coach — and Ronnie Swiggert, so I'm gonna have to rely on Cody who's a good guy but probably not as self-confident at investigatin' as Swiggert, truth be told. Cody and Mabel already radioed in the wife's apparently not at the house. I got Judd chasing down a warrant and Bodie heading up there to get them in and waitin' on word from the city police as to her whereabouts. They had a house in town, apparently." He heaved a sigh. "I gotta get up there soon too 'fore forensics gets there."

"I just can't believe that nice, young Frenchman's dead." Pearl shook her head in disbelief as she held the coffee pot up into the air, making sure with a quizzical glance that her husband truly intended to skip his beloved daily ritual of a cup of her delicious coffee. "And his poor wife. I can't even imagine, when she gets the news."

"We got all hands on deck — 'cept Ronnie and Buck at the moment I guess — tracking down family, next of kin, if there's anybody here related other than the wife. We'll get to the bottom of it. But that phone is gonna ring soon and I can't do much if I can't keep my eyes open." He considered his toothbrush, but decided he'd shave and clean up after he'd slept and headed into the bedroom, pulling the shades, tossing the damp towel on the chair and falling onto the bed with a groan.

"Pearl, baby, if the phone rings, tell them I'll have a statement later and refer them to the station, Rudy might still be there, and the new shift's in, gonna brief them this morning. As sheriff, I'm declaring myself chief investigator on this, so they won't be able to tell 'em much 'til I get on it. I'll be up and outta here in an hour to meet with the force, check out the house, then goin' out later today to start talking to folks who had dealings with this guy."

"Spike, do you really want to head this thing up with all the other stuff you got going on? I mean there's budget issues you told me about, an election comin' up next year and all."

"That's exactly why I want to be in charge. A murder in my little county, on my watch? There's no way I ain't gonna have my finger on every little detail of this investigation. This county deserves answers from the top."

Pearl shrugged her shoulders. No point in dragging out the conversation right now. "I'll make sure to get the phone it if it rings. You sleep." Pearl planted a light kiss on his forehead and wandered out after making sure he'd closed his eyes.

"Oh, I forgot, jeez," Spike called out. "If the medical examiner calls, I will definitely need to talk to her."

"Of course, dear. You'll need to know if he was already dead when he was placed by the side of the road."

Huh? Spike didn't recall giving Pearl any details, just that the guy was found roadside. But then again, maybe he had, he mused as he tumbled into a deep, dreamless sleep. Pearl woke him an hour later when Deputy Talon radioed in.

Spike walked around to the rear of the Rooster and knocked on a windowless, black metal door covered with dust from the dirt parking lot. A muffled voice from within called out, "it's open!" Spike found Marcus McGrath, owner of MMG Enterprises, bent over one of several large packing boxes edging a bubble-wrapped laptop into it. He gave Spike a quick smile, finished gently tucking the bundle into a corner of the box and straightened up. He was a big, bulky man, bearded, with thick, bushy eyebrows over jovial, blue eyes that radiated merriment even if the rest of his expression was serious. Everyone who knew him liked him for his easy going manner and quick Irish wit.

"Can't say it's good to see you, Sheriff." He stuck his hand out and Spike shook it. "Heard the news down at Farrin's store this morning. I figured I'd see you sooner rather than later." He tossed his head back with a light laugh.

Spike didn't smile, glanced around the office. "Mind if I sit, Marcus?"

"Not at all. Let me clear some stuff off that chair." He took a stack of black folders off the chair and moved them to a windowsill, then half sat on a corner of his desk, folded his arms and waited for Spike to speak.

"Well, now, you know we're investigating Mr. Daniel Perrault's death, Marcus. We're waitin' on the medical examiner's full report but we got a definitive ID. We're talking to anyone and everyone who had any doings with him, got an APB out for his wife who's missing."

"Beth is missing?" Marcus asked, a frown deepening on his forehead.

"Correct. Chief Deputy Talon drew up a list of persons of interest this morning. And it's pretty well-known out here that you and Mr. Perrault butted heads over construction projects and ended up suing each other. You want to tell me what exactly the problems were?" Spike opened his little notepad and patted his front pocket unsuccessfully for a pen. Marcus opened a desk drawer and handed him one.

Marcus nodded. "Basically, it was very good, so good that I moved my construction business out here from the city, as you know, to take care of all his building needs: his house in Scarcity, the restaurant in Nickel, those artists' ateliers, the produce store, everything. Even better, the plan was, once I'd finished up all that work, he'd continue to use me for other buildings he had his eye on to buy and fix up, basically go into an informal partnership with me. But after I got in really deep with him, he fires me and then proceeds to sabotage my business, trashing my reputation, so I couldn't get any jobs out here. None of the local subs wanted anything to do with me anyway; I was toxic because of Daniel Perrault. They all disliked him because of his miserly, bad-tempered ways. Thought he was the worst kind of outsider.

"I've tried for the past year and a half to rebuild what he tried to take away from me, but I lost my shirt, he didn't pay me all that he owed me, and, yeah, I'm suing him, or I guess his estate now. He'd already sued me for breach of contract. I went bankrupt, had to move my office to this building for the cheaper rent and give up my house. I'm wearing out my welcome staying with friends until I've wrapped things up here. I blame Daniel Perrault for all of it."

"Enough to kill him?"

"Of course not."

"Why'd it turn sour?"

Marcus sighed and sat in the swivel chair at his desk. "Dan — that's what I called him after he corrected my pronunciation of his name for the umpteenth time — 'Marcus, accent is on the last syllable, not the first — DaniEL!' — called me the very Monday after he and Beth came back to the city after their weekend out here. He told me he was buying a couple of hundred acres outside Scarcity with some long-abandoned structures he wanted me to completely renovate."

He swung around so he faced the window. "I'd gutted and renovated Beth's townhouse in the city and they'd really loved it. I put in a beautiful, modern kitchen — the place was 80 years old — and redid all the bathrooms, brought in some beautiful Honduran mahogany for bookshelves and floors. I mean that place was a true showplace."

"What'd he say when he called?"

"'Marcus, your future is with me in a place called Scarcity.' Ha, I should have taken that name as an omen." He shook his head. "Don't get me wrong, Sheriff. I like it here a lot, but I can't make a living and now I've lost my toehold in the city, so basically, I'm screwed. I filed for bankruptcy protection last year. As you see, I've sold off most everything and going back to work in town for a friend's small construction company. It's a huge step down. Dan ruined my life."

"Go on."

"I met Dan and Beth at the site a couple of weeks after he called…"

• • •

"Marcus, look at this!" Daniel spread his arms wide and turned slowly taking in the 360-degree bowl of the property. "It's got to be almost as beautiful as Périgord! Of course, I know you haven't been there, but trust me, it is very similar." He pointed toward the house and outbuildings.

"I want you to modernize, beautify what is there and connect all of the structures together so they look like they are a united front but fragmented at the same time, does that make any sense?"

"Modernize and beautify, yes; the rest, I think will come once we start the process. Can we go in?"

"Yes, yes, of course. Let's go in."

Marcus noticed Beth seemed a bit on the glum side and hung back to walk into the house with her instead of pairing ahead with Daniel. He and Beth had become close friends during the townhouse renovation. He stole a sideways peek at her as they walked.

"You're keen on this too, aren't you?" he asked.

"Of course I am, Marcus. I'm just afraid Daniel is moving too fast with his grandiose plans. Once the house is underway, I should warn you, he plans on buying up a building in Nickel and turning it into a restaurant and gallery and whatever, I mean, he's really determined to make a big splash out here."

"And you don't find that exciting? Are you worried about the expense?"

"No, no, it's not that at all. I'm very pleased he's found something to feel passionate about and throw his energy into. And the money isn't an issue. It's just…" Beth stopped before mounting the steps, watching Daniel through the doorway as he opened windows with a flourish. "I see too many times when he'll be out here, and I'll be in the city working. It's hitting me that we're going to be separated by this project, at least for the time being, and I guess I can't say I'm not bothered by that."

"Will you quit your job, do you think, if all this works out for him, for you?"

"I don't know, Marcus. I'm a city girl at heart. But if he wants to do this and live out here, I guess I will." She gave him a faint smile. "We'd keep the townhouse, of course. I couldn't bear to give that up."

'Well, it isn't that far away, you know. The city, I mean. I'll be commuting from there to work on this — if he hires me, that is."

"True, but it's more than that. Even in his blackest moods when Daniel complained about the turbine thing not working out, and he started talking about maybe returning to France, at least then I had him all to myself. I'm selfish that way. Now, I have to share him with this place he's become so quickly infatuated with, or at least the idea of this place."

"I don't think Dan would do anything you weren't happy with."

"You're right. Why am I like this? I mean I'm the one who found this area and encouraged him. He was like a little kid basically when I said let's do it. He's got big ideas and he's cheerier than I've seen him in months. I don't know why I went on like this with you, Marcus. Daniel will wonder why I'm hanging back or whether we're having an affair." She blushed. "I don't know why I said that either, jeez, sorry."

"No worries." Marcus looked away and up to scan the roof of the house. "I think we've already lost Daniel in the bowels of the place, frankly. But yes, I'd best follow along to see what he envisions."

"And, Marcus, of course you've got the contract for the work. That's the number one thing I will insist on."

He gave her a respectful nod and jogged up the steps into the house.

Marcus spent the better part of the summer obtaining the necessary permits to begin work, he hoped, in the fall. He liked Daniel and had never had a problem with him during the city townhouse renovation, but of course that had mainly been Beth's project and she'd been easy to work with. Looking back after things started to turn unpleasant with Daniel in Scarcity, he remembered Daniel's occasional disparaging comments about his guys' work, the grade of faucet for the master bath, the cleanliness of the site, little things. He'd stand in a doorway, arms crossed, a look of disdain on his face and blow out his lips in the Gallic way. When Marcus queried Beth if Daniel was unhappy with the way things were going, she would tell Marcus Daniel was just frustrated with himself for failing to get the wind project going. It had nothing at all to do with the crew or the work, she swore.

Ultimately Daniel gushed to their friends and neighbors who stopped by for a look at the progress that there was no better contractor in the U.S. or France.

"We'd be waiting every day for French workers to finish their *saucissons* and red wine lunch. No hurrying *them* along on the job," he'd say. "Marcus is absolutely top of the line, hardworking and focused, just what we needed."

But the Scarcity project frayed nerves on all sides from the start and Beth let Daniel take charge almost immediately. He hired an architect from a neighboring county and spent several weeks going back and forth with him on the details both on the phone and at the site until he was satisfied with a design. The project, with Daniel's idea to run elevated bridges from the main house to the outlying structures, turned out to be more complicated than Marcus had anticipated. In August, Daniel bought the abandoned building he'd seen in Nickel, an old apple packing operation, for his restaurant and gallery idea. He wanted Marcus, along with his main man Sam, to rehabilitate it at the same time as the house. He began scouting around for other buildings for a grocery store/farmers' market. Like a kid dazzled in a candy shop, he found so many commercial places for sale or about to be, he could pick and choose, flirt with them all or play one owner against another. Beth found the multiple projects too time-consuming for her to even consider immersing herself in and begged off involvement for the time being.

"I don't have the luxury just yet of running back and forth to Scarcity as you do, Daniel," she said one Saturday morning in September as they prepared to drive out to check the sites one more time before Marcus started work. "I still have a job, you know, and I get tired of that little inn we have to stay at every time we go out."

"Don't come out, then. You stay home and rest while I take care of what I'm hoping is our future, a glamorous and exciting future." He shot her an angry look while looking over the architect's blueprints and designs on the kitchen table. When she said nothing and turned to the sink to rinse the morning coffee mugs, he softened, rolled the plans and came up behind her, wrapping his arms around her waist.

"Look, Beth, I know the Scarcity house seems a bit isolated for you now, but it will become a social mecca when we get everything done. The restaurant will be a draw for people from our neighborhood in the city even, they'll come from all over the region for good, French, country food, and the artists out there will clamor to get into the gallery spaces. You will see, it will be fantastic." He cupped her breasts and nuzzled the nape of her neck, then turned her towards him and kissed her passionately. When he undid her belt and slid his hand into her jeans she swatted him away.

"The neighbors, Daniel, they'll see us!" He pulled back and looked at her with the imploring, child-like blue eyes that never failed to melt her resistance.

"Come with me, Beth. I can't, *won't* do any of this without you by my side all the way." He pressed his cheek lightly against hers. "These plans, this crazy idea, is for us, for our future. I need your guidance, your style, your *savoir-faire,* for it to work. And, of course, I have nothing else going on for me right now. I truly, truly need this."

Beth felt him sigh deeply and she stroked his hair tenderly with the tips of her fingers. For all his pedigree, money and good looks, deep down Daniel was essentially insecure. His father had always outshone him, and Daniel desperately needed to prove himself. Perhaps his big plans for Scarcity and Nickel were the only way he believed he could.

"You know I'm with you. I adore you, Daniel, you know that, too. But this is your venture and you should be completely in charge. I will support you any way I can, I just won't be with you on every single trip out there. When the time comes, I'll make it our home and we'll live there, I promise." Daniel lifted his head and slowly started to undo the buttons on her blouse. Fumbling with them and then her belt, he became the vulnerable, dependent, little boy persona she found so endearing. If she said the word and he gave up on this undertaking, then what? He'd revert to the aimless grumbler he'd been last year, that's what. It's quite possible their relationship would change for the worse. And, of course, failure to succeed in something here would completely crush his pride. She didn't want to know where that might lead.

It was best to accept Scarcity and what it meant to Daniel, for them. Positive things, she hoped. Their lips touched, and she gave herself to him.

Marcus was still tying up projects in the city and couldn't give Daniel an exact date as to when he would start the major renovations on the main house and annex. He hoped he could get the smallest structure, which he'd already gutted, refurbished before year's end so Daniel and Beth could stay there instead of at the inn when they came out to oversee work. Beth liked the simplicity of it and, surprised by how much she had warmed to Scarcity over the autumn, was excited about creating a modest office there, somewhere she could work for a quiet weekday or two while Daniel darted about. The permits on the other two buildings were taking forever, though, since they were registered as historic properties.

Marcus thought the smallest structure had once been a sharecropper's house. When he cut through to add more windows, he found the walls stuffed with old newspapers for insulation, and later discovered the remnants of pilings which must have held up a front stoop. There was no crawl-space or bathroom, and after exploring, he found vestiges of an outhouse in an adjacent field. There was a small fireplace and the floors were of the cheapest pine, but it was a well-built structure, though showing the neglect of decades.

Marcus rounded up a handful of local subcontractors to help him, and threw himself into what he loved to do most, rejuvenate from the studs out. He installed six new windows and replaced the flooring with reclaimed, random-width oak planks from an historic preservation project he had recently completed. He added a small wing in the back for an elegant, European-style bathroom and a second door to the west side that would eventually open to a bridge connecting to the center building. Using the old piling outline, he planned to build a front porch with slate flooring and Douglas fir planks for the ceiling. It would be large enough for a porch swing and a cozy breakfast nook with room to spare for more seating if Beth wanted to entertain there.

Daniel was out every weekend, often without Beth, buzzing around, looking at more buildings for sale. The locals murmured among themselves, wondering what he was up to. He hired a couple of high school kids to clean out the apple packing building — mostly old crates and rusted bits of machinery — and waited impatiently for the architectural plans to be finalized and approved, though the county, he was learning, moved at a glacial pace. With not enough underway to suit him, and little else to do, he set about repairing and replacing the fencing on the property with the help of neighbors, two brothers, Garret and Quinn Kelley, whose brawn was renowned throughout the county.

He threw himself into the project buying a brand-new, red pickup truck, a tractor, a couple of augers, spools of wire, enough fence posts to replace what had rotted or fallen over, and other supplies. Never did he think he would enjoy physical labor as much as he did, sweating and exerting under a cloudless, blue dome with the golden and red hues of autumn winking at him from trees around the house and woods. Daniel felt at home for the first time, his yearning for Périgord finally slipping away. His enthusiasm and energy level were at their peak as he relished the plans forming in his mind for his property and the town. He wanted to spend more and more time in Scarcity and, as autumn eased towards winter, he began to lose patience with MMG Enterprises. He threatened to scrap the contract and go with another firm if Marcus didn't pick up the pace to start on the main house soon.

"I don't want to wait much longer, Marcus, to get started with this. I can't get serious about all that goes into creating a restaurant and the art studios if I haven't got anywhere to live yet. People won't even talk to me unless they see I'm committed to this place."

"I know, Dan. Beth and I have a few more details to iron out, but her office should be finished and habitable except for painting and a few other minor things by year's end, as I promised. But for the bigger projects, maybe you should go with a local construction group out there. Just the driving time to get back and forth every day is going to eat into productive time for you. I'm sorry, I really wanted the work. The house is going to be fantastic."

"*Merde*!" Daniel clicked off his cell phone and pondered his options. Marcus did really good work and Beth liked him so much. He had, in truth, talked to two other small construction companies in Wayne County, but was very unimpressed with the people. He felt stuck; it would be hard to start the process all over again with firms from the city. He called Marcus back.

"Okay, you win. But I've got an idea for you. I want you to move your business out here. I've got plenty of work for you right now, plus I'm seeing a lack of competent construction people out here. You and I together could buy some of these empty buildings in Nickel, and even Scarcity, fix them up, maybe sell or rent them out. An incredible opportunity for you, Marcus. You'll have work for years!"

Marcus was pleased and accepted without thinking through the possibility Daniel could ever turn against him or his work. Still, it took another few weeks to make the actual move and the weather was bad — it snowed more than usual for the region. But by early February, Marcus was sure he could be set up temporarily in nearby Poppins Creek where he'd found cheap office space and a small, rental house where he could live.

Beth proposed she and Daniel spend the Christmas holidays with his parents in Périgord. She could see how agitated he was with Marcus, and she wanted to get his mind off the delays and annoyances, to recapture the joy of their last visit when they honeymooned there. Plus, in their absence, Marcus could work nonstop on her office interior and its veranda so it would be done when they returned, she hoped.

Marcus was happy to hear he wouldn't have Daniel pestering him day in and day out while Daniel and Beth were away. He didn't hesitate to move into the space as soon as they left so he could be on-site, work twenty hour days if he had to. He installed a small cot and threw an old sleeping bag over it, and warmed himself with a little space heater he bought in town. With Sam, who came out for a few days as an extra set of hands, Marcus worked the whole month of December except for a brief break on Christmas, spent with family in Wisconsin.

Upon their return from France, Beth marveled at Marcus's work and devoted her free weekends to decorating the interior. She and Daniel wedged a small bed in one corner so they could stay there instead of the inn while other work commenced. The fireplace, along with the space heater, provided enough heat to be snug. Meals were simple, mostly leftovers reheated in a microwave they installed in the bathroom, along with a tiny fridge and coffee maker. She painted the walls pale gray with the barest touch of lavender and bought an antique, mahogany desk with floral inlay designs on the drawers and legs as well as a pristine leather writing surface. The six new windows on three sides of the house stayed unadorned to take full advantage of the light and views. It was a beautiful space and quite comfortable.

Work on the main house and other annex crawled along as frequent inspections found one little thing or another that had to be changed. The plans for the second floor called for a huge master suite, a bath with a free-standing tub and open shower and a his-and-hers walk-in closet. The kitchen and living room on the first floor would have the finest wood and stone elements for a contemporary yet homey feel, and for the shelves in his office on the ground level, Daniel wanted the highest quality Brazilian mahogany. The middle structure housed Daniel's library, music and entertainment center, with two guest suites on the second floor. With all of that going on, Marcus also had to run back and forth overseeing his subcontractors at the Nickel site where the major work of building out the kitchen for the restaurant was underway. As if that weren't more than enough for one contractor, Daniel bought the closed general store in Nickel and wanted it updated as well, preferably at the same time the other projects progressed. Then Daniel announced he wanted a swimming pool and cabana built at a site where some sizable trees would have to be removed. This was turning into a huge, big-time project for MMG Enterprises. Marcus hoped he could handle it.

Moving the business to the area and renting a house for himself so he wouldn't lose time going back and forth to the city meant Marcus could get to know the area. He took a little time to immerse himself in the history. He was interested in the background of the property, and spent a Saturday at the town historical society researching the records thinking Daniel would be interested in the narrative. Instead, Daniel showed irritation at the distraction.

"Come on, Marcus. Enough playing around with my wife and her little house. It's time to concentrate on the important work, the main house and entertainment center, the pool, the bridges without even getting into the delays with the restaurant. And what about all the digging for the geothermal? When will your people be ready to start? This is most important. You've got to get that underway, and hopefully done, before cold weather starts again. We need to get going on this — I don't want to wait forever!"

• • •

"Daniel was right about that, and right to be worried. That geothermal project is what killed me," Marcus told Spike. "In the middle of it, some major problems were popping up at the restaurant site, so I'm running around like a headless chicken. It was a major headache finding the company that could do the geothermal which delayed getting that part underway by several months. Same thing with the pool, finding the right company in the middle of nowhere. Dan was apoplectic even as we had plenty of other work going on for him. The bridges connecting his buildings were also a real challenge, on top of the restaurant and other structures he'd bought. But the geothermal was a fiasco, I admit." He pointed to a box on the floor already sealed with tape. "That box has nothing but the legal papers on that. Once he sued me for breach of contract, everything slowly fell apart. He had trouble, but he eventually found a new contractor to finish my work. Can't tell you how that burned me up. He turned out to be a mean-spirited jerk. My work prospects slowly dried up until now, obviously, I can't make a living at all."

"What about his wife, didn't she say you were assured to have the work?" Spike asked.

"Yeah, she felt bad, but she'd already let Dan run the show, and she actually agreed with him that the geothermal should not have been such a mess to get going."

"I worked on the main house and secondary building all that spring and summer but nothing satisfied him. It ended up being a complete gut of both, so, yeah, it was taking longer than I'd hoped. Dan had some things shipped from France including a gorgeous old *poêle au mazout* he wanted in his office downstairs, and a La Cornue stove/oven in Provençal blue — stunning — which cost $10,000 plus shipping. I will say, the man has impeccable taste. Everything is of the best quality, and quality in this day and age takes time — finding the right sources, shipping, getting it out to the boondocks here, et cetera. We were way behind schedule, and the geothermal was a major project in and of itself. I was clueless enough to think it would be easy to get a geothermal crew out here to knock the project off in a couple of days. It was much more complicated than that — getting the equipment and expertise to drill several hundred feet down through rock, then getting the pipes laid; it's as involved as putting in pilings for a building. I learned the hard way. Felt pretty damn stupid on that front. Daniel was really pissed off he had to rely on the old furnace and buy a bunch of electric heaters, felt it ruined the aesthetics of the place. I couldn't disagree."

Marcus stood and pulled a thick three-ring notebook from a box that hadn't yet been taped up. "These are the materials just for the geothermal. It was my first time with this, and it was a little daunting. By the time I moved outside to oversee that work as well as focus on the bridges for connecting the houses using his architect's design, he threatened to take me off the project entirely. His attitude, frankly, was turning ugly. Finally, one day, he actually blocked my access to the site with a tractor."

• • •

Daniel parked his tractor at the first fence line to keep Marcus and his crew off his property. He was sick to death of the man and his mistakes. Granted, the quality of what he'd done was good — the kitchen and bath in the main house were top of the line, sleek and modern — but Marcus hadn't followed his directives in other areas. The roof line wasn't what he wanted and the bridges connecting the houses were horrible and disappointing aesthetically. He'd have to have them ripped out and redone eventually. And the fiasco of the geothermal, *ridicule*! If he'd known Marcus knew next to nothing about this kind of system, he never would have put him in charge.

He sat and waited for Marcus to show up. It was a perfect May morning, nearly two years since Daniel had set foot in Scarcity. Though close to completion, there were still little things to wrap up with the properties; he wanted the highest quality, copper gutters, rewiring for speakers from the music room/library to the rest of the main house plus some clean-up outside. He didn't need Marcus for that and he certainly had no intention of continuing to use him to finish up the work on the restaurant. It was basically ready for final inspections anyway, maybe a tweak here and there. He was planning a fantastic Bastille Day opening night, invitation only: friends and acquaintances from the city, a handful of local people he knew had money, weekenders he targeted by querying a couple of realtors, and of course artists he wooed for the studio spaces. His parents even planned to fly in and attend the festivities along with a group of his old Périgord buddies.

He surveyed his land and breathed in the fresh smell of his fields. He and Beth had moved into the main house last Christmas and Daniel never went into the city with Beth anymore, telling her it depressed him there. She returned a couple of times a month to the townhouse which she wanted to keep for now, though she'd cut back to part-time work and did most of it from her office in Scarcity. She could see there was no going back. If she wanted a life with Daniel, it would be in Scarcity.

Daniel couldn't be happier. For all his carping, he loved nearly everything about the house and the two annexes. The pool and cabana were just what he'd envisioned, but Marcus hadn't been involved in that work at all, Daniel ultimately hiring another company for the work. His office was the picture of tranquility with a plush carpet, subdued colors and soft lighting. His desk, facing the Zen garden beyond the sliding doors, was imposing — an intricately carved piece that had belonged to his grandfather in the Louis XIV style, a little fussy but Daniel liked the commanding impression it presented. Beth seemed happy enough too, although she'd made few if any friends in the area yet. Daniel, however, was out and about nearly every day, talking with people, explaining his plan, touting the restaurant, making contacts and (he hoped) friends to secure their support for his ideas for the town and beyond.

His parents visited last year in the spring and pronounced his *grande propriété* — his "homestead" — as beautiful as anything in Périgord. They toasted his success with a rich Bordeaux wine and *foie gras* from Daniel's home town. His father admired the fencing

Daniel was installing throughout the property and even assisted as best he could with the pieces that still needed work while Quinn and Garret looked on, chuckling to themselves at the greenhorns. "I mean, the guy's father's wearin' shoes with little tassels on 'em," they snickered. It had been physically exhausting but rewarding. Daniel admired it now sitting on his tractor with clear views in all directions.

The barn turned out to be a diamond in the rough. Daniel was familiar with barns in Périgord, which were built of stone and plentiful in the region. The one on his property, though in some disrepair, was built in the old post-and-beam, Dutch style with a steep, gabled roof and large, double Dutch doors, very rare for the region. Once he and the brothers had cleaned out years, maybe decades, of cobwebs and general debris — old tractor parts, crumbling ropes, bridles and heaps of mildewed hay — he saw how much usable space there was. It got him thinking about what he could use it for. Could he try a bit of farming without losing focus on his plans for the restaurant and store in Nickel?

The first summer, while he and Beth were still staying at the inn and waiting for Marcus to start work, Daniel started poking around the county to find out what the local farmers grew, what livestock they owned. He had pastures galore, almost two hundred acres of land where he could put just about anything he wanted out to graze and forget about. This was the main reason he had plunged into repairing the fences, which he could easily electrify later if need be. His closest neighbor, Thorne Tate, had a bunch of cows he occasionally caught sight of on the next ridge, so peaceful to look at especially in the late afternoon sun. Beth loved trekking up the right-of-way through their property that led to Thorne's and photographing the idyllic scene as she chronicled their "rural experiment," as she called it.

Daniel's back started to hurt, and he stood and stretched, then sat and leaned forward onto the tractor's steering wheel, massaging his forehead on the hard rubber surface. He had a headache. Typical of Marcus to be late. His thoughts turned to the bleak days after their holiday in Périgord that first winter when Beth returned to the city to work and he headed straight out to the Scarcity work site.

Daniel saw that Marcus made good on his promise to move full speed ahead while they were in France. He had nearly finished renovating the building for Beth's future office. There was no furniture and the walls weren't painted yet, but Marcus had left an orderly site in what was now a bright and cheery room and an elegant bathroom. Daniel admired the work done thus far on the porch, and imagined how excited Beth would be envisioning a garden around it. Marcus's cot and sleeping bag were still there as well as the space heater. Daniel wondered where he was and what progress he'd made in moving the business out here to speed up work.

He tried his cell and left a message, "Marcus! I'm at the house but I don't know where you are. Call me right back!" Then he tried Beth and got her voicemail. In the meantime, he inspected the rest of the property, and the restaurant, and saw that little else had been accomplished in his absence. In a fit of exasperation, he sped up to Thorne's and announced he was ready to go out with him to buy some cattle, right then and there.

"I don't have anything else to do! Both my builder and my wife are missing in action and I am really, truly sick of the do-nothings. Let's go find some cows!"

Thorne calmed him down and promised to go out with Daniel early the next morning. They met at Farrin's for breakfast — Daniel turning up his nose at the runny eggs and greasy bacon — then went straight-away to a breeder Thorne bought from and recommended. Daniel braved the frosty air, petulantly observing the bulls, stamping his feet in the cold while the crisp air numbed his fingers and reddened his nose. He claimed money was no object and wanted the biggest and best bull on the lot. He bought a Black Angus Thorne pointed out as the healthiest looking, if not the biggest, and arranged for the delivery of two dozen cows in a couple of weeks once the bull had adjusted. The bull, which Daniel named Grand Teton, was delivered to one of the newly fenced pastures on the other side of the right-of-way. His cell rang as he watched the unloading. It was Beth.

"Where have you been? I tried to reach you all day yesterday, Marcus too. I don't know where he is, and I had to sleep last night on his dirty old cot and sleeping bag. I want you out here with me so we can get the room set up."

"He's here in town and following me out tomorrow. After work, he and I went to select paint colors and he gave me the lowdown on my office with pictures. I didn't have my phone and didn't want to call you back too late. We did some furniture shopping, too, this morning. I'm so excited, Daniel! I think it will be beautiful, can't wait to see it."

Daniel's mood immediately blackened. "You're with Marcus? What the hell, Beth? He should have his ass out here by now. He knew I was coming directly out here to go over the next stages."

"He's been gathering his next round of supplies and preparing to move the office out there like you wanted, Daniel. This stuff doesn't happen overnight."

"Why hasn't he returned my call?" Daniel shouted.

"I'm sure he was going to call you. Maybe he thought it better to see you in person first," Beth replied softly. Where was this temper tantrum coming from?

"Fuck that!" Daniel howled in spasm of rage. "And why aren't you fucking here? I'm making important decisions here. I'm buying livestock!"

"Livestock! But, Daniel, we don't know the first thing about farm animals!" Beth exclaimed. It was clearly no use trying to defuse his anger. "How are we going to take care of them or know what to do?"

"You've got to decide what you want, Beth, because I'm not waiting for you much longer," Daniel said through clenched teeth. "I'm trying to build our home, start a restaurant and get a farming operation and art studios going while you are doing what? You're nothing but a government bureaucrat, *merde!*" Fuming at the thought Marcus and Beth were in the city together, Daniel couldn't control his anger and sarcasm. He heard Beth start to sputter a response, equally angry. They'd been so happy in Périgord, she was shocked at his sudden antagonism. They skied with friends in Courchevel, and Daniel bought her an exquisite Cartier, white-gold watch, though she protested it was far too fine for country life. Now here he was on edge again. She was starting to dislike what Scarcity was doing to his moods.

"Look, Beth, I'm not feeling very happy with you or Marcus right now, so I'm going to go look at my new bull. I bought cows, I bought them for you. We'll discuss all this when you come out." He clicked off the phone and stomped angrily back to the annex. He took Marcus's sleeping bag, folded up the cot, and threw both into his pickup truck. He drove to the barn and tossed them in one of the stalls.

He smiled as he sat back and waited for Marcus, remembering. When Beth hurried out later that day after their phone conversation, anxious and contrite, he fucked her from behind in the barn on top of that sleeping bag like a hungry dog. No man would ever have his wife like he would.

Later, feeling horrible remorse for treating her so badly — she'd looked so bedraggled and cold, her cheeks wet with tears dribbling to her chin, falling in drops onto her black parka, bits of hay clinging to her hair — he took her out for a nice dinner and promised he would help make the annex comfortable if she would just stay with him, cut back on work and help him. He needed to keep a watchful eye on her and Marcus.

"I want to try some cattle farming, maybe sheep and chickens this spring. This is a magical time for us, Beth! It was such good luck finding this little Scarcity crossroads. I pined for it while we were in Europe. My loyalties have shifted, and I want you to love it as I do."

"I do love it, Daniel. I'll feel better when my little office is finished. It will give me the flexibility I'll need. And I won't mind collecting a few eggs from time to time, but what about everything else? I mean with the house, restaurant/art gallery and a freaking farm to run, we'll never be able to go anywhere or do anything."

"Haven't you learned anything since you've been with me? Money changes everything, ka-ching, ka-ching." He rattled some coins in his pocket. "The brothers may be dumb as rocks, but they know how to farm. I'll hire them to take care of everything."

When Daniel saw the dust kicking up from Marcus's pickup truck at the cusp of the hill bordering his land, he pulled his cap down and stood up on the tractor to face him.

"Hey, Dan, what's up?" Marcus leaned out of the driver's side window.

"What's up is you're off the projects now. I don't need you or your crew anymore."

"Um, what exactly are you saying?" He opened the door and jumped out of the truck.

"I'm saying you are now fired."

"Fired from what, from everything?"

"Yes, my friend. I don't need you to finish the stuff that still needs to be done here and I especially don't need you to continue with the art studios. I've found another crew for this."

"Whoa, wait a minute, you owe me a lot of money on the geothermal you haven't paid up yet. I need to pay the guys for all the infrastructure work on that."

"Marcus, you know how unhappy I have been, with how long this has taken, with the mess digging for the geothermal that shouldn't have been such a disaster, and little things. I am not paying anything further for your work. We are done here and now."

"Why you son of a bitch, you can't do this!"

"I can, and I am, Marcus."

Marcus signaled to his crew pulling up behind his truck to stay put. His face twisted in a rage, he marched around to Daniel's side of the tractor and grabbed his ankle.

"Get down off there and tell me this to my face!"

"I'm done here. Now get out or I'll get the police to take you out."

"Where's Beth? I need to talk to her. She would never allow you to treat me like this. Dan, I've spent two years on this, you can't do this."

"I know about you and my wife. I know you seduced her, took her to bed. All your fun little afternoons working on her office, meeting in town," he said with a sneer. "I should have kicked you out a year ago."

"You're crazy! I never touched your wife. She was always a good friend, nothing more. She can confirm that."

"Get off my property."

Marcus pulled Daniel off the tractor by his leg, knocking him off balance and pushing him to the ground.

"I'll fucking kill you!" He straddled Daniel and started to choke him when he saw Thorne barreling down the road from the opposite direction in his pickup and let him go.

Thorne screeched to a halt roadside and leaned out his window. "Jesus, what's going on here? Daniel, you okay?"

Daniel stood and brushed himself off. "I will be when this poor excuse for a builder leaves my property."

"Okay, DANiel Perrault. Have it your way. I'll see you in court. I'll sue your ass for fraud, breach of contract, you name it. You are not done with me yet and you will pay what you owe me." Marcus spat on the ground at Daniel's feet and marched off to his pickup.

• • •

"I'm not proud of those few moments in my life. Fury is not too strong a word to describe what I felt at him right then. That guy was a demon as far as I was concerned. At that moment," he paused, "I know it sounds like I wanted to kill him, but I had absolutely nothing to do with this." Marcus opened the door for the sheriff, who had stood and handed Marcus his pen.

"You understand I can't rule you out as a suspect. You'll have to stay in the county until we get further along in the investigation, Marcus, I'm sorry."

"I hope it won't take too long, Sheriff. It's already taken too long to get on with my life. I've been trying to get my business back on track for a while now and failed. You understand. I can't say I'm surprised it came to this. He was the worst kind of person. You'll find out for yourself, though."

Spike hesitated at the door and turned to face Marcus. "One more question. Were, or are you, in love with Beth Perrault?"

Marcus blanched and shook his head. "I once might have been, but no more."

CHAPTER FOUR

AS SHERIFF STRYKER finished his report and headed home to catch a little rest after discovering the body early that morning, his deputies, Mabel and Cody, radioed in there was no sign of the wife — or anyone — at the house. Mabel wanted to know if they could enter and search it without a warrant?

"'Course you can, we got to find out where she is and what she might know. All reports say she's been living there with him since they bought it. There may be another body in there for all we know, hers. These are emergency circumstances and I'll get Detective Koons to get a warrant approved ASAP. In the meantime, I take full responsibility should it come to that. Let me get back with you." Spike cut off Mabel and radioed Bodie.

"We gotta go in, do what you gotta do. Koons'll come through for me. I'll get up there soon's I can. Get another call into forensics if need be before I get there."

"Roger that."

The local newspaper had already called, having picked up the story on the police band; it wouldn't be long before the story got out to the bigger papers and TV people. Nobody at the sheriff's department wanted Mrs. Perrault to find out about her husband's death that way. But where was she?

The property was a long way from the main road, and Mabel and Cody started to wonder if they'd taken a wrong turn when the house finally came into view. The sun was just coming up over the eastern ridge of mountains and the gently curving road spilled onto a scene of peace and tranquility, bathed in the sun's golden, early morning light, enriched by the autumnal colors of the fields and woods.

"Wow," Mabel drew in her breath. "This has got to be one of

the prettiest spots in the county. Had no idea it was this beautiful back here."

"Me neither," Cody responded. "Don't think we've ever had cause to come back here."

They turned off the right-of-way onto the gravel drive leading to the front of the house. It was quiet, and a front light was on.

"This house is awesome! Look at those passageways to the other two buildings." They peered out the patrol car windshield at the three, sparkling-white houses strung together by what looked like a shimmering necklace drifting on the air.

"It's different, takes full advantage of the views, that's for sure." Mabel admired the plantings around the house and their design as a keen gardener herself. She did a cursory survey of the driveway, shrubs and front steps; no sign of disturbance or any blood. A white Lexus SUV was parked off to the side and a green sports car, an Aston Martin, was parked around the back of the house. Cody aimed his flashlight into the SUV but saw nothing unusual and the car was locked. Mabel checked out the sports car which was also locked and looked clean.

On the front steps, preparing to knock on the door, the duo exchanged glances.

"I've never had to do this before," Mabel confessed.

"Me neither."

They listened for any sound from within the house but heard nothing.

"Let me do it," Mabel said. "If she's there, she's probably asleep. A female's voice won't scare the bejesus out of her." She checked her watch. "It's 6:42. Note that." Mabel took a deep breath, knocked hard on the door and counted to three. "Mrs. Perrault, this is Mabel Crone from the Wayne County Sheriff's Department. Could you please open the door so we can speak with you?" Nothing, no sound but the early twittering of wrens or nuthatches.

"Let's check the other structures," Cody said. "Maybe the bedroom is in one of them." Mabel nodded and headed around the outside to the end building while Cody made his way in the opposite direction around to the back of the middle building. He scanned the Asian-style garden and sliding doors at the rear of the main house, then the pool area, and saw nothing out of the ordinary. He heard

Mabel rap at the back door of the smallest house and call out for Mrs. Perrault. She turned from the door and called out to Cody.

"Seeing anything?"

"No, there's no door on this side to the middle building, just a stretch of lawn all the way to the pool and woods back there. Looks like to get in, you have to go through the main house or where you're at, and come in on the bridge."

"We're gonna have to radio Sheriff Stryker and get permission to enter the premises. You got your camera?" Cody's hand went to his belt and he nodded.

After talking to the sheriff, they waited in their squad car for Deputy Talon to arrive.

"Hard to believe anything bad could happen here or to someone from this place, it's so calm and serene," Mabel said, rolling down her window.

"Yeah, looks like the place has been taken care of. I'm gonna hate breaking down the door."

"Too bad Swiggert's out sick today. He's so good at breaking locks."

Deputy Talon, looking as beat as Sheriff Stryker felt, pulled up and indicated with a nod as he exited his vehicle they had the go-ahead to enter the premises. He knocked once more on the main door and requested the door be opened. Nothing. Cody tried the door and found it unlocked. They wouldn't need to break down the door after all.

"Let's do it," Talon said.

Talon led the way with guns drawn as the three went room to room and across the bridges to the other buildings. Clearly someone had been in the house the evening before. A light was on over the kitchen sink where there were dishes soaking, and an empty bottle of wine sat on the counter. In the master bedroom upstairs, the bed was unmade, and clothes were piled on a chair. The rest of the house seemed orderly, a few moving boxes taped and labeled. A damp towel was hanging to dry in the pool cabana and the pool was open, dotted with leaves and other debris from nearby trees. No sign of the deceased's wife.

"It's odd, the door's unlocked and there's a security system, but it hadn't been turned on. Whoever was here last night wasn't planning on being gone long," Deputy Talon observed. "The phone's blinking with a message or messages and there's no evidence of any cell phones. Get some pictures, Cody," Deputy Talon said indicating the office below. "Forensics'll want the computers, prints." He radioed Spike.

"Can you tell when's the last time someone was there?" Spike, freshly shaved, hiked up his pants and buttoned a clean shirt, shouldering his radio. "Forensics will have to do a thorough going-over. We gotta see what's in the fridge, the trash."

"Pretty clear at least one person was here last night, I'm speculatin' it was Mr. Perrault. There's only one used wine glass on the counter, we'll take it in for testing. No sign of Mrs. Perrault. House was unlocked, so whoever was here was planning on bein' back quick, I'm thinkin'."

"Roger, Bodie. Get a picture of every nook and cranny. I'll be there straightaway and forensics team's on the way."

Running on little more than adrenalin, Pearl's coffee and a batch of hastily ingested scrambled eggs, Sheriff Stryker left the forensic team inside the Perraults' various dwellings to finish and cruised up the right-of-way. He wanted to get the lay of the land and see what any of the next-to-non-existent neighbors might know or have seen.

Beth Perrault was not at her townhouse in the city, that much was now known, and alerts were out for her car, a cobalt blue Mercedes E class as well as Daniel's red pickup truck, also missing. Airports and train stations were on alert. Media from as far away as the city started calling in, including a reporter from the French TF1, as Daniel's father, François Perrault, was a well-known entrepreneur in southwest France and beyond. All Spike could tell them was the investigation was in full swing and ongoing, that no one would rest in his department until whoever who was responsible for Daniel Perrault's death was apprehended, that Mrs. Perrault will be tracked down quickly, that FBI's assistance might be requested.

He'd had the unpleasant task of calling Daniel's parents in Périgord, asking Monique, a local caterer from France, to be on the line with him to translate. They would fly in immediately and no, they hadn't heard anything from Beth. Spike would never forget the anguished howl Madame Perrault emitted before apparently collapsing onto the closest chair.

The right-of-way ended at the base of Madison Ridge and the only neighbor Spike knew of beyond the Perrault property was Thorne Tate, an old acquaintance, a farmer and volunteer fire fighter. He'd seen Thorne recently when the old Regan house burned to the ground after a lightning strike, luckily when no one was home. Locals really pulled together on that one, finding the family temporary shelter and raising money so they could rebuild. That's what he loved about the place; every local knew every other local, and their business, for that matter. Neighbor helped neighbor, there weren't many secrets. It's why this possible homicide was so puzzling. Who was so angry at Daniel Perrault that he was murdered that way? That usually meant sex or money in every investigation he'd ever read about. Someone must know where this came from, it wasn't out of the blue. And Judd could be right, remorse after an act of passion.

Of course, just because everyone knew everyone's business didn't mean they'd share it with cops. Spike knew from experience getting into people's homes and getting them to talk was sometimes like getting a cat to swallow a pill, near impossible. He thought of Hester whose panicked call had sent Spike to her and Otis's little domestic dust-up — *Jesus was that just a few hours ago?* — but it led to nothing more than them hanging their heads and apologizing for calling.

With this case, he'd have to use all his skills, together with a big dose of patience, to wring information from people. He wanted the story and he intended to get it. No stone would be left unturned.

He knew Thorne as a decent man, hard-working, and an upstanding member of the community. He'd been farming, mostly beef cattle, all his life, and owned the whole parcel from the Perraults' to the ridge line. After a little sleuthing, Deputy Jenks found out Thorne had helped Perrault get his farming operation set up. Thorne was a known drinker, his wife left him years ago, and his son moved away to take a job in another state, apparently not interested in continuing the family farm.

It was well into mid-morning, after Spike had fielded phone calls and brought the department up to date on the situation, when he found Thorne sitting on a rocker on his front porch with a mug of black coffee.

"Get you some, Sheriff?"

"No, thanks. Got enough in me to keep me awake through the day."

Thorne Tate was a big, powerful man with close-cropped, gray hair and a neatly trimmed goatee and moustache, a ruddy complexion (no doubt from the demands of farming in all types of weather), and a large, bulbous nose. In years past, Spike remembered how tobacco-stained both his fingers and moustache had been but knew Thorne had quit smoking, and he didn't appear to have started back up.

"Have a seat." Thorne indicated a straight-backed chair Spike pulled closer to Thorne and sat on with a grimace. *Worst kind of chair for comfort.*

"'Course you know why I'm stopping by, Thorne."

He nodded. "Can't believe this about Daniel and it's real upsettin' about Beth. Saw the ruckus over their place from my barn and drove down to find out what was going on. Your deputy didn't want to tell me much other than it was a possible crime scene." He took a swig from his coffee mug. "Rodney from the Rescue Squad called to ask what I knew, and told me about Daniel's body on the side of our main road and that Beth hadn't been found yet. Couldn't believe it. Jesus." He set his mug on the porch railing with a grunt. "Any leads on Beth?"

"Not yet." Spike noted Thorne seemed more concerned about Beth than what had happened to Daniel. "When's the last time you saw Daniel or Beth Perrault?"

"Haven't seen Daniel in a month of Sundays." Thorne started rocking and looked out towards his fields. "Last time was sometime midsummer, maybe. He left most of the farming and farm chores to Garret and his brother. You talk to them?"

"Not yet. What about his wife?"

"Today's, what, Tuesday? I think it was a Sunday, no a Saturday a coupla weeks ago 'cause I had to go help Liam with one of his cows Sunday. Saturday, she walked here, up the road, and gave me some of her photos to keep including a nicely framed photo — big one, blown up — of one of my cow pastures in the snow, the cows lookin' like little splotches of black ink. Nice of her, I thought. She'd gotten into photography since she'd been out here. Told me how much she loved the countryside since she'd been here, laughed about once thinkin' she'd always be a city girl. She looked happy, happier anyway. I hadn't seen her in quite a while, not since spring, as I recall, when she drove right by me on the right-of-way like a bat outta hell without waving, looking like one sad sack, very upset. Don't know where she was coming from or why she looked so distracted, but I didn't see much of her the rest of the summer. 'Course I knew the restaurant was gonna close, maybe permanently, and figured she was troubled about it. I'd heard the property was on the market; she told me when she stopped by it'd already sold.

"Anyway, she came up here with the pictures, a nice surprise, and we sat and talked awhile. She was sorry about having to sell and move away, said the new owners of the property sounded nice and would surely stop up to introduce themselves soon's everything was final. She promised to keep in touch with me too. She left and gave me a hug and kiss on the cheek. Last I saw her." Thorne sighed. "Damn, I'll miss her. Him too, I guess."

"She mention her husband?"

"Not that I recall, said she was organizing everything for the move, back and forth to the city place quite a bit. She thought she might sell it too, but decided she'd hang onto it for the time being. Told her I'd help her if she needed anything. She just nodded and gave me one of her beautiful smiles saying 'thanks'."

"Notice anything after that? Lights on at odd hours, new or strange vehicles?"

"No. I can't see the house 'cept from my barn which is up the hill a bit. Can't even see it from the right-of-way. You may have noted that comin' up here."

Spike tapped his pen on his knee in irritation. "Nothing at all?"

"Well, I did see her pull her car out last Saturday — that blue car — when I was movin' some hay around in the barn. It was early, guess about ten o'clock or so."

"Did you see her come back?"

"No, like I said, I only glimpse the house from the barn and I wasn't out there very long, maybe thirty minutes."

"Tell me about your relationship with this couple. It's known you helped Mr. Perrault with his farming, advised him. What else? You've been neighbors for three years, did you socialize?"

Thorne reached for his mug, drained the rest of the coffee and set the mug back on the porch railing. Spike shifted awkwardly in the hard chair and waited for Thorne to start talking. *Sometimes these folks are so damned tight-lipped but I gotta be patient, hard as it is. Swiggert oughtta be doin' this interview with his bony ass in this chair.*

"Beth was a good person, heart of gold, brought me soup once when I was sick, first winter they were in the house, I think. Nicest person you'd ever want to meet. Daniel was interesting, smart as anything, engaging even. But stuff happened with him and I pretty much cut ties with him six months or so ago."

"What stuff happened, Thorne?"

"I met them both soon after they bought the property. They walked up here to introduce themselves, handsome couple, and told me about some of their plans for the house and the old Flanagan property, plus the idea for the restaurant in Nickel. Sometime late that first summer, I think, Daniel drove up here in a brand-new pickup. Sat right where you are now. He was complaining about the builder, Marcus McGrath — you know him, he's still around. Daniel was upset at how long it was taking him to get going, at the slow pace of the permitting process. Told me Marcus came out from the city every day. I remember lookin' at Daniel and asking why the hell he didn't use one of the local contractors."

· · ·

"Because most of them can barely add, Thorne! You think I want one of those guys in charge? I'd have to follow him around like a kindergarten teacher, manage the subcontractors myself. *Non et non.* I know Marcus's work and he's as good as I've seen."

"Then get him to move his business out here, for Christ's sake, at least for now. You've got enough work, sounds like, to keep him busy for years with your big ideas for this little ol' county. You might get a few nasty looks from some of the locals, but I guess that's a price you don't mind payin'."

"Superb idea, Thorne! I'll press Marcus a bit more, dangle the idea I'm going with another contractor and then offer the idea about moving here. I know he wants my work. He'd be dumber than I thought not to grab at a partnership with me when I tell him about my long-range plans. If nothing else, he'll do it for Beth. I think he's a little in love with her, actually."

• • •

"You'll want to talk to Marcus, Spike. They had a vicious relationship at the end. Marcus near to killed him right out on the road there."

"Was there anything between Marcus and Mrs. Perrault in your opinion?"

"Hard to say, but I don't think so. They were close friends; Beth talked about him often, worked with him on designs, paint colors, especially for her office and over at the restaurant. Daniel had a temper and sometimes worked himself up into a jealous state of mind, but he imagined a lot of things that never happened or made stuff up. She was head over heels for Daniel. I don't see her two-timin' him. He's a whole 'nother kettle of fish, however."

"What do you mean?"

"Just stuff I've heard, don't know anything specific."

"Go on."

"Well, he was pretty darn itchy to do something, bored once he'd bought the property and the Nickel site while waiting for work to begin. We chatted some. He liked to come up and ask me questions."

"About?"

"Mostly what to do with his acreage. Told him I'd help him if he decided to buy cattle. He was frustrated, had a high energy level and nowhere to direct it in the beginning."

• • •

"People who need to make decisions go at a snail's pace here, Thorne," Daniel complained. "No wonder Wayne County is a wasteland, stymied by bird brains, worse than the *imbéciles* in France! Nothing moves forward, and Marcus isn't helping my frame of mind with his excuses."

Thorne's offer to teach Daniel the ins and outs of raising cattle sparked Daniel's interest in farming and the farmers in Wayne County. He was in the middle of farmland, after all, so he may as well learn something about it. If he made some decent contacts, some of the farms might be important suppliers for his restaurant later on. He approached the issue with zest, tearing around his property in his pickup, assessing every corner, bouncing around to various farms to observe or ask questions. He studied the fence lines that already existed on his property and read up on how to repair and install new ones.

By early autumn, he had all the equipment he needed to start work, with the added muscle power of two brothers who lived just off the main highway on the right-of-way, Garret and Quinn. He loved the work more than he thought he would, and came out every weekend, sometimes even during the week for several days, staying at the inn. He got enough posts into the ground before the soil got too hard that he could envision the contours of his pastures.

The first sign of trouble came when Thorne noticed a new fence line infringing a couple of yards onto his property. He confronted Daniel the next day, driving his tractor right up next to where Daniel had parked his pickup truck to string wire.

"Don't you know where your property line is?"

"I have a general idea. Is there a problem?"

"Darn right, there's a problem. You're on my land with this."

"But you're not keeping anything here, it's just grass. The fence is following the slope of the land so it's sturdy and in an undulating line that looks good, beautiful even, like a wave breaking, don't you think?"

"It's my hay field. This is where I do my haying."

"Looks like there's plenty of room to do this haying. Do you have to nitpick about a few inches of property? In Europe, we don't worry so much about this kind of thing."

"Well, this isn't your goddam, socialist France here, mister. This is my property and I don't want your fencing on it. I would appreciate it if you would move it onto your land. Or I'll have to call in some-one who will." With that, Thorne revved up his tractor and pulled away, leaving Daniel in a cloud of dust and diesel fumes.

Daniel didn't understand why Thorne would be so upset about a little strip of scruffy land, but by the end of that week, he had the brothers come and move the fence onto his own land. He didn't want to lose Thorne's good will since he needed his advice on cattle. In spite of his annoyance at Daniel's carelessness — really a self-ish disregard for property lines — Thorne liked him and wanted him to succeed. Daniel was close to the same age as his son, and he harbored a genuine affection for him, a fatherly feeling of devotion that surprised him.

• • •

"Didn't see much of him after that — they weren't living at the place yet — until sometime after Christmas. He burned up the road late one afternoon after dark and banged on my door. He was carrying on about how little got done around here, how he was a hustler and didn't have time to sit on his arse, wanted to go out right then and there and buy cattle. I had to calm him down and promise to take him to look over some cattle the next morning."

• • •

Thorne cautioned Daniel about what he was taking on.

"You don't want to farm. You want to do this as a hobby, I'm guessin', so how are you going to operate? You can't just throw a bunch of cows together. You gotta plan, know what you're doin'."

"That's why I came to you, Thorne, and you're right, I don't want to farm! I want to look at them, maybe make some money. I'm going to hire Garret and his brother to take care of everything. I want to be what you call in this country a 'gentleman farmer' — that's the expression, isn't it?"

Thorne gave a curt nod. "There's still stuff you have to think about and prepare for, you know. What about water and adequate hay through the winter? You haven't completed your fencing either, I see. There're large gaps along your back pastures. And calving? I don't know if those boys have ever done that kind of work."

"They'll have to learn, won't they? Once I offer them more money than they'd make in a year anywhere else, they'll be falling over each other to work for me."

"Well, I'm fine giving you advice if you want it," Thorne muttered, "but I'd do better by you to make sure you've got the name of my vet handy."

Daniel and Thorne set off early the next morning after breakfast at Farrin's, where Thorne liked to hang out with his fire-fighting buddies, for Bobby Egleston's farm, Thorne's source for his own bulls through the years. While Daniel wanted the biggest bull he saw, Thorne dissuaded him, explaining big didn't necessarily mean best.

"Most important is pedigree and health. Since you're doing this for fun, you don't want a bull that will sire large calves endangering both mother and calf. Calving problems, I've seen more of those than I care to and it's not a pretty sight."

"You mean I have to buy a small bull?"

"No, but you need to talk to Bobby about what kind of success he's had with which bulls and make sure that's what's best for the operation you want to get into."

"This is complicated! I thought you bought whatever you wanted and then off they went into the sunset."

"How 'bout if Bobby and I do this for you, son?" Thorne squinted at Daniel and gave him a wink. "We'll do good by you."

Daniel agreed that would be best and, following their advice, bought an Angus bull, naming him Grand Teton. He put an order in for a dozen cows Bobby was ready to sell, maybe a dozen more for the spring.

"Can one bull really handle all the females?" Daniel laughed.

"My friend, one bull can handle thirty or more in a season. You'll have to remove him after he runs with them awhile or they'll be calving all year. Not good."

"*Mon Dieu*, I do have much to learn. But this should be great fun to watch! We should all be as lucky as this guy!"

• • •

"Turns out he didn't learn much of anything except how to look at them. Garret and Quinn did the best they could, but Daniel let that bull run all that first part of the year with the cows, so calving went on from September all the way into the new year. He lost a bunch of calves and even a couple of cows. Very irresponsible."

"Didn't you help him at all? Or didn't he listen?" Spike asked

"Sure, I helped. But he seemed indifferent to the problem, distracted by too many other things. He did better by his animals the second year, after he saw the carnage from his recklessness. And he didn't know a thing about keeping the genetics of a herd strong. I couldn't teach him everything."

"What else? Why did you cut ties with him, like you said?"

"For starters, his fencing wasn't complete by the time he brought in more cows, so they were wandering over onto my property, into the woods where Garret, Quinn and I had to round them up 'fore they hurt themselves. And the worst was when his bull got in with my cows, broke through a part of the fencing that wasn't secured and started messing with my cows."

• • •

But Thorne nurtured a soft spot for Daniel even then, and forgave him for being a greenhorn. He admired him for trying to start something in Nickel, the restaurant and all, and didn't blame him for treating cattle farming as a spectator sport. He watched Daniel help the brothers from time to time the first spring, checking the herd and the water supply.

Before Daniel's parents came to visit the first time, Daniel plunged even deeper into livestock, buying a couple of dozen sheep and several hens. Thorne sensed Daniel needed to impress his father with his accomplishments in the U.S. With the house not yet done and the restaurant far from ready, he wanted to show something tangible, something at which he'd succeeded.

Beth invited Thorne for drinks one night before they went out to eat with Daniel's parents. It was a balmy, early spring evening, peepers just starting their mating calls and the barest blush of green brushing the fields and trees. They gathered on the front veranda of Beth's office, imbibing wine and pâté, though Thorne was a beer man. Daniel's father was exuberant, recounting his hours in the field with his son helping with the fence posts. Thorne felt out of place, a country boy with these sophisticated Europeans, Daniel's parents, François and Marie Claude. But Beth made him feel comfortable, translating and extolling Thorne's invaluable knowledge about cattle and how much he'd helped them understand the ins and outs of livestock.

Thorne, not used to wine, got a little tipsy and fawned over both Daniel and Beth, wrapping a massive arm around each and proclaiming to the elder Perraults there was no nicer pair on the planet.

"These two are God's gift to this place," he declared. "Best neighbors, best farmers and," turning to Beth, "best-looking people in all of Wayne County!" He clinked his glass with François and beamed widely, planting a light kiss on Beth's cheek.

"*Santé*!" they all responded.

• • •

"It's one of my happiest memories, to be honest, at least lately." Thorne smiled slightly at the memory. "They were so nice, so goddam good-looking, all of them. François and Daniel made fun of each other digging in fence posts, hopping around and laughing.

Beth seemed so happy. It was a downright delightful evening and I was sorry when it ended." Thorne pursed his lips and fell silent.

"What all happened after that to have you turn against him, as you've said?" Spike was anxious to wrap up the interview. He needed to get over to the builder, MMG Enterprises, then head back to the station to see what any of his deputies had found out. And where the hell was Beth Perrault?

"Everything was good for a while. He lost nearly all his hens early that summer to fox or coyotes, so I helped him install a sturdier fence, electrified, to keep 'em out. Same with the sheep, didn't know up from down until Garret convinced him to buy either a llama or a donkey to protect them. Think he lost four on one day, so he wised up."

• • •

Daniel appreciated Thorne's help with farm questions and enjoyed listening to him ramble on about country ways, the local people and their histories, at least in the beginning. Thorne would stop by, or Daniel and sometimes Beth went up to visit with him. But once Daniel became preoccupied with opening the restaurant and art studios and less involved with the farming, he started to get annoyed at the impromptu visits. Thorne would tool up on his four-wheeler, his sexed-up golf cart, "the Mule" he called it, any time of day, just to shoot the breeze.

Once, on a chilly March afternoon a few months after he and Beth had moved into the main house, Thorne knocked on the front door. Daniel and Beth had been arguing over Daniel's plan to fire Marcus. They were in Daniel's office going over costs and what remained to be done. Beth knew how unhappy Daniel was with the delays on the geothermal — he talked non-stop about it — but she thought Marcus deserved better treatment than to be summarily dismissed. Daniel lashed out, accusing her of not standing by him and even of being in love with Marcus.

"I know how he feels about you, it's all over his face when he sees you. You haven't forgotten your times with him in the city, then clucking together in your little office for hours every day last year, have you?"

"Oh, stop it! Yes, I like him, he's become a good friend and I'll be mighty sorry if you let him go before work is complete."

"I have my suspicions about you two, it's true. I always wondered how far you went together, Beth. He had ample time to seduce you either at the townhouse or here while I was out." He narrowed his eyes into slits and glowered at her.

Beth looked incredulously at Daniel.

"How can you think like that? That's insane! You need to get control of yourself because I don't like what I'm hearing." She rose to go upstairs to the kitchen and prepare dinner.

Daniel grabbed her hand, suddenly regretful. "I didn't mean any of it. I'm on edge, everything is coming to a head and I've got problems mounting with the restaurant and artists, even the store. Everyone seems to blame me for one thing or another." He put his arms around her and his lips to her ear. "Let me show you how I can love you, it's been too long." It was true, their passion showed signs of waning. She thought of her mother's long-ago cautionary opinion on love: "They don't last long, those days of wine and roses." Daniel was often preoccupied or too tired and he lurched unpredictably from one mood into another. Was this the new normal with him?

"Remember what it was like, chérie? Remember when we used to make love to Ravel's 'Bolero'? It was always perfect. It's a part of our early romance, isn't it?" Daniel grabbed his cell phone from his desk and searched for the music. The soft, opening bars of the piece filled the room, the gentle tapping on the snare drum followed by the mesmerizing, melancholy notes of the clarinet.

Beth stood with one foot on the step, puzzled and wary. Why was Daniel behaving so badly? It happened too often now. He was different even from last fall when they'd watched the first calves being born, sharing in the wonder of the bloody babies licked clean by their mamas and standing within minutes on wobbly legs to go for the teats. It was captivating, and Daniel had been as enthralled as she. But when they lost three calves and one cow during difficult births, Daniel blamed the brothers and then turned on Thorne, saying he'd given him bad advice. Though things simmered down after a while, Daniel's mood was often testy and irritable. Between Marcus and the problems getting his other projects finished, his frame of mind was decidedly darker than during their first year in Scarcity when he felt the world was his oyster.

"Beth, I'm sorry, I swear I didn't mean it. You have to understand what I'm saying about Marcus and his work, though. You must agree with me on this. Let's forget it for now, please."

The music always sent chills up her spine and it was hard for her to resist Daniel when he was at his most remorseful. They'd made love to "Bolero" many times. It was the perfect piece for it, gentle foreplay as the music drifted like an airy arabesque for several dreamy minutes, then moving at a crescendo to the final orgasmic crash of the finale. She let Daniel lead her to the couch, his lips skipping across her face like a dancer on ice. Afterwards, clothes strewn across the floor and their bodies sticky with sweat, they heard a knock at the door.

"Ignore it. It's Thorne. I knew I heard the Mule on the gravel drive," Daniel whispered. They lay still, throbbing in post-coital bliss, until Thorne peered in the sliding glass doors from the Zen garden. Beth shrieked, and Thorne backed away, then turned and rushed up the stone garden steps as fast as his 240 pounds would allow.

• • •

"I was going to tell Daniel I'd seen coyotes sniffing around his hen house again, and it looked like they'd done some digging. Believe me I felt stupid, looking in on them like that. I knew what they'd been up to." Thorne blushed as he relived the embarrassing scene in his mind.

"What else can you tell me, Thorne?" Spike asked. "Sounds like you were still friends at that point."

"We were, but like I said, he started to lose interest in the farming that summer, even as he came to understand the basics of livestock better. He gradually turned all the work and upkeep over to the brothers, which was fine. I knew he was getting more involved in opening the restaurant and art studios, so I let him be. He didn't come around as much as he used to and I sorta stopped going by as much. Seemed less welcoming. I tried to ignore it."

• • •

Thorne was surprised when Beth told him Daniel was going to fire Marcus. Sure, it was taking awhile to wrap things up, but the spread was beautiful. Each room on every level was unique. Beth had given him a tour when they moved in and his favorite was a guest room over the library, sponge painted in a light forest green over pale yellow, so it felt like you were sleeping in the woods.

Beth remained friendly with Thorne even as she got busy helping Daniel with the design and decorating of the restaurant. Opening the restaurant, despite the problems in the beginning, was an elixir for her. The pride in having her taste admired by her city acquaintances when they came out to see the restaurant was gratifying, and when *La Bonne Cuisine* magazine did a spread on the dining room and kitchen, she and Daniel felt all the hard work had finally paid off.

She brought Thorne eggs nearly every week in the summer — he'd never been interested in raising chickens. Sometimes she'd stay and have coffee with him. Thorne thought during the summer after Marcus was fired and the restaurant opened, she seemed less happy, confiding one day that Daniel was making a mess of things and taking it out on her. She tried to help, but disliked his hostile attitude and drew away from him, tending more to the house and garden. She admitted she was lonely, though she had made a few friends and still had consulting work to keep her busy on a daily basis. But she missed the old Daniel, she said, the charming and buoyant personality she'd fallen in love with.

"She hinted in more ways than one to me she wanted a child and Daniel didn't. She didn't dwell on it, but she definitely wasn't the perky, upbeat woman I'd first met." Thorne paused and took a deep breath before continuing. "Well, I might as well finish the story. I guess it was sometime around Christmas last year, I'm seeing all these tire ruts in one of my fields. We'd had a lot of slushy snow and the ground was downright spongy. I decided to walk around and see where they'd come from and where they went, prepared to file a report for illegal hunting on my property."

• • •

Thorne followed the trail of red clay furrows up towards his back woods where he saw Daniel's pickup parked just inside the woods. Furious at his continuing lack of respect for private property, he marched at a rapid pace to get to the driver's side window to see if he was in there and what he was doing. When he got close, quite out of breath, the windows were steamed up and he couldn't see inside. He banged on the driver's side window, cupped his hand to the glass and to his shock saw Daniel's head shoot up as well as a second head, female, appear. Daniel started the engine, backed up at light speed and tore off, leaving Thorne standing sickened and distressed. He didn't know whether to get in his own truck and run him down or confront him later. He knew he didn't want Beth to hear anything from him.

But the last straw for Thorne came when he went to the restaurant to present Daniel with the bill for the damage to his pasture.

• • •

"That son of a bitch thumbed his nose at me, told me I was mistaken, that he'd never been there, that I was nuts. I told him I wanted a check then and there to repair my field or I would tell Beth. 'Course I never would've done that since I liked her too much. But that worked. He paid me, then told me to get out of his restaurant and not to come by anymore." Thorne's voice caught, and Spike could tell he was a little choked up. "Still, I was sorry he had to shut that restaurant down. A real failure as it turned out, for him and Beth."

"Why didn't you tell me this in the first place, Thorne? Who was the girl?" Spike had a feeling maybe this whole thing had to do with her.

"Didn't get a good look, no idea."

"Jesus H. Christ." Spike shook his head and blew an exasperated breath out the side of his mouth.

"It sure pissed me off, though. My daughter had a no-good husband, too, who mistreated her."

"Thorne, I thought you only had a son?"

"She died. Of leukemia. When she was around Beth's age."

Spike stood. "God, I'm awful sorry. Sorry to have to put you through this, but we got to find out what happened to him."

"I know, Sheriff. I did treat Daniel like my own son. That's why his behavior hurt me so. And I'm sorry about him. And Beth..." Thorne couldn't finish the sentence and turned to look away from Spike.

CHAPTER FIVE

SPIKE THOUGHT LONG and hard about the picture Thorne and Marcus painted of Daniel as he drove back to the station from MMG Enterprises. He hadn't ruled them out as suspects, but the altercations were so far back in time, it would be odd they would ignite a murderous act now, he felt. Unless something else had occurred lately, which was, of course, possible. But this Daniel fellow was hard to figure. He had every imaginable good quality — smarts, vision, energy, charm — yet he seemed to turn spiteful, hostile even, towards those who wanted to help him. A real Jekyll and Hyde. Did it start when he came here? Or was it always with him? Both Thorne and Marcus saw the worst side of him, mean-spirited behavior he apparently couldn't control. Who did that push far enough to kill him? Could it have pushed either of those two men?

He'd stop to see if Rudy or Bodie was still working and had anything to report, then go home for a good night's sleep. Tomorrow would be hellish; media types would be calling again with their questions about progress on the case, wondering why Sheriff Stryker had no leads yet, or motive. And then, of course, there was the question of Beth and the missing vehicles.

The department was surprisingly quiet this late in the day, and for that Spike was grateful. He was too dead tired to write up his report on the interviews with Marcus and Thorne, and handed his notes to the deputy on duty to lock in his desk drawer. He'd have Rudy or Mabel decipher it in the morning and write it up later for the Daniel Perrault file.

Bodie had gone home, exhausted, but had left an abbreviated medical examiner's report with Rudy to give to Spike.

"Assume no news yet of deceased's wife?" Spike took the report and flipped through it. He didn't have the stomach just yet to read the details.

"No, but forensics has the computer found in the house and are searching it. They're also analyzing the flip-flop and the rest of the items, like that tied-up lock of hair, found with the body. No weapon has been found yet. The landline had two recent calls, one from a local number on Monday at 7:19 p.m., lasted forty-eight seconds, the other a voice message on Saturday at 10:16 a.m. from Maine. We're checking on deleted messages."

"And?"

Rudy checked his notepad for the details. "The local number was from a Wilford Shanahan listing on Grindstone Mountain Road. I was going to go over tomorrow soon's I got the okay from you to see who those folks might be, with Mabel or Deputy Crawford, as back-up if you'd let me. The other was for Mrs. Perrault, female, said to call her."

"Cell phones?"

"None at the residence and no apparent ability to trace locations."

"Gotta be turned off, maybe even battery removed. Killer may have done it to Perrault's phone, but what about Mrs. Perrault? Why doesn't she want to be found?" Sheriff Stryker grumbled. "This is a real puzzler."

"Tried calling the Maine number but no answer. Didn't want to leave a message, asked the local police up there to go by and check out the house. Registered to a Sophia Lambert, possibly Beth Perrault's mother. Should hear back from them any minute on that."

"Excellent work. And I appreciate you wantin' to go up to the Shanahan place, but I'll want Cody or Deputy Swiggert to go, Bodie probably as back-up. You're just a little bit green to lead an interview just yet." Rudy frowned but nodded agreement. He felt he should get more experience on his own and was disappointed but understood even a small sheriff's department had its rules and regulations.

"What about the mailbox folks who lived up the road from where we found Mr. Perrault, Marconi's right-of-way, anybody know anything, or know him?"

"Bodie and I talked to them all and no one knew anything about him or could figure why he'd be left there. Everyone was pretty shocked about it. Everything seemed legit."

"By the way, anyone talk to Deputy Swiggert this afternoon?"

Rudy shook his head. "Not that I know of."

"Goddam, biggest thing that's ever happened around here and he's in bed drinkin' tea!" Spike knew Ronnie's father from working with him in another jurisdiction before moving to Wayne County and running for sheriff. He'd promised to nurture the boy, plucked him out of boot camp, brought him into the department and taught him all he knew. Ronnie was a quick learner and showed promise when it came to investigations. And a murder! This would test *all* their skills.

"Well, leave a note for whoever gets in first thing to check on him. I got more people to talk to tomorrow than I got fingers and toes, and I could sure use another deputy."

Rudy winced but nodded his understanding. *Why couldn't he be more involved? A murder investigation!*

Spike suddenly felt extremely spent. He'd only had a couple hours of sleep in the past thirty-six hours and his middle-aged body was drained. But also, the enormity of his responsibility — to Daniel's parents, the community, the press, and to his force — felt like a punch in the gut right now. He had two daughters himself, one a physical therapist in Bristow, the other in Florida training to be a pilot. He was so proud of them, he and Pearl. Whoever or whatever Daniel was, he owed it to everyone, especially his parents and his widow, to respect his legacy and bring closure by being relentless in his search for the truth.

Pearl had dinner waiting — her signature pot roast that made the whole house smell so good. She had washed and ironed his shirts so he'd have a fresh uniform to put on tomorrow. She knew the gravity of what was at stake and wanted to ease the edges for him. Spike shoveled in his food gratefully and downed a beer — pot belly be damned — then tumbled into bed right after, having barely uttered a word to his wife about the investigation.

He was up at first light with a cup of coffee and the medical examiner's written summary. Cause of death was an acute subdural hematoma. Death would have occurred within minutes without medical attention. Bruising and lacerations to the face and eye suggested the deceased had been hit, possibly twice, with a male fist, DNA testing requested. Chances were good the attacker was left-handed. Impact apparently caused the deceased to fall backwards, hitting his head on a hard object, indications being a rock, due to dirt and residue in the wound and the shape of the affected area. Significant alcohol was present in deceased's system, no drugs. Left foot scraped on left side and missing other shoe. Some post mortem bruising and lineaments of blood on the back of the neck suggested the possibility of an attempt to stem the bleeding. *Judd was right about that*, Spike thought. He skimmed over some of the more technical details until one item caught his eye: The victim had reddish, purple bruises on each of his inner thighs, ascertained to be fresh erythemas; in other words, the medical examiner wrote, hickeys. He read further, "deceased appeared to have had intercourse one to two hours prior to death as evident from penile swabs taken from the body."

Spike dropped the report like a hot potato and leaned back in his kitchen chair, reddening and emitting a whoop of surprise.

Pearl, who'd had her head in the refrigerator retrieving eggs and a packet of bacon, turned and retied the sash of her robe.

"What?"

"Well, I'll be goddamned," he muttered.

"What? What's it say, Spike?"

"This stays inside this room. Mr. Perrault, we know, was not killed in his home but somewhere else, that's a fact. It seems from this report here that he might — and I emphasize *might* — have been with someone who was not his wife on the night he was killed."

"What'd they find?"

"Let's just say it's pretty clear he was active sexually close to time of death and that could be mighty important news."

"How'd they know?"

"Pearl, honey, there are ways of detectin' these things. The medical examiner wrote it right here in black and white." Spike's thoughts were spinning. Daniel Perrault was killed sometime between 11 p.m. and midnight at an unknown location. He apparently had intercourse around 10 p.m. or so. That'd be Monday night. Beth Perrault has not been seen by anyone in the county, as far as he knew, since Saturday morning when Thorne saw her leave in her car. Thorne seemed to think Daniel was with a female in his pickup truck as long ago as last Christmas. Could he be involved with someone not his wife? This put a whole new light on the case, could blow the investigation wide open!

Sherriff Stryker dropped the report into his range bag and zipped it closed, then rushed in to shower and dress while Pearl fried up two eggs and three strips of bacon for his breakfast, though he protested he ought to start having granola and get his waistline down.

Once he'd left the room, Pearl listened for the sound of the shower at the kitchen door, then fished out the report and flipped through the few pages to read with shock the concluding paragraphs. Something she'd heard a couple of weeks ago from a woman she didn't know at the annual Rescue Squad fundraiser had her mind combing for a scrap of that conversation. They'd chatted briefly when Pearl brought her potato salad into the Squad kitchen for the pot-luck dinner. Pearl had rolled her eyes at a skimpy outfit one of the teenage volunteer helpers was wearing. The woman caught her eye and gave a little shake of her head, pursing her lips in disapproval. She'd said something about teenage morals these days. And then she'd said in passing, almost under her breath, "...reminds me of (so-and-so), who's crying to my daughter the French guy can't go to their little love nest anymore."

What was the name she said? Don't suppose it will help much if I can't remember the name, Pearl thought. She decided she might ask around a bit herself before mentioning it to Spike. He'd find Pearl's input idle gossip, nothing he could follow up on, unless she could put a name to it. And, of course, Mr. Perrault might not be the only Frenchman here in the county, though she didn't know of any. Still, if she could supply a name, that would really help Spike going forward, wouldn't it? She put the report back and settled on calling Ann Teitjen who was on the Rescue Squad, and pick her brain about the woman at the fundraiser and who she might have been talking about.

As soon as Spike got to the station, one of the deputies informed him Mrs. Perrault's car had been located. "We just got a call it's parked at the house in Maine where the phone message came from. Police up there are investigating."

"Son of a gun. She high-tailed it up there awful quick, didn't she? And?" Spike noted it was unlikely Mrs. Perrault was Daniel's sexual partner on his last night alive unless her car had wings.

"There was no answer at the door, but they've left a phone

message they need to talk with her. They're waiting now on a warrant to get inside. The owner's car is missing — we assume it's her mother's — so they're thinking it's possible she might not be there at all. They've got patrol officers on the lookout for the other car."

Spike was on the line to the chief of police in the town where Beth Perrault's car was found before the deputy had even finished talking.

"Put me through to your chief of police. This is Sheriff Stryker from Wayne County." He waited impatiently, drumming his fingers and casting an agitated scowl around the room. He caught sight of John Winowsky, editor of the local paper, coming through the front door and motioned with his eyes for the deputy to deal with him. He covered the receiver and whispered, "Give him the 'we're working night and day and will get to the bottom of this.'"

"Yeah, Chief Branly, Sheriff Stryker concerning a person we want to interview about a homicide here in Wayne County. Yeah, that's right, Beth Perrault. I'm gonna need your help handling this situation with Mrs. Perrault. First, I want your officers to wait at the house until she returns, which she will. Second, I'm going to need her accompanied to Wayne County to be interviewed in the earliest possible time frame." Spike nodded and made a few grunts before ringing off, saying he appreciated the help and to keep him posted on any developments.

When the rest of the deputies got in, he brought them up to date. "Seems like things are starting to move along at a good clip. We know where Mrs. Perrault is, and we'll be able to get her story soon. Plus, it's possible, and I mean *possible*, Daniel Perrault was with someone not his wife on the night he died. Might be motivation, I don't know, but we need to find out if that's the case."

He dispatched two deputies to track down any employee of the now-closed restaurant and interview them: wait-staff, bartenders, kitchen staff. "Find out anything they may know about Mr. Perrault's activities over the last few months, and I do mean anything."

Spike slapped the medical examiner report on his desk. "All right, Cody. I would've like Ronnie in on this but apparently he can't drag himself outta bed to get in here. I need you to read over this report so's you know what's what, then go speak with the Shanahans and find out why someone from their house would be calling the Perraults."

Spike navigated his vehicle slowly and carefully onto the Waterloo Road right-of-way, and crept along to avoid kicking up too much dust. He hated driving on gravel roads. He gingerly pulled into the circular driveway in front of Turkey Hill Farm, owned by Bernard Melchoir, former chef at Mr. Perrault's restaurant, and his father, both known to law enforcement for a number of reasons.

The day was chilly. A cold front had moved in overnight, and frost sparkled on the grass and glazed the windshield of a parked, black Audi. Spike popped a stick of gum in his mouth and checked his watch: 8:22 a.m. Deputy Swiggert had responded to an ugly altercation between Daniel Perrault and his chef last spring, after another one the Christmas before. Melchoir was fired soon after that, he knew, and apparently the restaurant limped along without a regular chef until closing about a month ago.

The old clapboard farmhouse had clearly seen better days: front porch sagging in the middle (due, no doubt, to the wooden floorboards rotting away), peeling paint, landscaping run riot. Turkey Hill had once been a thriving nursery and orchard with greenhouses full of plants, vegetables for sale, and acres of fruit trees, but nothing had been tended for a couple of years and Mother Nature had taken over. The whole farm was nothing but wild and uncontrolled growth. *A shame,* Spike thought, shaking his head as he exited his cruiser and surveyed the property.

The house was painted in whimsical colors, a bright saffron yellow, the trim and gutters in a coral red with cloud-like puffs of white. There were all kinds of things hanging from nearby trees, bird feeders and wind chimes, and pinwheels stuck in the grass here and there made a whirring sound as they spun in the morning's occasional gusts. Views of the mountains Spike could glimpse through the trees were spectacular. The old timers really knew how to choose a homestead site. He mounted the steps and rapped loudly at the front door.

From within, Spike heard the loud thumping of someone with heavy boots rapidly descending a staircase, then a clatter of stumbling and cursing.

Melchoir opened the door slightly, and frowned. He was tall and wiry with a boyish face and a shock of improbably white hair worn long over the collar. Dressed in a plaid flannel shirt, jeans and work boots, he could almost pass as normal — which Spike knew he was not.

"Saw your vehicle pull in from upstairs. I had nothing to do with Daniel's death. And I have nothing to say about it."

"Whoa there, son. I'm sure you want us to find out who might responsible for Mr. Perrault's death. And I'm also sure you can help enlighten me a little on who might have been angry enough at him to be capable of this. So, I want to come in and ask you a few questions. You're already on probation with a suspended sentence for a felony, aren't you? So it's probably in your interest to cooperate with me, or I might find some reason to arrest you for 'contempt of cop.' Now I'd like to come in." Spike unzipped his jacket and put a thumb around a pair of handcuffs hanging from his belt.

Bernard Melchoir grimaced but opened the door to allow Sheriff Stryker to enter. The state police had raided the house earlier in the summer with a warrant for his father's arrest for passing bad checks and fraud, but he'd already fled and was still a fugitive. Authorities had been unable to locate him. Bernard claimed at his probation hearing he didn't know where his father was and hadn't seen him in months, which everyone assumed was a lie. Sheriff Stryker knew about both father and son through the courts.

The inside of the house was crammed full of stuff, but was more orderly than Spike anticipated, judging from the outside. The walls were painted in bold colors, yellows and oranges, and artworks and sculpture, some exotic looking, were scattered about. Shelves were laden with books, and the rooms were furnished with a hodgepodge of furniture styles: early American, Shaker, Caribbean. Bernard led Spike into the kitchen, and indicated a chair beside a small, wood-burning stove. Large, double French doors opened in warmer months onto a west-facing deck with an uninterrupted view of the whole mountain range in the distance, seemingly close enough to touch. A few pearly clouds hovered beyond.

"I'll just get a little fire going in here. I don't have central heat and it's a bit chilly in here this morning." Bernard collected a couple of small logs and sticks of kindling, some newspaper from a copper bin in another corner of the kitchen and put the lot into the stove. He set a match to it, and in no time a small fire crackled. "Get you anything, Sheriff?"

"No, thanks. Let's just get right to it, Bernard." Sheriff Stryker peeled off his jacket and sat, appreciating the cushion and pillow on the chair. Bernard remained standing and leaned against the kitchen counter. He wanted a smoke desperately, but settled for asking Spike for a stick of his gum.

"As Mr. Perrault's chef at the restaurant, you spent plenty of time with him."

"Yes, Restaurant Perigeaux. Daniel named it after the region he was from."

"Can you tell me where you were, Monday into Tuesday around midnight?"

"Oh, come on, Sheriff. You can't possibly think I had anything to do with this! In some ways, I loved Daniel. He's, or I guess *was*, a lot like me: fiery, impatient, driven. I liked that about him. I had no reason to go out and kill the guy. I learned from him, he paid me well. I admit we had our differences. I'm sorry it ended in scorched earth for both of us, but I haven't seen him in months. Wouldn't know his whereabouts if I wanted to."

"So, where were you again, around that time?"

"Right here. I'd sell this place and move if I could. I want to go back to Quebec. You, of all people, know I can't until my probation period is over. I went shopping for food and spent the evening reading, went to bed early. I heard the news from Fleur, an artist who rented studio space from Daniel. She called to tell me yesterday afternoon. She could barely get the words out, she was so broken up about it. She's a little ditzy anyway."

"Okay, let's move on. He fired you for your, can I say, bizarre behavior? He had trouble finding a permanent chef after you, and eventually closed because of that, I understand."

"It wasn't my fault he closed! Daniel made some stupid mistakes, pissed people off. He had too many things going on at once!" Bernard started pacing the kitchen, agitated. "You know his first chef, before me, left almost right away and went back to France? Daniel's first mistake was his grand opening before *il maîtrisait la situation*, got his ducks in a row as you say."

"All right, then, let's start with that. Then I want to hear about your time as chef. I'd especially like to hear about what brought one of our deputies out there, not once but twice."

"Daniel planned to open with great fanfare on Bastille Day, this was last year. The place was nearly finished; he'd fired his original builder and had some local contractors complete the little things under his direction. Beth was very involved too at this point. They were happy and excited."

• • •

After firing Marcus, Daniel spent every day in June inspecting each nook and cranny of the restaurant right down to the fixtures in the bathrooms, which were Hansgrohe, the highest quality. The open kitchen gleamed with modernity and professionalism, and Beth's selection in dining room tables and chairs blended elegance with country rusticity perfectly. The tufted, medallion chairs in dove gray with carved oak in a smoky, lilac finish complemented the gray-lavender wall color, though Daniel fumed for a week that Marcus and Beth had picked the same color for her office, together. It worked beautifully, he finally conceded, with the billowy, snow-white curtains hanging from wooden rods at the tall windows around the room.

The refurbished oak floors exuded a rich, warm, cozy, country feel and the exposed ceiling beams with tracks of subtle, pendant lighting created a perfect balance for the eye. And the bar! Daniel designed it himself, in the same rich oak. It curved in a seductive crescent to the left as you entered the dining room, and he hired a woodworker from the city to carve floral motifs and dentils, topping it with black granite. Reviewing the whole picture from the entrance, Daniel found the entire panorama infinitely pleasing. No way this would *not* be a destination for hundreds of miles! When work was completed on the side veranda, he planned to add outdoor dining.

He pinched the sous chef from the restaurant in Scarcity — Gerald Labossier, a former café owner from Bordeaux who knew the cooking Daniel was after — from the Dordogne region, his beloved Périgord! They were working on the menu together; Gerald had many contacts in the region who could supply the ducks and geese for dishes that would dominate the menu. Daniel insisted any fowl be fed the same diet as those in Dordogne and he visited the farms from which Gerald sought supplies to verify. He began buying wines from the Dordogne and the Bordeaux regions using his connections with wine merchants in the city.

As he stood admiring his — *his*! — Restaurant Perigeaux, he felt a tap on his shoulder. He turned to see with displeasure Sally

Higgins-Jones, the British woman with whom he contracted to organize the art studios, round up the artists and manage that part of the enterprise. She was an older woman and had the yellowed, crooked British teeth he found so off-putting. Was it all the tea they drank? But she was a savvy businesswoman and he needed her relationships with the many artists in the area. Plus, she was keen on the idea of connecting the restaurant with the artist studios, and had signed a five-year lease with Daniel to rent studios to artists, take her cut from the rent earned, and pay Daniel his share. It was a perfect arrangement, as Daniel wanted to concentrate on the restaurant but needed the cachet of an artists' atelier.

"Sorry to disturb, but I've got a group of potters thinking of coming in who really would love it if you could put a kiln into one of the studios. It would diversify the offerings, Daniel. Painting and photography are one thing, but having pottery going on would really round things out, I should say."

"What is this, a kiln?"

"It's where you fire a clay pot. I know it's quite expensive, but clearly it would be worth it. It would add another dimension to the whole enterprise. Nothing like this exists in the county."

"Ah, *un four*, I understand. This is quite a large thing, isn't it? It would take up an entire studio we could charge an artist rent for, *non?*"

"Yes, it would, but we still have four studios unrented as I speak, and this might fill them by the time the restaurant opens. I think it would be quite brilliant on our part. We could rent time to outside potters for its use. I really don't think we would lose any substantive money on this."

"All right, as long as you get me a good price, and charge a good price for its use. Why wouldn't the potters who rent space pay for its use too?"

"I'll work on this, thank you, Daniel. This is going to be so wonderful for the artists in the region. Many of them are my dear friends, and I know just how pleased they are this is happening."

"Yes, well, Sally, I've got much to do so..."

"Of course. I'll be in touch, luv."

Daniel pivoted back to admiring the artistry of the bar and the shelves displaying his selections of liquor — all the highest grades

— illuminated by under-counter lighting. He'd ordered a top-of-the-line, French espresso machine, stipulating that it have a pressed-tin façade for the look he wanted. For dishes and platters, he scoured the internet for the colors he wanted and settled on a fanciful array of rustic lines from both Alsace and the Dordogne, to be offset by the finest Parisian crystal and cutlery. He liked the contrast, and thought the dichotomy would work very well on the tables. The opening fête would be phenomenal!

Bastille Day dawned hot and dry. Daniel left his parents, who had flown in a few days earlier, for Beth to entertain, while his friends, who had come in from Périgord, slept off their jet lag at the local inn. Beth's mother had broken her leg sky diving and couldn't make the trip, and her father had died in a car crash when she was a child. Daniel wasn't too sorry his mother-in-law wouldn't be there, as his relationship with her, a stony New Englander who distrusted him, was frosty at best. She once told Beth handsome men — especially Frenchmen — always stray, and tried to make her think twice about marrying him. Even at their wedding reception, she didn't lighten her humorless demeanor, in marked contrast to Daniel's sunny family and friends.

He hurried to Restaurant Perigeaux to make sure all preparations for the grand opening that evening were in place. Gerald and the kitchen staff were already at work concocting the appetizers for the evening: house-smoked salmon on a mini corn muffin, topped with a dollop of sour cream and a sliver of black truffle, *foie gras* in a Sauterne aspic, and *escargots* in walnut butter. Dinner would be *confit de canard,* accompanied by potatoes sautéed in duck fat, and a salad. For dessert, Daniel had decided on walnuts dipped in dark chocolate, all specialties from Périgord. He'd selected the wines for the evening, reds from the Bordeaux region and whites from Alsace. The bar was spotless, surfaces gleaming in the sunshine, the bottles in their myriad colors creating a kaleidoscope of hues. While the liquor license application he submitted nearly two months ago wasn't technically approved yet, he reasoned it would be shortly, and wasn't worried about opening without it on hand. He called the Alcohol Beverage Control people frequently, urging action. He usually got the same guy with an annoying twang, a slow thinker in his opinion, Jonathan Jagger, known as Jinx. As Bastille evening approached, he lost patience in a final phone conversation with Jinx calling the whole process absurd and unreasonable, and the ABC agents a bunch of has-been law enforcement officers.

He never bothered to get what the state called a "banquet license" for Bastille Day evening, thinking it completely unnecessary. Why would adults drinking at a private party require some stupid application (and another fee, after he had spent thousands on his application so far) to be sent to the state for approval? He knew of no such cumbersome requirements or exorbitant fees in France, or anywhere in Europe for that matter. And this silly obsession over underage drinking, blah, blah, blah. From a young age, Europeans understood wines, and by extension, alcohol, and they drank in moderation, unlike immature Americans who drank themselves into a stupor as soon as they could get their hands on a fake ID.

The dining room looked glorious in the morning sunshine. Mini French flags festooned the tables along with small bouquets of wildflowers. Daniel expected fifty or so: his family and old friends from his town in France, of course, as well as a few friends from their days in the city, local people who served on county agencies whose goodwill he needed, a few of the artists he cultivated to join his atelier experiment, and Sally Higgins-Jones. He'd made inquiries and persuaded a handful of wealthy weekenders to attend for good measure.

• • •

"Gerald told me later, after the fiasco, it was a huge success," Bernard said. "The newspaper ran an article the next morning."

"Tell me about the fiasco."

"Well, the evening went super. Gerald outdid himself and every dish, I'm told, was perfect, as wonderful as any Parisian establishment could create. He was the real deal. The wine and champagne flowed, and the evening went late. Of course, no Bastille Day is complete without a somewhat wine-infused rendition of "La Marseillaise," and the crowd, I'm told, got quite jolly, with Daniel and his father and friends belting the thing out more than a few times. The artists, mostly women of a certain age I must say, were happy as clams and joined in the fête. Everyone was in high spirits. But Daniel had ignored the state liquor laws and the next day — we don't know even now if the ABC was alerted about the event or word got out from the newspaper — but the very next morning, a citation was slapped on the front door of Restaurant Perigeaux for dispensing alcohol without the proper permits."

. . .

Daniel arrived at the restaurant early the next morning to congratulate Gerald on his exquisite cuisine and the impeccable service (Gerald had brought in seasoned wait-staff from his connections just for the special opening evening). Daniel also wanted to plan for the rest of the week, only to be blind-sided by the notice affixed to the window.

He ripped it off the door and stared in disbelief. "What is this *connerie*? What is this?" He rattled the paper in the air in frustration. Gerald rushed to the door, clearly upset.

"An ABC agent was here earlier. He told me the restaurant dispensed alcohol without a license and you'll have to go to a hearing. Your permit is officially on hold, he said. You can't serve any alcohol at all! This could take weeks, he said, and I don't know what to do! Should we open? I've got a hundred pounds of duck being delivered this morning, and at least that in vegetables. What am I to do with this?" Gerald was in an agitated state, red-faced and perspiring. He handed Daniel the card the agent had left with him.

"ABC Inspector Jinx Jagger," Daniel read. "That same idiot! This is pure folly, madness! I applied for a liquor license and was told it would probably be approved in time for our opening — this week! Last night was a private party. They cannot do this to me! Everyone knows Perigeaux is opening this week, people are excited, we have reservations! *Merde et merde*, I'll get this guy on the phone and figure it out. It's a simple misunderstanding! It's got to be." Daniel raced in to use the restaurant phone while Gerald threw his hands up in exasperation, and sat down heavily on one of the dining room chairs.

Daniel took a deep breath and asked for Agent Jagger. "This is Daniel Perrault from Restaurant Perigeaux. Please, there must be a misunderstanding. My application to serve alcohol is in and was due to be approved for our opening this week. Last night was a private party. I didn't think it would be a problem." Silence while he listened.

Gerald could see he was getting increasingly flustered and angry. "I don't see the crime here! This is a horrible way to act and unfair! You're going to put me out of business with your idiocy!" Daniel slammed down the phone in fury.

"What did he say, Daniel?" Gerald asked.

"We are being punished by an empty-headed bureaucrat from a useless agency enforcing a petty insignificant law! It's wicked but he's got me by the *couilles*." Daniel paced while he fretted. "I have to go to some hearing about this and can't serve alcohol until we resolve that, then resubmit our liquor application. I can't tell how long it will take."

"*Mon Dieu*! We can't run a restaurant that way! No wine with the meal, *ce n'est pas possible*! We are a French restaurant *nom de Dieu*." Gerald sank his head in his hands. "And what do I do with all the product coming in this morning? Eh? You have answers?"

Daniel continued to pace. "Gerald, we are opening. We will explain the situation to our customers and hope they understand."

"What are people going to drink? Coca Cola?"

"There's nothing I can do about it. The alternative is to close until we have the permit and I can't risk that. I'm not canceling any reservations! *Merde*. I'm going to have to hire a lawyer to deal with this. This Jinx character said something about I might never get a liquor license with my attitude. This is bullshit!"

• • •

"Gerald was miserable," Bernard continued. "His reputation was at stake as well, you know. You're either a fine dining establishment or you're not, in the restaurant world. He looked into getting his old sous chef job back at the Scarcity restaurant, but they wouldn't take him. So the restaurant opened without a liquor license, and they could only sell water and soft drinks. Bookings fell off once the word got out about the problem Daniel was having with the ABC, and of course he was a raving lunatic over it, calling Jagger non-stop to complain, threatening to sue, you name it. He was losing so much money. Special events that had been booked were canceled, and his suppliers were screaming."

• • •

Jinx Jagger couldn't believe what an asshole the French Frog, as he and his fellow agents called him, turned out to be. He broke so many ABC rules and regs it wasn't even funny. He mocked the process and ignored the law from top to bottom. He not only never bothered to take the license issue seriously, he didn't buy his wines and alcohol from state stores, as required by law. Jagger had seen the boxes from fancy city shops and stores when he went by the morning after the party. If anything had happened the night of his so-called opening party that was alcohol-related, he'd be sitting on his can in prison for a good long time. He insulted and threatened, a real bad egg. There was no way his license wouldn't be slow-walked now.

Just to stick it to him, Agent Jagger frequently stopped in Restaurant Perigeaux to spot-check that all the liquor, beer and wine was locked up. Daniel was running on a very short fuse, hanging over Gerald's every move to check portion control and waste. He simply couldn't let the restaurant hemorrhage money at every seating until he could finally start serving money-making alcohol. He couldn't keep his contempt for Jinx Jagger under wraps either, and bristled when he saw him swagger in with his badge and uniform, so self-important.

"Do you have a right to come onto my property without warning?"

"You bet I do, Mr. Perrault."

"What a waste of everyone's time! With all the criminals running around in your country, this is what you find important? It's laughable." Daniel stormed off into the storeroom so he wouldn't go too far and make matters worse. Having his beautiful, new bar sit there empty was killing him. Gerald understood completely, of course, but warned Daniel his attitude might work against him.

"You know, these swelled-head types sometimes never get a liquor license to serve alcohol. There's protocol involved here," Jagger insinuated to Gerald in his laggard manner of speaking when he came by the restaurant a few days after the party. Once Gerald heard that, he knew he'd never be able to continue with Daniel. This could be catastrophic for his career, and he didn't want to put his future on the line with a local nutcase. He quickly made up his mind if he couldn't return to his old position, he'd go back to France.

After the euphoria of the Bastille Day event, the chaos created by the ABC for his restaurant opening pitched Daniel into the depths of gloom. His parents and friends were puzzled by the setback but figured everything would eventually fall into place for Daniel. His father told him if all else failed, he could return to the wind turbine business with him in Périgord. *Never*, Daniel thought. His friends left with an encouraging pat on the back.

Meanwhile, Beth could hardly contain her annoyance with Daniel for being so indifferent to state laws and for making it worse by intentionally provoking the agents at the ABC. They faced each other in their kitchen a few days after the French contingent returned to Périgord. Daniel had just ignored yet another phone call from Sally Higgins-Jones who was demanding to know what was going on, and he was visibly annoyed.

"I don't need your little wide-eyed looks of shock that this is the way it is right now," he sneered. "It's not as though you're not part of the problem, you know."

"What? I've been nothing but supportive on this. I assumed you were doing what was necessary to get the permits in order. I had no idea you were being so flippant about the whole thing!"

"Oh, so now it's all my fault your country has such stupid, stupid laws. These people are all morons and they need to know that's how I feel."

"You'll never get anywhere by whipping them up and getting them angry. Stop calling and threatening them, please, Daniel!"

"Beth, this restaurant will fail if I don't get these licenses soon. And don't think it won't be bad for you too, since we could lose a ton of money going forward in this way." Daniel looked at Beth with scorn. She was only too happy to cavort around while he worked his fingers to the bone and lay awake night after night worrying. "Why don't you just get out of my way?" He pushed her against the stove, jabbing her with his elbow for good measure, stalked out of the house to his Aston Martin and sped off.

He felt he had no choice but to get his lawyer to pursue his interests with the ABC, and called him *en route* to his office in the city. Daniel wanted to file suit against the ABC and their agents for unjustifiably holding up his liquor license.

"I don't care about the cost, Bret. I need to win this against them. Withholding my license is groundless and maybe illegal. We've got to set a standard here, put this useless bureaucracy back in its place."

Though his lawyer suggested the ABC might dig in its heels and make this a long and costly ordeal, Daniel wouldn't budge and wanted quick legal action.

• • •

Sheriff Stryker didn't know Jinx Jagger but he had friends at the ABC and had heard about the lawsuit at the time. It wasn't particularly relevant to his investigation, he didn't think, just a legal dust-up that, while leaving bad feelings all around, didn't amount to anything he needed to look into. Or could there be more bad blood there than he thought?

"Let's get to where you come in, Bernard." Spike glanced at his watch. Bernard's constant pacing around the kitchen and keyed-up mien were tiring to watch. The morning was getting on, and he hadn't heard anything yet from the station about Beth's whereabouts or what Cody had found out at the Shanahan residence concerning the Monday evening phone contact with the Perraults' house. And he had to track down the investor in Daniel's art studios, this Sally person, and get her statement.

"I'm getting to it, Sheriff. But you've got to understand the stressful situation I came into so you can appreciate my patience and good-will in going to work for Daniel Perrault."

CHAPTER SIX

THE NEXT FEW WEEKS after Restaurant Perigeaux opened without a liquor license were bumpy and often chaotic. Daniel had anticipated a slow period over the summer, and thought it would help the restaurant find its footing and make for a smooth launch. Several special private affairs, mostly groups from outside Wayne County, were booked and Daniel was counting on their success to spread the word about the upscale elegance of his creation. The artists would generate business as well. At last, Daniel would realize his dream of bringing sophistication and French *savoir faire* to this sleepy little backwater. People would come from far and wide to savor the food, wines and décor. He would be a local sensation!

Instead, Daniel felt assailed on all sides and from everywhere at once. Important bookings were canceled, and reservations he secured never filled the dining room. The wait-staff, comprised mostly of local young people, was inexperienced and mistake-prone. Daniel wandered the dining room nightly, making notes of errors and admonishing the culprits at pre-dinner meetings the next day. He watched the kitchen workers like a hawk, checking portion control and monitoring waste. Gerald was under so much strain he had chest pains and found himself screaming at Daniel to leave the kitchen to him and stop meddling.

"I've never worked like this before! I need to do things my way and not have you, of all people, who have never run a kitchen, tell me what to do and how to do it." Gerald faced Daniel with a look of exasperation and disdain, then turned to continue sautéing onions for the evening's French onion soup.

"Look, Gerald," Daniel said through gritted teeth, while grabbing him by the upper arm and forcibly turning Gerald around to face him. "I don't care how you've worked at other restaurants. I'm in this business to make money, and, right now, we're not making very much. You'll operate on my terms, or not at all. I'll be in the kitchen as much as I want to be and..."

"That's it, then! I will not continue like this. It is very bad for my health, and I refuse to allow you to make me ill." Gerald threw the wooden spoon he'd been using to stir, sending it clattering into the sink. He untied his apron and threw it on the counter. "It's official. I quit!"

After Gerald's departure, kitchen underlings filled in as chief cooks as best they could, but the food was not of the same caliber, and reservations continued to dwindle. At the same time, Daniel's legal fees to fight the ABC were mounting and his revenue couldn't keep up. His main supplier of ducks and geese, the basis of many of the entrées and his *foie gras,* was unhappy with the cutback in orders. He'd doubled his number of fowl in anticipation of a robust partnership. Sally Higgins-Jones was hounding him daily about the lack of pedestrian traffic through the art studios, which she hoped the restaurant and the special bookings would have drawn in.

"I can't go on much longer this way," he complained to his lawyer.

"Then let me suggest you follow my advice. Transfer owner-ship of the restaurant to your wife, and let her apply for the liquor license. It's you the ABC wants to screw. If your wife applies, there's no reason she wouldn't get approved in the normal time frame. Issue resolved."

Daniel felt as though his manhood was being ripped away. Turn two years of planning, money, headaches, hard work, stress — blood, sweat and tears! — over to Beth? Beth, who'd always questioned his projects, preferred city life if you scratched the surface of her, and was probably dallying with that sleaze, Marcus. It galled him no end to give up his huge accomplishment to her, even though she would be out of the picture as soon as he had the licenses he needed and was up and running the operation again. But it further eroded his admittedly waning affection for her — she'd begun again on start-ing a family, a boring, wearying subject. At times, he couldn't even look at her without contempt, and spent most of his time alone in his office when he was home, avoiding her useless efforts to seduce him. Let her take charge! Eviscerate him like everyone else if that's what she wants! He wouldn't give her one lousy fuck if she got on her knees and begged him for it.

With no chef and no liquor license as well as legal fees edging to six figures, Daniel announced to Beth they would close the restaurant until he hired a new chef. When ownership transferred to her name, Beth applied to the ABC, and Daniel created an ad for the local and regional papers for an experienced, seasoned chef. He asked the wait and kitchen staff to have faith — if not in him, in Beth — that Restaurant Perigeaux would reopen very soon. Most of his workers would be laid-off temporarily; maybe one or two could work a few hours at the store Daniel had planned to open later in the fall, but now hastened to complete. He'd bought the closed general store in Nickel at the same time as the apple packing warehouse, and Marcus had cleaned it up and finished putting up oak shelving before he was fired. Hard-pressed to find workers to finish the job, he turned to Garret and Quinn for help. They hauled refrigerators into the storeroom, polished the wooden floors and threw out hundreds of dusty cans of processed foods and sundries. They unearthed an antique, pot-bellied stove ensconced deep in the storage room and installed it, in fits and starts, in a corner of the store. Daniel was pleased with the result, seeing it as a charming and homey farmers' store, the quintessential rural market but with French flair!

With time on his hands while he waited to reopen, Daniel tapped into the handful of local farms supplying the restaurant with produce and dairy and started planning how to stock the store. He didn't want too much clutter, too many items and kept the layout simple: two aisles, a large produce counter across the back and a refrigerated display case on the right side where purchases were paid for, filled with cheeses, yogurts and he hoped eventually sandwiches on French baguettes and — yes! — wines. It was a bright, airy room, cheerful and the perfect size. There was a small front porch Beth planned to embellish with potted plants. She'd chosen a spring-green color for the brick and yellow for the shutters, and the formerly drab and cheerless building now stood out on Main Street like a pretty piece of confection. In fact, Daniel referred to it as his *bonbon*, and savored the changes he believed he was bringing to the town.

He stopped at Farrin's general store for a copy of the local paper to see how his ad looked. A handful of folks from the hollows and subsistence farmers were gathered around the coffee machine at the back, a popular socializing spot. When Daniel strode in, some eyed him suspiciously while a few nodded in his direction, then turned back to continue their small talk and ignored him. Daniel knew they'd probably heard about the ABC mess, and secretly enjoyed the hubbub surrounding the restaurant. And he knew there'd been talk about how 'froufrou' his new store looked in town. He didn't know any of them and figured he'd never see them frequent it, or his restaurant, anyway. He hastened out to his store to see when it looked like it would be ready to open.

Neeraj Pantoja was in charge, recommended by Gerald who'd bought apples and peaches from his orchards. Neeraj also owned a vineyard a few miles away that he'd started when he moved to Wayne County from the West Coast, and Daniel was impressed with the wines he was producing, though they were young. He seemed to have good managerial skills and understood the ins and outs of stocking a small store. Plus, he knew the region well, and could flesh out new sources for Daniel over time, while Daniel was busy running the restaurant. Seemed like a good match.

It was September, two months since the Bastille Day party and a month since Restaurant Perigeaux closed after Gerald's departure. Daniel knew they'd open within a couple of weeks, maybe within a few days — they must! — and October would be its glorious rebirth. The menu was already taking form in his mind. The season called for dishes of wild boar and rabbit, pheasant and quail and of course duck. Walnuts and truffles! Desserts, *tarte aux noix, massepain!* All he needed was a chef, *merde!*

He parked his pickup in the small lot behind the store. It was a warm day, with the first hints of fall in the leaves and fields as the light shifted toward the equinox. The field he'd passed outside of town was awash in yellow goldenrod and the purple of bobbing heads of thistle. He felt good, better than he'd felt in days, optimistic things really would work out on all fronts. He and Beth were even getting on a little better, at least this week. They'd made love last night; she was indispensable to him right now. She owned the restaurant, of course, but assured him she'd be a bit player, a supportive wife, when it reopened. That suited him. She got on well with Sally Higgins-Jones and managed to get her out of his hair for now. That helped. Yes, things were looking up.

The back door was open, as the day was warm, and he knew Neeraj was expecting delivery this afternoon of the refrigerated case. Neerja's car wasn't in the parking area behind the store but there was a green Jeep. Daniel ambled across the parking area and stood in the back doorway to admire the layout of the store, which would soon be bustling, he knew it. A young girl was stocking the shelves with some of the artisanal pickles, tomato sauce, spices Daniel had found in the surrounding counties, as well as items he'd ordered from Périgord: dried mushrooms, walnuts, chestnuts, olives, and canned *foie gras*, of course. She had her back to the door and was stooping to access a lower shelf. Her hair was black and long, down to her waist, and tied at the nape of her neck with a red ribbon. She wore snug blue jeans that accentuated a perfect, little, rounded rear end. Her sea-green, peasant-style blouse was loose fitting, with embroidered flowers along the neck line. Daniel didn't wish to startle her and knocked softly at the open door. She straightened up and pushed a strand of hair from her face with the back of her hand.

"Hello. We're not quite open yet, next week, I think."

For one of the first times in his life, Daniel was tongue-tied. There was something about her mouth and jaw, an innocent voluptuousness, and he'd never seen a more perfect nose. Her eyes were a mesmerizing green, an unusual grass-green, and her skin color, café au lait. Her high cheekbones, long neck and willowy body intoxicated Daniel immediately. He felt an erection growing, and actually started to perspire with a surreal desire. Who *was* this creature?

"Ha, ha, I know. I own this place. Who are you?"

"Oh, you're Mr. Perrault? I'm sorry, I didn't know! Mr. Pantoja is a friend of my mother's, and asked if I could help him out this week to get things organized here at the store. He said you want to open next week. My name is Cocheta, Cocheta Shanahan." She smiled at him with a quizzical look, thrusting her hands into her jean pockets, a pleasing act of shy vulnerability.

"Cocheta, difficult. I will call you Conchita." Daniel studied her carefully. "Very happy you work here. I'll tell Neeraj I'm very pleased." His erection was palpable, his palms moist, and tiny beads of perspiration tickled his hairline. "Well, carry on. I'm sure I'll see a great deal of you in the future." He reached out to shake her hand, and ran a finger across her inner wrist, feeling the texture of the little veins.

"Yes, of course." She smiled self-consciously, and Daniel noted the slight gap between her front teeth, thrilling him. Back in his pickup truck, he put the fingers that had touched her to his nose and breathed in her scent, an animal earthiness. He drove away in a state of bewildering arousal.

• • •

"Bottom line is Beth got the liquor license quickly, including one for the farm store," Bernard continued. "Daniel with his attitude was the problem all along. Everyone knew it. Gerald later told me if he hadn't acted so haughty and patronizing, there never would have been an issue. He was a complete boor when his temper exploded, as I found out.

"Anyway, I answered Daniel's ad, and he hired me. We reopened with a grand flourish in mid-October. Everything was in place — the bar fully stocked, the wines and champagnes flowing, and I was the head chef churning out the most wonderful entrées you can imagine. Daniel and I worked well together. I have cooked in many places, most recently in Quebec City, and know the trade well, but I definitely learned quality control from him. How come you never ate there, Sheriff?"

"Our records showed Deputy Swiggert was called to the premises around Christmastime of that year. What happened, Bernard?"

"I'm not happy about that night. Everything had been going along well. I told you Daniel was a lot like me, we didn't always see eye to eye. He had a lot of catching up to do to recoup the losses since the fiasco. He pushed me to cut costs non-stop, always on my case about portion control and waste. He seemed on edge about every little thing, and even sometimes quite distracted or troubled. I hadn't been sleeping well, and made some mistakes with the sauces, over-salted, and some dishes came back from customers. He came storming back with the plates and berated me in front of the entire kitchen staff. Everyone could hear him in the dining room and basically, I lost it.

I left in the middle of dinner service and went out to my truck and got my ice hockey stick — I used to play, you know, tried out for the Nordiques, back in the day. Anyway, I bashed his outdoor front lights to smithereens with the stick. Daniel came running out understandably livid, bolted back inside and called you guys.

• • •

Deputy Swiggert and his partner, Mabel Crone, pulled into the parking area of Restaurant Perigeaux. They noted people milling around in the dark and cold on the front deck of the restaurant, diners they presumed. Deputy Swiggert put his spotlight on to illuminate the scene. Some seemed quite upset at the ruckus, had on their coats and were starting to head to their cars, while others had their napkins in hands, shivering in the frosty air, wanting to get back inside and finish their meals. Swiggert got out of the car, followed by Mabel.

"What's going on here, folks? Anyone hurt?"

"The chef just broke all the lights out here, officer!" a man standing on the steps to the deck shouted. "There's been a fight in the kitchen, I don't know what happened." He pointed to Bernard, still in his chef garb and holding the hockey stick, looking upset and confused.

Daniel came storming out of the restaurant. "Please, you can all return to the dining room. I will talk to the police." He held the door open and some, but not many, of the diners returned to their tables. Daniel watched a large knot of people hurrying to their cars, knowing they hadn't paid their bills and probably would never return. He scowled and turned to address Deputy Swiggert.

"Look at this debris! My lights have been shattered by this, this idiot!" He made to advance towards Bernard, but Deputy Swiggert inserted himself between them.

"Whoa, there, mister. I see the damage. Let's not make it worse. Is there somewhere we can all talk inside?"

Daniel glared at Bernard, then at the deputies, and indicated the door. He followed them inside and led them to the small office/storeroom off the kitchen. The kitchen and wait-staff stared in stunned amazement as Mabel and the three men marched through, uncertain whether to carry on as if nothing was happening. Daniel returned to the dining room, waving his hands as though shooing chickens to get them back to work. He pulled out chairs for returning diners, murmuring apologies, promising their meals would be cleared and new dishes brought out if they desired. "So sorry for this little disturbance. Dessert will be on me!" he exclaimed with a wide smile and outstretched arms. It was hard to resist his charm, and a few diners applauded.

Deputy Swiggert was taking Bernard's statement when Daniel rejoined them. All three were standing in the cramped space, and Daniel was left in the doorway, blocking the kitchen staff from access to items in the storeroom. He wanted this over quickly and to his satisfaction.

"Officer, please, my chef must offer to pay for the repairs to the lights. You've seen the results of his childish behavior, the mess he's made of the evening. I want justice. What were you thinking, Bernard? How could you do this to me?"

"How could *I* do this to *you*? You insulted me in front of everyone. Anyone can make a couple of mistakes in the kitchen, you don't know the half. I was willing to accept responsibility, but you wouldn't let it go, dogging my every move and criticizing every step!" Bernard turned to Deputy Swiggert. "*He's* the one you should issue a citation to!"

"Okay, let's settle down here, now. Name?" Swiggert looked at Daniel, his pencil poised over his notepad.

"Name? You want my name? How could you not know my name? I own this beautiful restaurant! I've been in this county for over two years. Everyone knows who I am!"

"Name, please."

"Daniel Perrault," he huffed.

"Okay, I'm going to issue a misdemeanor citation to Mr. Melchoir here. He'll have to appear for a court hearing and you'll probably be called to make a statement."

"Statement! I just want my lights repaired quickly and paid for. I can't wait for a court hearing on this!"

"There'll be a court hearing for Mr. Melchoir whether you can wait for it or not. Nothing stops you from repairing your lights and, if he's found responsible, he'll have to reimburse you."

"This is absurd, of course he's responsible! *I* didn't do it. Look, he's holding the damn hockey stick he used to do it. There were witnesses!"

"Deputy Crone will get pictures of the stick and the broken lights."

"Great. I'm the injured party and I'm stuck with the mess. What a corrupt system!" Daniel considered Deputy Swiggert. He was tall and thin, and his uniform hung on him. His hair was cropped short under his hat, no facial hair, young. He had clear blue eyes, freckles across his pug nose, thin lips. An all-American, small-town-boy face. "You don't know anything about the restaurant business, do you? How much work, planning, day-to-day crises there are? I don't have time to go tell some little judge that I need my lights fixed by the person who broke them, maliciously, I might add." He sent a withering glance in Bernard's direction. Bernard hung his head.

"Mr. Perrot..."

"It's Perrault."

"There's a process here. Mr. Melchoir has a citation for a misdemeanor and a date to appear, and I'm sure things will wrap up quickly."

"So, I spend my own money if I want my lights fixed?"

"Yes, sir."

Many diners had finished their meals and departed, but some remained, listening to the back-and-forth next to the kitchen while staff hung in the corners and the kitchen workers silently began the evening clean up.

Daniel thought of Jinx Jagger and the small-mindedness of the ABC, and in his frustration, assumed a sarcastic tone. He reached for, and held up, a bottle of red Bordeaux wine. "I guess you wouldn't know how much something like this wine costs, or how it is different from a Burgundy. You local-yokels who have never been anywhere can't possibly understand what I am creating here. Your lives are *insulaire*, while I'm trying to bring sophistication and good taste to this county. I feel I'm being unjustly and constantly punished for employing people, feeding people. It's beyond *stupide*."

Ronnie Swiggert reddened in anger, but refused to allow a schoolyard war of words to escalate. He was certainly seething at the insulting tone and ridicule in front of his partner and others and toyed with giving him a citation. But he was a professional and would conduct himself as so. In the end, he decided to take the high road and snapped his notepad shut. "I'll see you at the courthouse, Mr. Perrot, when your chef's hearing takes place. You have a good evening." He straightened his hat and walked out of the restaurant without a glance at anyone, Mabel behind him.

"Why did you let that guy talk to you like that, Ronnie? Even I was ready to slap some cuffs on him for disrespect," Mabel asked as she took pictures of the broken lights.

"'Cause he's a small person, Mabel. I didn't want to bring myself down to his level. I'll tell you one thing, though. He's treadin' on thin ice if I find him talking to me, or any deputy, that way again."

"Proud of you for handling it that way, Ronnie. I wanted to give him a good kick in the you-know-what!"

"Wasn't any need to add fuel to the flames. Spike taught me to stay stoic when faced with hostility. To a point, that is."

The next day, Daniel wrote a scathing letter to the editor of the local paper complaining about the unjust treatment he thought he'd received at the hands of the local deputies, without naming names. It wouldn't be hard to figure out who he was referring to, though, since a few of those who were in the restaurant probably knew the deputies in question were Ronnie Swiggert and Mabel Crone. The incident, and Daniel's alleged indignity, were the talk of the county all week afterwards. Swiggert was upset about the force getting a bad name in print, but Sheriff Stryker told him to just ignore the gossip. "Folks'll be onto somethin' else in no time," he said.

• • •

"So, you got a misdemeanor in December, and you were ordered to make restitution to Mr. Perrault. What was your relationship after that, Bernard? You kept working for him until you were fired in April, four more months. And now you've got a felony on your record." Spike was getting warm, sitting so close to the wood-burning stove. He got up to move the chair further away and decided to remain standing. He was keen to get to the end of Bernard's story, as he pretty much knew how it ended, and have him come around to the station later for a statement.

"Daniel cooled down fast and said he expected me to continue working for him. He was boxed in, though, because the holidays were around the corner and he needed me. He knew deep down I was the best chef around. To be honest, after that, he seemed to step back a bit from the day-to-day operation. Staff had become more established and everybody loved working at Perigeaux. There wasn't much turnover. Christ, I was happy I had that job. And when Daniel was in a good mood, that place sang with joy."

"And yet, it ended badly. Tell me why."

"Like I said, he gradually seemed less involved and spent more time overseeing the farm store and the art studios. He let me make most of the purchasing decisions. I'm not saying he didn't check up on things, but he didn't have his finger on every little incoming and outgoing thing like before. He actually liked some of the new recipes I wanted to try as we moved toward spring. And he and his wife, Beth, actually came out to eat at the restaurant for our special Valentine's dinner."

"Was his wife involved much?"

"Some. I mean, technically, she owned the place. She'd come and have a drink at the bar, they'd eat together from time to time there. But she never involved herself in the kitchen. She liked working with the artists and arranging special evening shows to attract diners to visit the studios. It seemed to suit her best."

"Did she ever say anything to you about her relationship with Daniel?"

"Never."

"Did you ever see Mr. Perrault with anyone other than his wife?"

"All the women loved him, the artists, the waitresses. He definitely appreciated them and liked the attention. One of the artists, the one who called me yesterday, Fleur — I think she was a photographer — seemed especially enamored with him, and would wander over to the restaurant as soon as Daniel arrived, just to hang out. Sometimes she'd take pictures of him. I mean, the *mec* was good looking and charming as hell, when he wanted to be. Any one of the females, maybe the males too, would have fallen head over heels if he'd made any kind of advance. But I never saw anything happen. He was driven, busy. All was good until he accused me of stealing."

• • •

Disturbed by his chef's violent outburst and, in his mind, the bureaucratic process to get compensation for the damage, Daniel nevertheless relied on Bernard with the hugely important holidays a mere few days away. A special Christmas Eve dinner, complete with *bûche de noël,* was planned and reservations were healthy. After New Year's, business would be slow — winter after all — and they'd see few visitors or weekenders venturing into the countryside. The local people who'd dined there a few times would probably hunker down until spring. There'd be a small uptick around Valentine's, but otherwise Daniel would have to rely on the bar income to offset his costs.

He was forced to let several staff go, at least temporarily. He considered closing mid-week but wanted the bar open every night — it was the only one within miles. He cut back on the number of dishes and managed to stay above water for the time being. The ateliers were all rented, and he spent part of each morning wandering through the spaces and chatting with the artists. They were ecstatic to a fault to be part of what they considered a cooperative where they could all work independently, yet share ideas and display their works in informal shows and special events.

With little choice, he kept Bernard on, allowing him more freedom to order supplies and plan menus. Maybe he had been a little overbearing with Bernard. He was extremely sensitive to any criticism, as most chefs were, and Daniel truly regretted berating him in front of the staff for his minor mistakes though he would never admit it to Bernard.

• • •

"When Daniel stormed into the kitchen early that afternoon in April, I couldn't believe what he was saying. I thought he was kidding," Bernard continued, shaking even now as he remembered the scene. "He told me two cases of red wine — a Pinot Noir and Cabernet Sauvignon — were unaccounted for, missing, and he actually outright accused me of carting them off for my own use. Of course I denied it, but he shoved a bill of lading in my face that showed my signature for receipt of the cases."

• • •

"Where are these cases, Bernard? We're talking about several hundred dollars here, *mon ami.*" Daniel was furious, realizing he probably never should have trusted Bernard to run the show these many months. "I'm going to have to review weeks worth of deliveries to see what else you may have stolen, and of course this will come out of your pay!" He rushed into the office to go through the paperwork.

• • •

"Well, I completely lost it, Sheriff." Bernard dropped noisily onto a kitchen chair and covered his face with his hands.

"I followed him into the 'office,' which didn't have much more space than a broom closet what with supplies and deliveries stacked along the walls. He was rifling through the file cabinet. I told him how unfair this was, I'd never touched anything for my own use except to taste my sauces. Christ! I never even ate a complete meal at Perigeaux! He turned toward me and looked like a person possessed in my mind, a demon! I saw red, and thought he was about to attack me like a wolf, snarling and biting."

• • •

Bernard, trembling in fear and flirting with a nervous breakdown, ran to the restaurant phone next to the bar — Monty, the bartender, wasn't in yet — and dialed 911. "Please help me! I'm being attacked! There's a mad dog on the loose here!"

"Are you insane?" Daniel dashed from the doorway of the store-room office to Bernard, who cowered like a hunted animal. Daniel quickly grabbed the phone and slammed it down without speaking into it. "But you've gone mad yourself! Nothing is attacking you and now we've got to deal with the law here again. Jesus, Bernard!"

Sure enough, they heard a siren in the distance, car doors shut forcefully in the parking lot, and finally the resounding stomping of boots on the wooden front steps to the restaurant. Deputy Swiggert, followed by Deputy Mabel Crone, entered the building and approached Bernard, now weeping with his face plastered against the granite counter of the bar. Daniel stood arms akimbo with a look of extreme annoyance on his face.

"*Oh mon Dieu, non!* I cannot believe this! You again?" Daniel turned his back to the deputies and cupped the back of his neck with his hands, leaning back in frustration and disbelief. He bent at the hips to calm himself, then pivoted back to face Swiggert. "This man needs to go home and get rest. There is nothing going on here that can't be resolved between him and me."

"We got a call there is a mad dog here. Is that correct?" Swiggert asked.

"Of course not. My chef here is under stress, apparently, and needs some time off. I'm not sure at all what he meant."

"Let me hear from this gentleman if he's the one who placed the 911 call. Sir? What seems to be the problem?"

Bernard whimpered something about 'unfair,' 'disrespectful,' and 'tired,' but was unable to lift his head and face the deputies.

"You see? He is unwell. Please, nothing is going on here. I would ask you to leave before our staff arrives for the dinner service."

"Sir? You have no statement to make?"

"No," Bernard mumbled.

"You see, please? Please, just go. We will deal with this issue ourselves." Daniel waved one arm to indicate the door and actually put two fingers on Swiggert's back to guide him out.

"If there's no statement we won't follow up on this, but — it's Mr. Perrot isn't it? — this is our second call in just a few months to your establishment. One more and we will have to initiate some sort of investigation as to what the issues are here." Swiggert glanced at Bernard, then focused his attention on Daniel.

"It's Perrault. There is nothing more here than a temperamental chef and a stressful job feeding people outstanding food and drink. I don't think there is any crime in this. Now if you would please go, both of you, we could get on with the evening's preparations." Daniel walked to the door himself and opened it for the deputies.

"Well, watch yourself," Deputy Swiggert muttered as he exited and descended the steps to his patrol car.

"Why'd you say that to that guy, about investigating him if there was another call to the restaurant?" Mabel asked as they slid back into their patrol car and switched off the flashers. "You know that's not true."

"Just wanted to get under the guy's skin, piss him off. God, there's something about him that really gets my blood pressure up," he said. "Such a little prick with an inflated attitude about his importance." He swung the patrol car out of the parking area and radioed in that the situation had been handled.

Meanwhile, Daniel told Bernard to get the hell out of the restaurant and he would be in touch if he wanted him back. He got on the phone immediately to the second-in-command in the kitchen, a local kid named Eddy, to get in early and be in charge of dinner prep at least for tonight. "Get out of my sight," he barked at Bernard.

When Bernard got home, his father, with whom he lived at the time, asked him what he was doing back at the early hour. "What the hell, son? Don't tell me you've gone and done something stupid! Did you get yourself fired again?!"

"Goddam, leave me alone. Like you're a saint. I've got issues to think about." Bernard, completely spent with emotion, threw himself onto the couch in the living room and flung his arm over his eyes. His pet cat, Slinky, jumped up onto his groin and began nuzzling his other hand, then bit his thumb when Bernard tried to shoo her away. The pain zigzagged through his body like lightening and he grabbed her by the nape of the neck and marched out to the back garden where he kept two male Alaskan Malamutes in a large cage. In a fit of fury, he hurled the cat into the cage where the dogs, normally docile, were caught by surprise and their killer instincts aroused. In short order, Slinky was torn to bits.

Bernard stood immobile and dumbfounded while his father, alerted by the yowling and growling, ran out and saw the carnage. "You fool! You complete and total idiot! What have you done? You just murdered the cat! My God, even if you are my son, I'm calling the police! You can't get away with this. You killed Slinky! Maliciously and on purpose! What's wrong with you?"

• • •

Bernard sobbed uncontrollably while Sheriff Stryker stood in silence, gazing out the double French doors at the mountains to give Bernard time to compose himself. "The judge charged you with a felony for that," he said quietly. After a long pause he added, "Cruelty to animals. And you already had a misdemeanor on your recent record."

Finally staunching his spasms of grief, Bernard rose unsteadily to his feet and staggered to the kitchen sink, where he doused his face in cold water. "I loved that cat, Sheriff," he said, drying his face on a kitchen towel. "There isn't a day when I don't think about what I did that night. I couldn't explain it then, I can't explain it now."

"You were taken into custody on the spot by the arresting officer who responded to your father's emergency call. Your father said at the time, according to the officer, you were delirious, unhinged and acting like a madman."

"I know," Bernard whispered. "I *felt* unhinged. First Daniel falsely accusing me of stealing, then my father all over my case like I was a kid again. I snapped, is all I can really say."

"Your father disappeared into thin air after that, not even coming to your hearing, where you pled guilty."

"I know."

"You claimed you didn't know where he was, but you did, didn't you, Bernard?"

"No! He left a trail of bad checks and the state police were onto him around the same time. He was no Boy Scout, my father, you know. I didn't want him there anyway. I pled guilty to get it over with. I wanted my sentence handed down and to move on. The verdict was six months in jail, all but ten days suspended, and six months probation. My dogs were removed, and I can never own another cat."

"And you were fired from the restaurant as soon as Mr. Perrault learned of the whole mess."

Bernard leaned on the kitchen counter, seemingly lost in thought. "I never spoke another word to Daniel after he booted me out of the restaurant that April afternoon. He sent me a letter terminating me with a paltry final paycheck. I'm sure he deducted the missing wine, unfairly, I might add."

Sheriff Stryker pulled on his jacket and zipped it up. "Bernard, I want you to come into the station right after we're done here and make a statement for the record. I can't rule you out as a suspect in Mr. Perrault's homicide."

"*Quoi? Non!* Why?"

"Motive, and no way to verify your claim you were here in your house early Tuesday morning. Your aggressive behavior in killing a cat. I could go on."

"I didn't have any reason to want Daniel dead! Yes, accusing me of stealing was horrible and I went a little nuts. But I've abided by my sentence. It wasn't my fault the restaurant only limped along last spring and summer after he fired me, then closed. He couldn't find another talented chef, or maybe nobody wanted to go work for him, I don't know. He had too much going on and couldn't give his full attention to anything. I haven't seen Daniel since last spring, I swear. God, I can't wait until I can return to Quebec and put this nightmare place forever out of my mind!"

Spike moved as though to leave, heading for the kitchen door. "One last question, Bernard. What was your reaction when you got that phone call telling you Daniel Perrault was dead?" Spike turned quickly and looked closely at Bernard's eyes to gauge the question's effect. A liar, or guilty party, in his experience as a sheriff, would almost always betray culpability in a barely perceptible shift in eye contact.

"Reaction? I guess disbelief. For all his quirks and mean-spiritedness, Daniel was larger than life. He could light up a room or suck out all the air depending on his mood. If this had happened last year, I would have wept. Now, I don't feel anything at all." Bernard never flinched looking at Sheriff Stryker, then dropped his eyes to stare at his hands.

CHAPTER SEVEN

JESUS, BERNARD WAS *tiring to listen to. All that pacing, play acting, weeping over the cat. He was a true question mark. Did he have an evil core to stalk and murder, or was he a garden variety, high-strung creep who blows a gasket from time to time?* He'd have Chief Deputy Talon take Bernard's statement at the station and get his opinion. He'd have forensics check the tires on the Audi to see if the tread matched anything they'd photographed at the scene of the body. He'd also have one of the deputies interview Bernard's cellmate while he was in jail, see if he'd talked about Mr. Perrault in a vengeful way. For now, he was a suspect. Spike would put in for a search warrant for his house and car, and interview folks on the right-of-way, ask if they heard a car go by early Tuesday morning, close to the time Mr. Perrault's body was dumped roadside. And they'd search his property for any sign of Daniel Perrault's still-missing pickup truck.

Spike checked his watch again: 9:34 a.m., too early to follow up with his deputies on what they might have found by talking with any former Restaurant Perigeaux employees they tracked down. Cody probably hadn't finished interviewing the people up on Grindstone Mountain Road to find out why someone from that house called the Perraults' early on Monday evening, Daniel's last evening alive. He radioed into the station he was going to poke around the shuttered restaurant and investigate the wing where the artists' studios were located.

"Sheriff, yer wife called, said to give her a call soon's you can."

"Roger." *She probably just wants to know what I want for dinner before she goes out shopping. Forgot to ask this morning, I was out the door so fast.*

Though the restaurant had closed, the studio complex was still open as far as he knew, its future probably uncertain under the circumstances.

He pulled into the parking lot and sat for a moment in his patrol car, reflecting. *It's a pitiable thing, an enterprising foreigner, French guy, coming to our little county, a place he'd never been to or heard about before, starting all this positive stuff, then having his life snuffed out, for what possible crazy reason?* He studied the façade of the restaurant through his open patrol car window. Forensics had gone through the place yesterday, taken some fingerprints and removed the computer. They hadn't found anything out of the ordinary.

The October light of mid-morning danced on the metal roof and the large, blood-red awning stretching across the front deck with "Restaurant Perigeaux" stamped in gold cursive, flapping in the breeze. Two large windows on either side of the entry door were covered on the inside with brown paper and a wooden sign hung from the top of the door: "CLOSED." Large, colorful, sky-blue flower pots placed along the edges of the deck were filled with neglected red and white geraniums, now wilted and bone dry, burned by frost. Spike had never been inside, much less eaten a meal there, but he remembered how long the apple packing building had been empty, deteriorating, practically rotting away until Daniel Perrault bought it. Looking at the building now, so clearly a labor of love and pride, he felt gloomy and low-spirited at the bad luck Daniel Perrault endured, even though he had brought some of it on himself. And to die here? Spike shook his head and, not for the first time, wished he'd gotten to know Mr. Perrault, taken notice of someone outside the county trying to do something *for* the county. It probably wouldn't have made any difference in terms of his fate, though. Spike sighed and put a fresh stick of gum in his mouth, straightened his hat square on his head and stepped out of his car.

There were three other cars in the parking lot, people working in the art studios, Spike assumed. The entrance to the ateliers was to the left of the restaurant's front deck and he proceeded, slow-paced, up the steps towards that entrance, the door of which was ajar. He knocked, announcing his presence.

"Hallo, Sheriff Stryker coming in. Anyone here?" He paused in the large entryway then ambled toward the hallway that led to the various art studios situated on either side, about a dozen, Spike calculated. Everything was wood or glass and fresh to look at. Three large, modern-looking chandeliers hung evenly spaced down the hallway, casting a bright, cheery light. *It certainly took some doing to fashion all this out of a run-down warehouse,* Spike thought. Studios on the left with windows to the outside had their own doorways and "windows" on either side, so visitors could easily see the artists' works or even the artists at work. The studios on the right, enclosed on three sides, seemed to be for exhibiting. Spike walked lightly down the hallway, noting only two studios had easels set up and artwork on the walls; the rest were locked and dark. An exhibit of photography on the right was lit up and a young woman sat at a desk, staring at a computer. She bolted out of her chair when she saw Sheriff Stryker.

"Oh, goodness, oh dear, you're here about poor Daniel, aren't you? I just can't believe it, it's too horrible." She held out a limp hand and Spike shook it. She was slim, gamine, with long blonde hair, pale skin and large blue eyes, red-rimmed from crying, apparently.

"I was just looking up to see if there is any news about what happened," she said.

"Can you tell me who you are?"

"I'm Fleur, Fleur DeHood. I've been exhibiting my photographs here since the gallery space opened last summer. Daniel created such wonderful ambiance for us artists. I just can't get my head around what's happened to him." Fleur sniffled and blinked back tears. "And Beth, my God, I can't imagine how devastated she must be."

Spike figured this was the photographer Bernard mentioned who may have been enamored with Daniel Perrault, but he decided not to query her further right now.

"Is anyone in charge here?"

"Well, Sally is here, in her office." Fleur pointed to the end of the hall. "She's been trying to figure things out. Oh, Sheriff, who could have done this?" She pulled a tissue from the sleeve of her jacket and blew her nose.

"That's what we're working on, miss, and we'll get to the bottom of it very soon, I'm sure."

He heard a woman's voice call from the direction Fleur had indicated, "I'm here, be right out!"

Sheriff Stryker looked around Fleur DeHood's space from the doorway and noted the array of photographs displayed on the wall. Many of them were of Daniel Perrault, Spike knew, from what he'd seen of the autopsy photos. He had a fine, strong nose, slightly crooked like one of the French actors Spike had once seen in a dubbed movie, with full, fleshy lips and engaging, deep-set blue eyes. In some photos, his white-blonde hair was slicked back to reveal a finely shaped forehead; in others, his hair was longer and wilder, looking the scoundrel. He thought of the moment he'd seen Daniel Perrault's tousled blond hair poking out of the sleeping bag, and shivered. Fleur had photographed him inside the restaurant as he checked on things in the dining room and kitchen and outside, overseeing the final touches to the exterior. There were a few more intimate ones: facing the photographer, toasting with a glass of white wine and a coquettish smirk, and one of him in profile at a window, shirtless, the setting, or rising sun, behind him. *Interesting,* Spike thought.

"I believe Mrs. Perrault was also a photographer. Did she ever display her work here?"

"No, Beth just took pictures for fun, for her own personal use. She was mainly interested in supporting all of us artists. Oh, God, how's she doing?" Fleur's eyes welled up again in sorrow.

"Sheriff, I'm so glad you're here," Sally Higgins-Jones said brightly as she strode confidently down the hall towards him and offered her hand, which Spike shook. She had close-cropped, snow-white hair, a narrow face with thin lips and a lanky build. Her black, below-the-knee skirt and what looked like a white lab coat hung on her frame in a frumpy way, but she spoke with authority in a clipped British accent. "We've been completely floored by this terrible event and want to do whatever we can to help find out who did this to Daniel, don't we Fleur?" She inclined her head toward Fleur who nodded mutely.

"Yes, ma'am that's precisely why I'm here, to find out more about Mr. Perrault's relationship with you and the artists, during his ups and downs." He spoke slowly and deliberately mostly as a counterpoint to her over confident air. Where was her grief for the loss of Daniel Perrault?

"It's looking like most of the studios are empty. When did that happen?" Spike asked, gesturing around him.

"Do you mind coming into my office? We can talk much more comfortably there. I could make you some tea, or would you like a glass of water?"

"No, thank you. Let's go sit. And Miss DeHood? I may need to ask you some questions too, so please remain in the building for a little while until we're done."

"Of course, Sheriff."

Sally Higgins-Jones had a small office in the corner with windows on both sides that looked out over the fields on the edge of town. Offering Sheriff Stryker a comfortable chair, she moved to stack some framed pictures against the wall out of the way. "My unsold watercolors," she mused with a smile.

"I won't take up too much of your time, Ms Higgins…"

"Oh, please call me Sally! Otherwise it's such a mouthful for people."

"All right. We know a little about the arrangement the artists, and you, had with Mr. Perrault and the restaurant, but we don't know much more than that, and we don't know exactly what went wrong. How's about you give me the background?" Spike removed his hat, placed it beside him on a small table and unzipped his jacket. Sally Higgins-Jones sat at her desk and clasped her hands in front of her. "And maybe a little bit about what's going on with this place now, empty as it looks."

"What's going on now, as you see, is a state of collapse. The whole arrangement started off on solid ground but by early summer, after Bernard the chef left, it was on life support. With Restaurant Perigeaux closing and now this…" She took a deep breath continued. "This is now a dead enterprise, sadly." She flushed pink, realizing her poor choice of words, then pursed her lips in disgust or regret, hard for Spike to tell.

"Daniel Perrault was the best and the worst thing to come into my life, ever," she continued. "His vision, his willingness to take risks, his French *panache* were his positive traits. Impatience, hardheadedness and, really, malice were his downfall. We had a foolproof partnership, I thought, until we didn't. Daniel's demands pushed me to the brink of personal bankruptcy. All of the artists I brought here, my friends, have left and don't talk to me anymore. When the restaurant closed, it was clear I was the one without a chair at the end of the party game of musical chairs. Of course, with his death, I'm sure Beth will free me from further obligations, the only good thing to come from this. How is she doing, poor dear?"

"So Mr. Perrault's death benefits you?"

"Sheriff! You aren't making an assumption I had anything to do with this, are you?"

"No, just statin' a fact, ma'am."

"I loved Daniel, we all did. But he drove a very hard bargain with me and I learned to dread him and the control he had over me, professionally and personally in the end. But I would never harbor any thought of... well, I just can't even think along those lines." Sally brought her hands to her face, then ran her fingers through her hair. "In many ways, the problems were my fault, Sheriff. I always considered myself an astute businesswoman, but I signed a lease with Daniel I should have considered more carefully. He needed me to run the art studios and I should have pushed for more latitude. But the man had such charm, such charisma, I couldn't resist the opportunity to work with him, and truly believed everything would turn out splendidly for us both. I couldn't imagine then that I'd end up crushed and in a very deep hole."

• • •

After firing Marcus, Daniel relied on a few local workers he corralled, friends of Garret and Quinn, to put the finishing touches on the restaurant. The artists' studios were basically complete, except for installing the doors and hanging the chandeliers Beth had found at an estate sale in the city. Finishing the space was one thing, but he hadn't had time to think about how to round up local artists and get them to commit to renting space from him. Beth might help dig a few out of wherever they were now if he asked her to, but he didn't have time to negotiate all the details, special requests or deal with them at all, he figured. The restaurant was paramount, the launch was Bastille Day in July and here it was June! It wasn't crucial to have the ateliers filled by then, but it would be nice to have the whole place buzzing with activity, luring people into the restaurant when it opened.

He enlisted Beth's help.

"Chérie, I need you for this part. You're artistic with your photography, you've got the artist's mindset. Can you make the rounds here and in Scarcity and pry a few of the best to set up shop here? It's a win-win, don't you think?"

"I think so, but you have to tell me what it's going to cost them. What's your plan for rent and all that?"

"I'd like someone in charge, one person to deal with. Sign a rental agreement with us, fill the spaces, collect rent from the artists. There must be someone around here who would want such a moneymaking deal. All I want is the monthly income, it'll help offset the cost of running the restaurant in the early months, that was the plan all along, *n'est ce pas*? If you do that part, I can devote myself completely to creating wonderful food and drink. Deal?"

"Deal." Beth gave him a playful smile. Daniel was so far along into his dream, how could she say no? Besides, it would do her good to get out of the house and meet new people. The anxiety of finishing all the building and renovating, along with Marcus's firing, had taken a toll on her. Her consulting work had become much less fulfilling since she'd adjusted to country life and with Daniel out so much, she was getting lonely. She felt she needed to get closer to Daniel again too.

Beth borrowed the pickup to make the rounds in the county, thinking the Mercedes or Aston Martin might send the wrong message to artists she wanted to woo for spaces at what Daniel had christened 'Les Ateliers de la Campagne.' She left her card with every artist she could ferret out, and followed with an invitation to an open house at the restaurant and adjacent studios. Daniel pressured her to get as many as possible to move in by July 1.

Sally Higgins-Jones, who dabbled in watercolor in a small studio in her house, drove over as soon as she met Beth and heard about her courtship of the artistic community. She found Daniel overseeing the installation of the pendant lighting.

"Hello, Mr. Perrault?"

"*Oui*?" Daniel turned to see a woman in a pink suit and high heels with large, dark glasses carrying a briefcase, an unusual get-up on a June morning in the middle of nowhere, he thought. What might this be about? "Carry on, Vincent," he said to the young man on a ladder. "But make sure the pendants aren't too low, *subtilité* is what I want. Can I help you with something?" he said to Sally.

"Mr. Perrault, my name is Sally Higgins-Jones and I think I could help you run your atelier. I've done this before, when I lived on the West Coast and before that in England. Would you like to discuss this?"

"Where are you from? Here?"

"I am now. I'm an artist and have been living in the county for several years. I'm originally from London, perhaps you can tell?" She smiled. *What a charming-looking man, and ambitious.* "The restaurant is looking quite beautiful and I took the liberty of strolling through the studios next door. Absolutely splendid, a wonderful idea to combine the two as you are."

"How can you help me?"

"I know every artist in the area. I met your wife — Beth? — and she explained the plan. You'll need someone to run the show, so to speak: first get the commitments, then take care of the logistics, do all the paperwork, arrange shows, collect the rental fees and take care of bills. I'm excited just thinking about the wonderful collaboration between your lovely restaurant and these many talented artists. The symbiosis will be unique, everyone will benefit."

"Let's go into my office to talk." Daniel motioned to a small alcove off the kitchen. She's a little aggressive, this one, he thought, and old-fashioned looking, dowdy really. How could she boost the glamour I'm creating? On the other hand, maybe a schoolmarm is what's needed to manage a bunch of self-absorbed *artistes.*

By the end of the hour, Daniel and Sally agreed to collaborate, the details of which Daniel's lawyer would work out. While her brashness and self-assurance grated on his Gallic sensibilities, he acknowledged she could run the art part of his venture and free him for other things. He knew Beth didn't want to get too deeply involved. Maybe this was his lucky day!

By July 1, Sally had filled half the studios with four watercolorists, an oil painter (the only male), and Fleur DeHood, a photographer. She couldn't help stopping into the restaurant to give Daniel a status report, and he began to resent the intrusions as he madly prepared for his grand opening.

"Sally, our deal was you were to run the show. For the moment, only come to me if there is a problem you can't solve yourself. Beth is able to help too, you know."

"Yes, of course, Daniel. But I do think in the beginning, you need to know the ins and outs of what goes on."

"In the beginning is exactly when I can't be involved in the day-to-day with all the other work I have. *Non*, I am relying on you. You need to work out the kinks, Sally. Why don't you give me a report once a week? When the restaurant is up and running, I will be up to my neck. Once things smooth out, I'll stop over more often. Agreed?"

• • •

"What exactly was your agreement with Mr. Perrault?" Spike asked.

Sally rolled her eyes, then focused on her clasped hands. "I signed a five-year lease with Daniel to rent the entire atelier for two thousand dollars per month. He wanted to motivate me to recruit only serious artists who would commit long term to the studio, hence the extended time frame. I, in turn, could charge as much as I liked to sublease the spaces which meant I could realistically earn triple what I paid Daniel." She fell silent.

"And I'm guessing it didn't work out that way?"

"Sheriff, I'm not blind to the fact I'm plain and getting on in years. My husband passed away five years ago — I was his second wife, we married late. I have no children. Teaming with Daniel was so enticing, I probably would have signed a ten-year lease with him. I wanted the prestige, the exposure, the local celebrity, really. It wasn't only for the money, you see. I was featured or quoted several times in the local newspaper. After the dust-up was over — the ABC issue and Gerald, the first chef, quitting — the reopened enterprise hummed along beautifully for a while. I loved being around Daniel; he had an aura, exotic and charismatic. Everything was festive when his mood was good. One of my happiest evenings in recent memory was his Bastille Day opening gala. We all had such a stupendous time! That was a glorious night. And Beth was a sweetheart. She didn't mind my infatuation with her husband. All of us were a little in love with him, I think."

"Go on," Spike pushed as she fell silent again.

"Well, having to close nearly right away until the liquor license was sorted out and Bernard was hired was very, very hard on all of us. The atelier was fully committed by the end of the summer, including two different potting groups who were very pleased to have an industrial-grade kiln on site. Of course, anxiety set in immediately, with everyone wondering if they'd made a huge mistake. Without the restaurant, foot traffic into the atelier came to a halt. As you can see, we're a bit removed from the center of town." Sally gazed for a moment out the window at the fields stretching away toward the Baptist church on the other side of the highway. Clouds were rolling in from the west, a chillier, damper afternoon and evening were predicted, grim harbinger of winter to come.

"I absolutely never lost faith in Daniel during those early difficult weeks, but I had to let him know the mood people were in and how precarious the situation was, for me in particular. I realized how much pressure he was under, his demeanor said it all. He accused me of stalking him — can you imagine? — only because I needed reassurance from him that all would soon be well. Luckily Beth helped a great deal, organizing special events and meetings, which drew a few groups of people in. She promoted the site non-stop as best she could. There's nothing an artist needs more than recognition. Finally, with the relaunch, we all breathed a collective sigh of relief."

• • •

Daniel had his hands deep in a carton of Yukon gold potatoes that Bernard would make into a delicious au gratin dish baked with French gruyere cheese and savory morsels of crisp local bacon. This would blend perfectly with the pork chops Bernard wanted to *sauté* with apple slices and a hint of sweetness, maybe cinnamon or a touch of molasses, a perfect fall dish. Beth and Sally Higgins-Jones meandered into the kitchen from the atelier together to peek at the evening's preparations. They each planted a kiss on Daniel's cheek and Beth grabbed a bottle of wine from the storeroom/office.

"Time to do a little celebrating, don't you think, darling?" Beth asked.

The relaunch of Restaurant Perigeaux in October generated much buzz, both locally and through Beth's contacts in the city where an article appeared detailing the phoenix-like comeback of a French restaurant, stumbling out of the gate but now righting itself. Both Daniel and Sally Higgins-Jones were interviewed, and people were drawn out from the city to have a look. Daniel needed as much business as he could muster as he'd been hemorrhaging money on the establish-ment as well as lawyers since the Bastille Day event. Sally finally looked less drawn in the mouth as the undercurrent of discontent among the artists started to dissipate. The lean weeks were over!

At the bar, Daniel, Sally and Beth toasted one another with glasses of Cabernet and mulled over the next few weeks.

"Bernard seems to be a good chef, as long as I watch for any wasteful habits he's picked up in previous jobs. Seems more steady than Gerald, more open to my know-how," Daniel said.

"Oh, yes," Sally chimed in happily. "He's just what you needed, Daniel, stability and solid talent. I know he's going to be smashing on the team."

Beth nodded and looped her arm through Daniel's. "Now you can relax a bit, maybe even take a little time for yourself, for us. We could plan a trip to Europe after the holidays, see all our old friends and your family..."

Later, after the restaurant closed for good, Daniel recalled that mid-afternoon aperitif, with October light filtering through the win-dows onto the crystal wine glasses creating rainbows on the table-cloths, the succulent smells coming from the kitchen as Bernard and his assistant chopped and diced, someone humming a silly ditty in the distance, as the last truly happy moment of his life.

He'd started thinking far too often about Cocheta — Conchita — and gradually a juvenile longing for her became nearly unbear-able, but to act on it would be ruination. How could it not be? As much as he sometimes found Beth tiresome and, yes, less desirable, he couldn't betray her. She'd put on weight since giving up the biking and running, her city exercise, for work around the house and farm. He loved her, she'd always supported him, *mon Dieu*, saved his ass from losing the whole project even though he'd resented her for it! *Non*, he'd have to keep himself under control when it came to Con-chita. She worked in his farm store, 'L'Esprit du Pays,' in the morn-ing until early afternoon when she drove to Bristow for community college classes. Maybe he could help her? He stopped frequently to check on things and, frankly, feast on her with his eyes. Afterwards, in the woods behind the parking lot, he imagined his face nosing into her long black hair and worked his penis to the brink, ejaculating in a spasm of anguish.

Daniel had plenty to keep him busy and focused his mind as best he could on anything other than Cocheta. Bernard proved to be a very good chef but cavalier about waste, throwing too much out, piling plates high with portions only a farmer could finish when farmers weren't even the usual patrons. He constantly pointed out ways Bernard could save him money: making soup from what was unsold the day before, throwing everything into a salad special before freshness became borderline, freezing some unsold cooked items. Instead of leaving bulk orders to Bernard, he oversaw every order himself, which wore on Bernard as the weeks progressed. He wanted the operation under his control with minimal interference from Daniel and feared that would never be the case.

By fits and starts, things fell into an acceptably comfortable routine, even when an occasional tantrum erupted. Daniel and Bernard were usually in sync — if they wanted to be — but when they weren't, everyone heard the sound and fury from the kitchen. In those instances, Daniel would step out of the altercation — "I'll be the big boy here," he'd say — then amble through the art ateliers to clear his head. A handful of people were always wandering around and he loved the outpouring of admiration when he revealed he was the founder and owner.

Over time, as things settled down, Daniel made good on his promise to Sally to get to know the artists and their works. He appreciated the enthusiasm in the ranks. Most of the artists were in every day of the week to work, lingering into the early dinner hours to keep their studios open for restaurant-goers who might wander through. Some of the older artists painted as a hobby, but others truly wished to sell their works and were thrilled at the exposure Daniel offered. Although he didn't find anything he'd hang in his own house, he bought several of the best pieces to display on the restaurant walls, indicating on the menu the works were for sale. Though only one painting sold during the months Restaurant Perigeaux was open, a rather stunning landscape of sunflowers and poppies under a stormy summer sky — very Van Gogh-ish — Daniel let the artist keep both what he'd paid and what it went for. This endeared him to the whole group. Sally was especially overwhelmed by his generosity.

"We couldn't have a better patron," she gushed. "Perhaps being a restauranteur will become fatiguing someday and you will become an art dealer!"

Daniel didn't have much use for pottery but liked Fleur Dehood's photography. She and Beth had similar sensitivities. Fleur begged Beth to exhibit her own photos in the studio, but Beth demurred saying she was a sorry neophyte.

"Mine aren't of your caliber, Fleur. I do it for fun and put them in an album. You, you're the talent!"

Beth's self-effacement surprised Daniel. She'd always been a confident, successful professional. Part of the reason she'd so infatuated him was her spunky intellect coupled with her unapologetic sexuality. But both were slipping away. She spent most of her time alone, walking around the property, tending to the garden and animals. The landscaping and flower beds were all from her designs and she hired Garret to plant a peach orchard and build a dozen raised beds for vegetables. Her consulting work had dwindled to a few hours a week, and when she went into the city to check on the townhouse, she didn't go into the office to solicit a project, but instead went shopping and cleaned the townhouse, dull, mundane activities. Daniel kept meaning to check and see if Marcus's truck was in front of his office on the days Beth went into the city. Anything could be going on while he struggled to put the restaurant on the map! And the weight gain. Didn't she see what was happening to her figure? God, she'd look like her mother soon enough!

When Fleur asked if she could do some photographic studies of him, his *amour propre* kicked in and he agreed. Fleur was cute and fun, a little waif of a thing, decidedly not his type, but he luxuriated in the obvious infatuation she held for him. Her eyes were full of longing when she looked at him, he could tell. Ha! He'd always loved leading women on, only to cut them off once he had them hooked. Conchita, he thought ruefully, could have been a different story *if* he'd been reckless enough to let his fantasizing become reality.

He began to study his own body carefully in the full-length mirrors he'd had Marcus install in their walk-in closet, and noticed the beginnings of a paunch despite the sit-up regimen he endured a couple of times a week. Through the warmer months, he made daily use of the pool, swimming laps at his favorite time of day, what he called *l'heure bleue*, twilight. Without that exertion, he noticed with dismay a new flabbiness in his arms and thighs. In short order, he bought an elliptical machine and weights for a corner in his office, and worked out four or five times a week before making his rounds of the farm. The work on the fencing last fall and spring had kept his upper body taut and strong but now, eating so many meals at the restaurant, he was too soft in the middle. He needed some manual labor!

Before the snows came, he hauled hay bales with Garret and Quinn, finished reparations on the fencing, and dug trenches around the chicken coop to keep foxes and coyotes out. He'd forgotten how much he enjoyed being in his fields or tooling around on his tractor and resolved to spend part of each morning taking care of farm chores. Beth was both pleased and relieved. She had long thought he spent too much time at the restaurant, or fretting about it when he was home, and needed to let Bernard have more control. Having him around more perked up her mood and she joined him with her camera, snapping away as they worked or aiming at distant vistas. "Harmonious" would be how she described those late fall days.

With Fleur, it happened just before Christmas. She asked if Daniel would walk with her in the woods near her cottage in the afternoon light, close to sunset, so she could do a series of photos of him in various poses. There was a contest she wanted to enter, "The Male at Ease." Her house was up one of the hollows, a run-down, caretaker place located on the property of a large farm with several old apple orchards. Daniel followed Fleur's beat up Baja in his Aston Martin which he soon regretted as the asphalt road turned to gravel and became steeper before they reached the turnoff to the farm. Luckily, there was no snow or ice yet, but he inspected the car when he arrived to make sure nothing had damaged it.

The cottage, really a sorry-looking bungalow, was pocket-sized inside, one room comprising a sitting and eating area, a tiny kitchen, a sleeping loft above reached by a wooden stairway. Daniel felt a twinge of pity. What a lonely life! Truly, the atelier at the restaurant was her life-blood. He would make sure to ask Sally to lower Fleur's rent.

Fleur wore cowboy boots, leggings and an over-sized man's white shirt. A tortoise shell clasp held her hair back in a long pony tail.

"Could I get you something to drink, Daniel, before we go outside? I thought I'd get a couple of shots of you inside then we'll walk to a little spring and waterfall nearby. I'd like a final shot of you by the window as the sun goes down. Look how gnarled the trees are, all knotty and twisted. With you gazing wistfully onto such a melancholy landscape as the sun dips behind the crest of the mountain, it will create the ephemeral longing I want to capture."

"Do you have whiskey?" Daniel felt ill at ease. Did he want to do this? The atmosphere was decidedly cheerless, and he wanted to get the process over as soon as possible. She did not have whiskey but gave him a glass of white wine, room temperature. He drank it in one gulp and turned to her with a "what now?" look. He wore a denim shirt and jeans — the look she had wanted.

"Here." Fleur showed him where to stand and positioned his arms, tilted his head, asked him to move naturally into different positions. She snapped at least a dozen pictures.

She'd asked him to wear his red-and-black, checkered lumber jacket for the outdoor shots. He retrieved it from the car and met Fleur outside on a narrow dirt pathway leading from the house to the woods. She wore a heavy, red knit sweater tied at the waist over the shirt. He followed her as they walked in silence. The path turned mossy where someone had cleared it of last fall's leaves and meandered to a small clearing where a stream spilled over rocks into a good-sized, greenish-brown pool. Ice crusted the edges.

"I swim here in the summer, and often come just to relax and think," Fleur said, and Daniel nodded. "There's a perfect pine tree stump for sitting a little further down." Fleur indicated the direction with her head. "If I could get you to walk towards it and sit, I'll get some shots of that, then some close-ups." Daniel did as he was told. Fleur kept snapping, then came close for profiles and frontal shots. She never asked Daniel to smile and he didn't. "Perfect! Now a couple of action shots. I'd like to get shots of you skipping stones into the pool and then if you could jump the stream a few times and walk back down the path, I'll get those."

"You want me to jump over the stream?"

"Yes. I can get your reflection in the pool as you jump, if we do this right. Should look very good."

After a good thirty minutes or so, Fleur said she had enough and they headed back towards the house.

"One last sequence, Daniel, please." He'd removed the coat and was heading to his car.

"Oh, right. The final inside shot. Is the light going to be right?"

"I've timed it perfectly. I know the ways of the sun this time of year. Should get a perfect set of shots with your profile against a winter dusk."

Daniel obediently went to stand by the window. Fleur came up beside him. "Last request. Could I remove your shirt? I think it would add to the drama of the shot and really get at the heart of the contest theme."

She unbuttoned his shirt while Daniel watched, then stepped behind him to gently slide it from his shoulders, letting it drop to the floor. Fleur ran her hands across his shoulder blades and down his arms, then came around to his front and drew her hands down his chest to his belt. "So smooth, so beautiful," she murmured. Daniel's heart was beating hard. *There was no mistake, this was all a ruse to seduce him, maybe a trick so she could tell Beth he was unfaithful!*

"No, Fleur! What are you doing?"

"Daniel, I've loved you for months, since I first met you. Please forgive me." She stood on tip-toe and kissed him on the neck. He pushed her away.

"Not a chance, Fleur! You're Beth's friend and she's my wife. I love her. Why are you doing this?" He reached for his shirt. Fleur stared at him in shock. *How could he refuse her?*

"Of course you love Beth. I love her too."

"Then why?"

"Daniel, I don't know. I wish I were Beth. I love you and have wanted you for so long." She sniffled and put her head against his chest, hugged him. *What a pitiable creature,* he thought. "Please, Daniel. I haven't been made love to in a long time. I want to give love. Let me love you, just this one time. I'll never tell Beth. I would never hurt her, she'll never suspect a thing. It would be once, Daniel, just to be close to you just one time. Then we'll go back to the way things have been. Please."

"I can't."

"Why?"

"I don't want you. Let me make this clear. You tried to seduce *me* and I am rebuffing you. Now, please, I would like to leave."

"Please! At least let me get the final shots of you!"

Daniel sighed deeply and tossed his shirt onto her couch. "All right, but let's finish this quickly."

Fleur took a series of pictures, the rapid camera clicks unnerving Daniel.

"Let me just undo your belt buckle for the final shot."

Before Daniel could stop her, Fleur had her hands on him and despite his resolve, he allowed her. Within a few seconds, her boots and leggings were off, her shirt ripped open, buttons bouncing across the wooden floor. He took her against the window frame, her legs wrapped around his waist. It was over in minutes, leaving both breathless and sweaty, without having exchanged a kiss or a word.

"This will never, ever happen again. If Beth gets wind of these few moments, I will make sure you regret it!"

He left her weeping on her couch, naked, hair stringy, the camera abandoned on the floor, her final shot accomplished. Daniel was sick to his stomach. This had never felt right. Beth was in the city for the weekend. She set this up to test him, he knew it! She was trying to get him to succumb so she could justify her own little trysts! Well, he'd tell her the whole story. He couldn't blame Fleur, really. He knew his effect on women. How humiliated she must feel! She will probably leave the studio, which would be a headache for Sally, but so what? What did he care?

When Daniel arrived at the restaurant that evening, the dinner service was well underway. His mood was black. When a diner indicated he wanted to return his dish, Daniel exploded at Bernard, who went berserk and tore outside to destroy the exterior lights with his hockey stick.

He went home late and hardly slept a wink, his mind swirling with the events of the past few hours — Fleur, Bernard and his crazy eruption, Swiggert's damnable obstinacy in following silly police protocol. He'd write a letter to the local paper about the injustice of it all!

First thing the next morning, he went to the farm store. Cocheta was sitting on a stool behind the register, blowing on a cup of something hot. She wore a white, lamb's wool jacket with a plum-colored scarf knotted loosely at her neck. Her hair was pulled back in a messy knot on the top of her head. She looked fetching, as usual.

"Mr. Perrault, so good to see you!" She put down her cup and hopped off the stool.

"Good to see you, too. I think business has been solid, hasn't it? I think we'll start the sandwiches again after the New Year. Mr. Pantoja's wife has some ideas for chutney and other new things. And I want to try and add some tropical fruit, people will crave it at that point in the winter." His hands were shaking, his heart ready to burst out of his chest.

Cocheta rounded the counter and looked closely at Daniel. Why were those eyes so mesmerizing? She zeroed in on the left side of his chin. "I think you cut yourself there."

"Yes, I believe I did, shaving this morning, I guess." She brought two fingers to the cut and made a sad face. Daniel grabbed her wrist.

"Just remember — you touched me first." He pulled her to him, noticing she was only slightly shorter than he, and held her for a moment. Then the dam broke.

• • •

"I happened to be in my office wrapping up some paperwork when I heard the shouting in the kitchen," Sally continued. "The next thing I knew Daniel was running out of the restaurant after Bernard and I heard something being smashed. I put on my coat and went outside to see what happened. It was a frightening and horrible scene, Bernard swinging his hockey stick at all the exterior lights Daniel had so painstakingly installed. Embarrassing for all of us as well, really. Most of the diners were too frightened to come back inside and had already grabbed their coats to depart. The police came, and I thought it best if I just left. There was nothing I could do."

"Bernard continued to work for Mr. Perrault until April. What was it like after the light mess?

"Well, Daniel was really quite stymied by the situation. It turns out those two months were the busiest the restaurant ever saw. And of course Daniel couldn't possibly replace Bernard in the middle of a holiday season. Somehow, they came to an understanding. Daniel knew Bernard was quite shaky, he recognized he was unstable, but he was willing to take the risk with him and get through the holidays."

"And after that?"

"Everything went well for a while but bookings for January were sparse. Daniel wanted to take a break with Beth and go to Périgord which they did for most of the month. He told me he felt maybe he'd been too hard on Bernard and should give him more control, so he drew back from the day-to-day once he returned from Europe. As a matter of fact, he seemed distracted for quite some time upon their return. I never queried him if something was wrong, whether it was Beth, health or financial issues. But, we had to face it — Restaurant Perigeaux started to decline in January. Something just seemed wrong. I don't know if it was the bad press about the personalities involved or if the food wasn't as top notch as it had once been, but it was a rare night when the place was booked after the holidays.

"The whole arrangement was so perfect in the beginning," Sally continued. "The art, the way Daniel promoted us; he came by more often once he turned more of the restaurant day-to-day operations over to Bernard, a mistake, as it turned out. I felt so valued by Daniel, so important, like a presence in the community. I guess I let too much go to my head. When the next horrible disaster with Bernard occurred, I could read the writing in the tea leaves — we were going south. Daniel tried to keep things going with the rest of the kitchen staff, but they truly needed Bernard's guidance and it wasn't long before Restaurant Perigeaux began its slow demise. I was quite in a fix, as it turned out."

"Go on."

Well, I had this five-year lease with Daniel, you see. Once it became clear the restaurant was failing and traffic collapsed, most of the artists I'd recruited, my *friends*, Sheriff, left for better locations and abandoned me! I could understand, to a certain extent; they didn't wish to be affiliated with a dying operation. I'm sad to say it ruined many of my friendships. As people trickled out, I couldn't give Daniel the rent money he demanded because there wasn't anything coming in. I went to him in desperation, but he turned out to be quite heartless about it. 'What do you want from me?' he said, throwing up his hands. 'You signed a contract, now honor it!' I was aghast at his hard-heartedness. Because of his refusal to let me out of a contract that had become untenable, I was in a deep, deep hole. With his death, I assume all is null and void."

"Pretty convenient for you Daniel Perrault is dead, isn't it, Mrs. Higgins-Jones? You can rip up your obligations for, what, four more years of monthly rent? You'd get off scot free."

"Yes, that is correct, Sheriff. But I am not a murderess, and this is not an Agatha Christie novel. You will find nothing but that I am completely above reproach and grieve Daniel's death, as anyone who knew him would." With that, Sally pushed back her chair, stood and put out her hand to Spike.

"I hope you find who did this horrendous thing, Sheriff. And if there is anything else I can help you with, please do not hesitate to contact me. Now if you'll excuse me, I need to prepare some paperwork for when Beth feels up to meeting with me."

Spike positioned his hat on his head and touched the brim. "Thank you, ma'am. If I have further questions, I'll let you know."

Leaving the building, he hesitated at the door to Fleur's studio. She was wiping off some of her framed photographs, wrapping them in packing paper and taping them closed.

"Are those your portraits of Mr. Perrault?"

"Some of them. I have hundreds I took over the past year, which I'll keep. He was such a good model. I entered a contest with a portfolio I compiled of him and won honorable mention. He was so embarrassed!" She smiled. "But he didn't hold it against me."

"Miss DeHood, were you in love with Mr. Perrault?"

"That's very personal, Sheriff! Put it this way, if he'd ever left Beth..." She stopped. "I adored him, but it was pretty one-sided. He was absolutely faithful to Beth." She turned to gaze at a photo of Daniel skipping pebbles in a mountain pool. "He was truly special, never to be replaced, in my opinion." She sat and gave Spike a blank look. "I can't believe he's gone."

CHAPTER EIGHT

SPIKE RADIOED IN he was heading back to the station. Rudy and Bodie were not back from tracking down former restaurant workers, not surprising since some of them had probably moved on to other jobs in neighboring counties or were leaving the region for good. The restaurant closed a month ago and all signs pointed to it never reopening again, even before Daniel Perrault's death. People couldn't sit on their hands for long and wait for a miracle. Plus, Spike wasn't hopeful any major lead would come from the people who worked for Daniel. After all, he was and would have been their livelihood — what were the chances a waiter or kitchen worker would want him dead? Unless there was some romantic thing. Unrequited affection? Didn't seem enough to kill for. Bernard was still a prime suspect, and this Sally Higgins-Jones could have hired a killer. She had the most to gain from his death. Her attitude and cool as a cucumber manner in the face of the trauma were suspicious and could be hiding something. He'd get a warrant to search her computer and cell phone, and probably her house. And the photographer — it seemed a little weird to have all those pictures of the deceased displayed on her studio wall. Could the two have pulled something like this off together? Spike released a groan of exasperation. The media types might be at the station this morning, and they'd stick a microphone in his face, wanting answers. Daniel Perrault had been dead thirty-four hours and Spike still had no clear suspect, not to mention any incriminating evidence. The media would push him hard as to why not.

After her husband left early that morning hopeful there'd be a break in the case, Pearl poured herself a second cup of coffee and stood looking out the kitchen window at the first frost of the season glistening on the grass, the last of her blue asters in the flower-bed bowing down in exhaustion, hostas scraggly and spent. She'd have to get out soon and tidy up before the first snows came. Every year the garden became more of a chore after a summer of weeding and watering. Past fifty, with ten extra pounds around the waist, she didn't get the same joy from it she used to, and Lord knows Spike didn't have time to help out now that he was sheriff. Pearl was proud of him, of course, moving up the ranks to the top job like he did, but he got tired too, night shifts especially wearing on him. And now a murder to solve!

He rushed out this morning determined to find out who poor Mr. Daniel Perrault might have been with on the night he died. He knew as well as she did he wouldn't get answers from the medical report. Someone had to blab, that's how things worked in the country. And to get someone to blab, you had to be a bit sneaky, catch them unawares. That's the way someone spills the beans without even knowing it. That woman at the pot-luck dinner knew something and Pearl had to figure a way to find out exactly what it was.

Would it be wrong if she called around, got a name, told Spike? She'd never officially met the Perraults, but her bridge club had splurged and gone for a celebratory dinner at the restaurant after winning a tournament last March, and Daniel Perrault was there. She remembers him greeting her group at the door and ushering them to their table, all the women tittering behind their menus how charming he was, how "easy on the eyes," as Laura Rollini remarked. Not hard to understand how a country bumpkin teenager from around here might fall hard for him, if she'd heard right at the Rescue Squad pot-luck. Did he take advantage? Could it be true?

Pearl tapped her fingernail against her coffee mug. Should she call Ann? She'd know who the woman at the pot-luck was, the one who'd said something about a French "love nest." But then what? How could she connive to get the name? Everyone knew about the death, and the sheriff's wife is calling? Nothing would snap jaws closed tighter than that. It wasn't that they wouldn't want to help; they're just welded to a deep-rooted clan mentality, us against the discord of the outside world. If you ask the right question, though, some might have an inkling as to what you're talking about and let the cat out of the bag, is the way Pearl saw it.

It was early enough, and she knew she'd catch Ann at home. What'd she have to lose? She'd either get a name or she wouldn't. If she did, it would sure make Spike look good, probably help solve the whole damn case by end of the day! She picked up the phone.

"Hey, Ann, it's Pearl. How are you?"

"Pearl! How's your husband holding up? What a terrible thing to happen here. I didn't know the fellow, but so sad."

"Yes, it is. He's fine, he'll get to the bottom of it 'fore too long; he's been interviewing lots of folks about what they know. Say, Ann, how'd you do at the pot-luck? Make as much as you'd hoped?"

"Oh, sure, we did pretty good. Lester got one guy to write a check for two hundred dollars! Should get us through the rest of the year, so that sure was good and unexpected."

"That's really good, Ann. Those evenings are so much fun, too. Nice way to make money and be out with people. By the way, I need a couple girls to help me out at a bridge party I'm having next week." *Easy little white lie,* Pearl thought. "There was a really nice woman I'd never met before at the pot-luck who spoke about her daughter, thought maybe I'd try her, see if she might be interested."

"You might mean Lynette..." Pearl heard Ann *tsking* to herself into the phone. "Now I'm drawing a blank on her last name. Husband just started with Rescue. Lemme ask Lester." Ann covered the mouthpiece with her hand and yelled to her husband for the new guy's name. "It's Davis, Lynette and Flint Davis. Now I remember, ha, pardon my senior moment," she laughed. "Yeah, they have a daughter, Tracy, believe she works over in Smedley in a jewelry store or something, goes to the community college too. Might not have time, Pearl, but you could ask. Believe they live out on Highway 909."

"Guess they'd be in the phone book?"

"Sure, should be. Surprised you don't know 'em; been around the county forever. Lynette used to be part of that little antique business in Scarcity, "Tin Drum." You must remember it, burned down 'bout five years ago?"

"Oh, I do. What's she do now?"

"Think she might work at the school, not really sure, Pearl."

"She might be hard to reach by phone then, I guess. She said her daughter had a real close friend too. Thought if I asked the two of 'em, they'd be more likely to help me out, what do you think?"

"You could try."

"Might be easier if I tried her friend first, don't you think? Know who it might be? I mean, if Lynette's at the school all day and her daughter's so busy?"

"Might be. Let me think. I think I recall Lynette worried Tracy was gettin' real close with that mulatto girl, the one lives up Grindstone Mountain Road, real pretty girl. She's a mulatto though, Pearl. Father's a Negro. Not sure if that matters to you. Mother became common-law wife to Wilford Shanahan, who managed Tillerson's farm operation before he died couple years ago. I think I recall girl's name is something kinda weird, Cocheta comes to mind."

"Cocheta, Grindstone Mountain Road. She go by Shanahan? That's real helpful, Ann. I'll see if I can lasso the two of 'em into some afternoon work for next week. Thanks so much."

"Glad to help. And Pearl, let me know if there's anything I can do, or Lester, for you and Spike."

"Thank you, Ann. Appreciate it. I'll keep you posted on any news if you want."

"That'd be good."

Pearl hung up the phone feeling goosebumps travel up and down her arms and around the back of her neck. *That's gotta be the girl!* Pearl knew of her from shopping a time or two at the farm store in town. Wasn't hard to put two and two together. If this Cocheta and the Frenchman were something — lovers! — then she'd probably been the one with him on the night he died. Stood to reason. But what if she's wrong? Wouldn't be any harm done. But if she's right, a big piece of the puzzle would fall into Spike's lap. Might break the case open even today and save Spike wear and tear on his body, not to mention his mind. He was looking so exhausted this morning, even after a good night's sleep.

She went in to shower and think on it. After she toweled off, she called the station and left a message for her husband to get back to her as soon as he could. When he hadn't called back in an hour, she called his cell and left another message.

As Spike pulled out of the Restaurant Perigeaux parking lot after his unsatisfactory interview with Sally Higgins-Jones, he saw a missed call on his cell phone and clicked to see it was from Pearl. Worried something might be wrong since Pearl rarely called his cell, he didn't listen to her voicemail and called her back.

"Pearl, honey, you okay?"

"Yes, Spike, sorry if I got you riled, but I think I know who Mr. Perrault's girlfriend is, or was. You know, who he was with the night he was killed."

"You *think*? How would you know who it is?"

Pearl explained the information she'd gotten from Ann and the connection with the Shanahan place up on Grindstone Mountain. "The girl's name is Cocheta, and it sounds like she and Mr. Perrault may have had a little love nest somewhere."

"I can't tell you this now, over the cell, but this makes a helluva lot of sense all of a sudden. Lemme get back to you." Spike deleted the voice message she'd left. Goddam, it takes my wife to put a few pieces together, he marveled. So, our Mr. Daniel Perrault not only had a little side interest, but they apparently used a secret place to meet. The call to his house on the night he died was from her, Cocheta Shanahan. Why? Lure him out? To what?

Spike checked his watch: 10:19 a.m. Why hadn't Cody radioed in from the Shanahan place yet? He must have talked to the girl by now. He radioed Bodie to meet him at the Grindstone Mountain place, then radioed Cody for an update, feeling slightly irritated at his silence. He wished he'd been able to send Ronnie up with him; he'd proven he could be a top-notch interviewer in difficult situations, more seasoned than Cody. Mabel had radioed Spike that Swiggert called to say he'd be in the station by lunchtime. Spike would make sure to have him get right into the case, starting with finding this supposed love nest place.

Deputy Cody Crawford threaded his police vehicle through the low-hanging hemlock branches along the narrow dirt road leading to the Shanahan property. They brushed against the car like green streamers and he hoped they weren't scratching the paint. He was plenty nervous about his first solo interview without Bodie, Mabel or one of the other deputies. This was one of his first real investigations, not to mention a murder investigation. Normally Sheriff Stryker would have sent Deputy Swiggert, a more experienced interrogator, but he was still out. Mabel offered to come as back-up, but the sheriff wanted her to swing by the Kelley brothers' place and get their statements on what they might have seen or heard the Monday night.

Grindstone Mountain Road lived up to its name. After the dirt road portion, it was practically washed out, disappearing into a stony, dry creek bed. Cody wondered how much further he had to go as the car bumped and jolted right and left. He was glad he lived right off the main highway and wondered why anyone would build up here. Even on a sunny day, this part was dark and menacing. Finally, a house came into view, a two-story clapboard painted white with a screened porch on one side and a well-tended front lawn. The house was landscaped with azaleas and backed up to the woods, where maples were beginning their autumn transformation into fiery reds and golds. Cody had to admit it was a peaceful, pleasant sight. When he exited his patrol car, he heard the rush of a nearby stream, probably the beginnings of the Spendthrift, he thought. A nice spot for a house, after all.

There was an old Dodge Caravan, faded blue, and a new-looking, green Jeep parked off to the side, both muddied, and the Jeep recently driven, judging from relatively fresh tire tracks in the grassy muck that served as a parking area. Cody glanced into the cars and studied the house. He noted a curtain in a second-floor window fluttering closed. A bird feeder by the porch was full of seed and blue jays were fighting off other smaller birds for the prize. Cody adjusted his shirt and tie, hat, and gently touched his gun in the holster. He walked up the front stone steps and tapped on the door with the high school class ring he wore on his right pinkie.

A woman opened the door a crack. "Oh, Officer. Can I help you, you lost?" She didn't open the door any further.

"No, ma'am, I'm not lost. Deputy Crawford here, I'd like to ask you a few questions. Anyone else in the home?"

"Deputy Crawford." Not a question, just a statement. The woman didn't open the door any further, simply peered out the opening at Cody.

"Ma'am, I'd like to come in and ask you a few questions," he repeated.

"What about?"

"Could you step outside, please?"

"No sir, I want to stay right where I'm at."

Cody saw a flicker of hardness in her eyes, colored an unusual light green. Her face was pale, and she wore no makeup; her hair was dark with flecks of gray and pulled back behind her head. He caught a whiff of the house, a subtle mustiness mixed with furniture polish, like the old pages of a book, a whole library of books.

"Okay. I would like to ask you a few questions, if I may." The woman nodded slightly but kept the door barely cracked.

"Mrs.?" Cody gave the woman a quizzical look.

"I am Skye."

"Okay. Skye. Do you have a last name?"

"What's this about, Officer?"

"I want to ask you about a phone call made from this house on Monday evening."

"A phone call? What about it?" She cocked her head and eyed Cody with suspicion.

"A phone call was made from your home phone to a land-line belonging to Daniel and Beth Perrault. Do you know why?"

"I don't know anything about that, it's impossible."

"Why is it impossible?"

"I don't know them."

"What about others in your household?"

"There isn't anyone else here."

"You live alone here?"

"Yes."

Cody took out his notepad and a ballpoint pen. "Ma'am, our records show this house is in the name of a Wilford Shanahan."

"He's dead," she interrupted.

"Oh, I'm sorry to hear that, ma'am. Would he have been your husband?"

"Officer, I haven't made any phone call to those people, so I don't believe I need to answer any more of your questions. There's no one else who could have made it either."

"Mrs...Skye. I respectfully ask that you step outside for further questioning. Otherwise I'll have to come back with a warrant to search your house." Cody was proud of his composure and authoritative voice.

She hesitated but opened the door, stepped out onto the landing and pulled the door almost to a close behind her. *What's she hiding?* Cody wondered. Slim, almost bony, with a pronounced jaw and thin, reedy neck, she wore a white T- shirt and tugged an oversized, black mohair cardigan around her as she emerged into the morning chill. Her slacks were silky-looking, lightweight, with a mix of colorful patterns and designs including a parade of little white elephants, trunk to tail, against a ruby-red, paisley background around the hemline. She was barefoot and stood with her shoulder towards Cody, hugging herself, a hostile stance. Her large, dangling earrings, strands of blue and red beads, rotated right then left with her slightest movement.

"Let me repeat my question. A phone call was placed Monday evening to the Perrault residence from your phone. Can you explain why that would be?"

"And *I* repeat, I have no idea, must be a mistake, didn't happen."

"Technology doesn't lie, Mrs. Skye. At 7:19 p.m. on Monday evening, a call from your phone was placed to the Perraults' home phone. Who else lives here?"

"I told you. No one."

"If you're lying to an officer of the law, that's a serious offense. Who are you protecting, and why?"

Skye pressed her lips together and looked at Deputy Crawford's badge. "I really can't help you. I'm sure there's a mistake here. Maybe crossed wires or something."

"I don't think that would be the case. I'm sorry if this is an inconvenient time but I'll have to ask you to come into the station and go on record, stating you did not make that phone call." Bodie had taught Cody to never take his eyes off someone's eye movements when interrogating. Skye's eyes darted for a split second to the upper right in the direction of the second story of the house. Cody didn't miss it. "If you would come into the station, you'll see your phone number in black and white on the Perrault phone log at the time and on the day that I stated."

"Officer, why is this phone call so important? I had nothing to do with…" Skye stopped.

"With what, ma'am?"

Cody stood ram-rod straight, waiting for a response. A brief gust of wind blew a few loose strands of hair across Skye's face, but she made no move to sweep them back. Cody sensed without looking that the trees behind the house started to billow, sending a handful of colorful leaves sailing into the air. The bird feeder swayed, scattering the birds, and the splash of the stream adjacent to the property seemed amplified on the waft of air.

Deputy Crawford took a deep breath and said loud and clear, "Mrs. Skye, sometime between 11 p.m. and midnight that same evening, Monday into Tuesday last, Mr. Perrault was killed, beaten and left on our main highway in a sleeping bag." He studied her face for any reaction and saw a brief flicker of pain.

From the interior of the house came a wail of anguish. For a moment, everything seemed to freeze in place. First to move in the split second that followed was Cody, who un-holstered his gun. Immediately, Skye screamed and pushed open the door. "Cocheta!" she cried. "Cocheta!" She ran toward the stairs and started up them two at a time, stumbling and catching herself with the bannister, Cody following briskly behind her. Skye reached the second-floor landing first and ran to a closed door. Locked! "Cocheta! What are you doing? What have you done?" she screeched, weeping now and clawing at the door.

"Stand back, ma'am," Cody ordered. He kicked open the door with gun drawn and stepped cautiously inside, Skye behind him. Cocheta was sitting on the bed, cradling her face in her hands, heaving uncontrollably. Beads of blood dotted her cheeks where she'd dug in her nails. Skye ran to her and wrapped her arms around her, pulling her head to her shoulder. The girl sobbed with abandon, stamping her feet, then tearing at her hair.

Cody approached her guardedly and waited silently for a full minute before speaking, hoping she'd calm down. When she continued to cry, albeit a more quietly, he spoke. "Miss, I'm going to have to ask you and your mother to come down to the station for questioning." He felt perplexed. *Why did the mother lie? Did she really not know about the phone call, not know Daniel Perrault? And Cocheta, something needs explaining here.*

Cody's handheld radio clipped to his belt snapped to life. He recognized the sheriff's voice, but the signal was too garbled to understand.

"Excuse me a minute. I'm going to have to ask you both to stay right where you are." Cody dashed downstairs and out the door, strode quickly to his vehicle and sat in the driver's seat to radio back to Sheriff Stryker.

"Cody, you still up at the Grindstone Mountain place?"

"Yes, sir. Got a bit of a bombshell going on here."

"I think I know what you're 'bout to say. That girl that lives there, 'cording to my sources, she was Daniel Perrault's lover, had a little rendez-voo place for their meetings. Bodie and I is comin' up, so sit tight, will ya? I got Detective Koons preparing a warrant to search their house as we speak."

"Roger that."

When Cody returned to the girl's bedroom, she was lying down and Skye was trying to offer her a glass of water. Cocheta's left arm was crooked over her eyes to cover them and the other hand clutched at her stomach. No longer sobbing, she alternated between groaning and sniffling.

"Ma'am, Miss, Sheriff Stryker and Chief Deputy Bodie Talon are on their way here. We'll have to respectfully ask you both to accompany us to the station for questions concerning the death of Daniel Perrault."

Cocheta cried out, "No, you must be wrong! He can't be dead, he *can't* be." She resumed sobbing into the bedclothes.

"Officer, I know nothing about this, or why the phone call. I'm in the dark here. I know Mr. Perrault owned the store where my daughter used to work, that's it."

"Ma'am, in that case, you'll have to explain at the station why you lied to an officer of the law about not knowing the deceased, and about your daughter being here in the house when you said no one else lived here."

"It was clear something bad happened, but I swear I had no idea what! I was trying to protect my daughter." Skye brought her fingers to her temples and shut her eyes tight, then turned to address Cocheta. "What haven't you told me? Is this why you came home so upset last night? Wouldn't get up this morning?" Cocheta only moaned and turned away from her mother to face the wall. Her long black hair splayed wildly across the pillow and bedclothes, her sky-blue shirt trimmed with a black and white fringe of beads across the shoulders had come untucked from her jeans. "Cocheta, you must look at me, tell me! Did you make this phone call? Did you kill this man?"

Cocheta sat up at once, frantic with grief and cried out, "No! Don't you see? I *love* him. He can't be dead, he can't be!" She collapsed again and wept into her pillow.

Skye threw up her hands in disbelief. "How can this be? You never let on, never said! Answer me this — you went to school, didn't you? You weren't skipping school over this and lying to me?" Cocheta shook her head. "Answer me! To my face!"

Cocheta lifted her face. "I went to school, Mama."

All of a sudden, Cocheta started to laugh in a distracted, wild-eyed way, hysteria setting in. She focused her eyes on Deputy Crawford. Through sniffles and hiccups, she managed to get a few halting words out. "I thought you'd come to arrest me because of the cabin, the abandoned house where Daniel and I went to meet." She heaved a huge sigh and continued with difficulty. "Not to see if I'd murdered the only man I'll ever love."

Skye leaned over the bed, pumping the mattress up and down crying, "Oh my God. A *house*, Cocheta? You hid this from me? How long, how is this possible?"

Cody heard the sound of cars on the rocks and gravel of the drive, heralding Spike's and Bodie's arrival.

"Miss, you and your mother will need to come to the station. We'll need a statement from both of you concerning Mr. Perrault's last hours, that phone call and, miss, details on your relationship with him." Skye plopped into a chair, fingered her earrings. "Why can't we answer your questions here? You can see Cocheta is in no condition to travel, especially to an unfamiliar place."

"Sorry, but we must get your statements on the record." A loud knock and heavy footsteps ensued as the sheriff and Bodie entered the house.

"Sheriff, upstairs here," Cody called out.

All three officers stood in the small room looking at Cocheta who finally sat up and agreed to a few sips of water from her mother. Her eyes were red and swollen, her cheeks flushed, and her hair and clothes completely disheveled. In spite of her current appearance, it was clear she was a beauty, with lush, raven-black hair reaching to her waist, an alluringly defiant mouth and jaw, and skin a deep, golden brown set off by stunning, almond-shaped green eyes.

"I think it's best we all head to the station soon's we can," Spike said, "and get your statements. We have quite a few questions for you both, I'm sure you can understand, concerning the circumstances of

Mr. Daniel Perrault's death."

Cocheta clutched her stomach again and tears welled in her eyes. "What about his wife, Daniel's wife?" she whispered meekly. "Does she know?"

"We'll go over everything at the station," Spike said. "Ma'am, we would appreciate it if you'd help your daughter downstairs and into one of the police vehicles."

By noon, mother and daughter were in the interview room at the station. Skye asked, and was denied, her request to drive herself and Cocheta so it didn't look like they were being arrested for anything should a neighbor see them in the sheriff's vehicle. "Deputy Jenks, or Deputy Swiggert when he gets in, will drive you back to your home when we're done. Please don't worry." Spike tried to sound comforting but he was itching to peel back the layers to Cocheta's story. He believed somewhere in it was motive for murder, but where?

"How did you meet Mr. Perrault?"

"I worked a few hours in the morning at his farm store, L'Esprit du Pays, in town until I went to school in the early afternoon. I usually opened it at seven in the morning." Cocheta clutched at tissue, trembling and shaky.

"He came by frequently, I assume, to check on things?"

"Yes, frequently."

"When did you and Mr. Perrault become involved with one another?"

"A few days before Christmas last year."

"And when did you start going to this cabin to meet in secret?"

• • •

Cocheta's fingers touching the cut on his chin electrified him. Daniel pulled her to him. "Just remember — you touched me first." With that he pressed his lips to hers, relishing their plump softness, gently guiding his tongue around them and into her mouth. She was receptive.

"Put the "closed" sign on the door and hop into my truck," he said into her ear. She did as he asked, and Daniel followed her outside and into the truck.

"But what will Mr. Pantoja think if he comes by? He usually stops by sometime early in the morning to check on me, see if I need anything, you know, change or something."

"I will call him in a few minutes and tell him I needed to close for a couple of hours to assess the merchandise. Not a problem when you own the store, don't you think?" He smiled and drew her close to his side, taking in her scent.

They drove to Daniel's house, as Beth was in the city for the weekend. Cocheta rested her head on Daniel's lap so no one they passed on the road would see her with him. He led her inside to the kitchen and asked if she needed anything to eat or drink, then took her jacket and hung it on the back of a kitchen chair.

"No, thank you. Your house is beautiful, so big. You built it, I know."

"Yes, I'll show you around." Daniel showed her his study, then the large library and entertainment area of the middle structure as well as the two guest suites above. "That's my wife's study, the last house." He pointed.

"It's nice, the porch is so pretty."

"Come, I'll show you the master bedroom. There are skylights." Daniel took Cocheta's hand and guided her upstairs. "Aren't the views incredible? You can see the entire valley from the bed. I love waking here and at night, studying the universe through the skylights."

"Is that a closet?" Cocheta indicated the his-and-hers walk-in closet.

"Yes."

"And your wife's clothes?" She ran her hand along them as they walked through to the master bathroom. "And a huge tub! It must be nice to soak there!"

"Yes, Beth likes to."

"Where is she, your wife?"

"My wife, fair maiden, is in the city at our other house for a couple of days. And so, Miss Conchita, we are all alone here." One at a time, Daniel slowly removed the bobby pins holding Cocheta's hair in its tousled mess, watching as her sable-colored tresses cascaded down her back and across her breasts. How long he had waited for this moment, to drink in this enchanting goddess? She was exquisite, exotic, luscious to behold. Daniel had been with many women before marrying Beth, but Conchita was by far the most bewitching.

Young, sensual, an eye-ful of beauty, she was. His hands shook, and he put both his hands in her hair and again sought her mouth with his, delirious with desire.

"Conchita, Conchita, what am I going to do about you?" he murmured. "I want you so badly and have for so long a time."

"You've wanted *me*? I can't believe you ever even noticed me! I've always thought you were really amazing — the store, the restaurant and everything. I respect you so much. And now I think I am probably in love with you!"

They embraced each other tightly, their bodies a perfect fit against each other, and Daniel led her to his bed. "How old are you, my Conchita?"

"Seventeen, but almost eighteen."

"And do you have a lover, have you had lovers?"

"I've been with a boy before, but I have no one now."

"Who could possibly ever let you go? You are not a trifle, you are a *star* and I will treat you so."

"Mr. Perrault, you're so nice! I'm just a country girl."

"Call me Daniel, *nom de Dieu*! I will take care of you and you will not be 'just a country girl' ever again." He began to gently unbutton her blouse, nuzzling her neck, his erection close to the bursting point. He unclasped her bra and her golden breasts spilled out. He lowered her onto his bed and his breath came hot and feverish as his tongue circled first one nipple then the other, savoring her scent, a mix of wilted flowers and vanilla. Her velvety pink nipples immediately blossomed into rigid nubs as Daniel began to toy and nibble. She groaned, an animal purr, he thought, further exciting him, if that was possible.

As he pulled his sweater over his head and began to unfasten his belt, he noticed Beth's hairbrush and a stack of books she intended to read on the bedside table, as well as a small photo of them on their wedding day in an antique silver frame. He dropped his eyes in shame and his desire for Cocheta vanished in a heartbeat. Daniel went over to the window and looked out towards the pastures where a few of his cows were grazing on the hay Garret and Quinn had spread for them sometime in the last couple of days.

"What's wrong, Mr., I mean Daniel? You don't want me after all?" Cocheta sat up and rebuttoned her shirt, embarrassed and concerned.

"Oh, yes, I want you, Conchita. Make no mistake about that. I just don't want you here, in my bedroom. It doesn't feel right."

"I understand. What should we do?"

"I have an idea. Come with me." Daniel sprinted down the stairs with Cocheta's hand in his. They jumped into his truck and he drove as far as he could along the right-of-way then up across one of Thorne's fields to the very lip of the furthest woods, inching in a few yards so the truck, he thought, wouldn't be seen. He parked and turned to Cocheta.

"Now."

They began again as before, and Daniel moved the bench seat back as far as it would go. Kneeling on the cab floor, he gently pushed up her skirt, slipped off her panties and spread her legs. There was no holding him back now! The goblet he had yearned to drink from for weeks was now before him, ambrosial and enchanting to behold. He kissed her soft pubic hair and flicked his tongue in and out of her until her whole body rose in a spasm of unbearable bliss. "Oh my God, oh, Daniel! I didn't know I could ever feel anything like this. Oh, God, come into me, please. I want you so badly. I love you more than anything." Her eyes closed, and she cupped his face, stroking his jaw line with her thumbs.

Daniel lay on top of her, barely able to endure his desire. They kissed, Daniel absorbing her taste and smell. He began at her hairline, moving down to her eyelids, her sublime cheekbones, the cusp of her earlobe, to the long slope of her sensual neck. His pulse throbbed beyond reason and he prepared to enter her, flooded with a craving he didn't understand and apparently couldn't control.

All of a sudden, he heard a rap on the window and turned his head to see Thorne's face cupped against the driver's side. He was using his sleeve to make a circle in the condensation on the window outside so he could look inside. Daniel sat up, pants around his knees, and revved the engine, backing up and taking off at breakneck speed before Thorne could even step back far enough to avoid a spray of mud against his overalls.

Daniel took Cocheta back to the farm store. Neeraj hadn't been by yet so there wouldn't be any questions, he didn't think. He walked her inside and slumped against the counter. Cocheta came up behind him and put her arms around him.

"Conchita, it's risky, for you, for me. I have a wife. I don't want to hurt her. You've charmed me, and I want nothing more than to be with you whenever I can be." He turned and placed his lips against her temple, savoring the gentle throbbing he could feel there, and the scent — citrus? pine? — of her hair. "But we must be very cautious. Do you understand what I mean?" Looking at her — God, those eyes! — he watched her silently nod. "We need a safe place to meet. I won't be able to see you for a while this way. The holidays at the restaurant will be very busy and I must oversee Bernard, my chef, who is turning out to be a crazy person. Then, Beth and I are going to France for most of January..."

"No!"

"Yes, it's been long-planned, my Conchita. We see my parents and friends, and ski. I'll be thinking of you every minute, wanting you, but we can't meet like this again. Maybe we could find a private place to meet, I don't know. My neighbor saw us, and this could be very bad."

"Would he say anything, do you think?"

"I don't know. He likes, really loves, Beth, so I don't think he would want her to know anything that would upset her, but still, this cannot happen again." He ran his hands through her long, silky hair and twisted it into a knot at the nape of her neck, kissing and nibbling her ear, reminding himself to collect and throw out the bobby pins he'd left on the dresser in the bedroom.

A car door slammed in the rear parking lot and they quickly drew apart, Daniel pretending to peruse products on the shelves, Conchita opening the front door to remove the "closed" sign and hurrying to her spot by the register.

Daniel realized he'd forgotten to call the store manager in case he saw the "closed" sign. "Ah, good morning Neeraj. I was taking stock of what items I might want to order from France while Beth and I are there next month."

"Very good, Mr. Perrault. Busy this morning, Cocheta?"

"Very quiet so far, Mr. Pantoja." She knotted her scarf around her neck and prepared to leave for school.

"I think because you forgot to remove the "closed" sign, no?"

CHAPTER NINE

DID MR. PANTOJA or Mr. Perrault's neighbor ever say anything? That they suspected you two were involved with one another?" Sheriff Stryker asked. He felt both repulsed and intrigued by the young girl sitting before him. Christ, barely out of puberty and sexually involved with a married man! He tried to push the medical report details out of his thoughts but couldn't.

"Never. At least the neighbor didn't know I was the one in the car that day. Daniel, Mr. Perrault, later told me the neighbor threatened to tell his wife he saw him with a girl in the car if he wasn't compensated for the damage to his field."

"All right, what happened when Mr. Perrault returned from France?"

Cocheta took a deep, sorrowful breath. "I knew about lots of empty houses, some completely abandoned, in the hollows. I pass them all the time. I thought if I found something, it would be the best place for us to meet. Daniel wouldn't want a paper trail, I figured, so while he was gone, I drove around looking for someplace."

Skye shook her head and whispered, "How could you? Behind my back, all this?"

Cocheta hung her head and wiped at her nose with a small wad of tissue. Deputy Jenks moved the tissue box closer to her, and she gave him a weak smile.

"I wanted somewhere pretty secluded, but not too hard to get to. We just didn't want to be seen or hurt anyone." She glanced at her mother.

"I found a place up Prattle Hollow, set back in the woods by a little brook."

• • •

Daniel didn't come by the store at all before he left for France after the holidays. He was looking forward to a break from the frenzied pace of the restaurant, and especially from Bernard. His confusion and remorse over both the unexpected encounter with Fleur and his sexual seduction of young Conchita weighed on him, putting him in a sullen and dispirited mood. Beth asked if he'd prefer not to go to Périgord or if he was simply tired of the tumult surrounding Bernard and the restaurant generally.

"Non, chérie, I most definitely want to go away. I want to see family, friends, be with you." He gave her shoulder a squeeze as he walked down the stairs to his study. He couldn't even look her in the eye, he felt so culpable, deceptive, which of course he was! And yet, what harm was done? Fleur's a lonely nobody who tricked *him*, corrupted *him*. He hadn't wanted her! And Conchita, Conchita — why is she so irresistible? He'd have to end it or drown, obvious to him even now. Périgord would clear his head, help him figure things out. He wouldn't hurt Beth, he couldn't. Time away from Conchita would surely weaken her mystique, wouldn't it? He thought of the moment before Thorne — damn him! — interrupted them, his whole body aching in agony for her, to be in her. She was everything he wanted. He wanted her now. He opened the sliding door to the Zen garden, stepped outside and waited until his erection subsided, taking deep gulps of cold air to assuage his torment.

Cocheta began to think the whole thing with Daniel had been a dream. His silence was hurtful, but he had warned her, and she didn't try to contact him or see him at the restaurant. Instead, she fantasized about him, reliving his kisses, his tender words. She loved him! A man, not a boy. She wasn't a virgin, but the one real boy-friend she'd had was a local twit who didn't know the first thing about girls, or what true intimacy meant. She was noticed, she knew she was pretty and she liked the effect she had on men, but she didn't flaunt it, preferring to be stand-offish, aloof.

Daniel was different: worldly, accomplished, talented, charming. She'd harbored a crush on him from the first time she met him, but the idea he would want her too had been unimaginable. And now! She never thought this could happen to her, a backwoods country girl with such a cultured, refined man. She was dying to tell her friend

Tracy about him, his manners, his beautiful house, but of course she couldn't, at least not yet, for fear word would somehow get out and ruin everything. Cocheta knew his wife too; she often stopped by the store, checking supplies in the stockroom or making notes. She liked her, but once she fell in love with Daniel, Beth became a shadow, a phantom with no significance and she never thought about her at all.

With the community college closed for the holidays, she spent most of her day at the farm store arranging and rearranging the shelves, running errands for Mr. Pantoja to gather ingredients for holiday cakes and pies his wife would prepare, purchasing wrapping paper, ribbon and cards for a special Christmas display. She bought gifts for Daniel, a picture frame with a photo of her in it and a wallet of real calfskin.

At night, she mooned over Daniel in her room. Christmas day itself was lonely, just she and her mother exchanging gifts, although her mother made an effort with a mid-day meal of honey ham, braised apples, onions, and potatoes she'd stored in the root cellar from their summer garden. Cocheta made a small chocolate *bûche de noël*. "The farm store has an easy-to-follow little cookbook," she told her mother who was surprised her daughter could make anything so delicious. Later, they visited with Skye's relatives over the mountain, deep country folk whose talk centered on weather and local gossip.

She wasn't sure when Daniel left for France and asked Mr. Pantoja if he knew the date he would be back.

"Oh, I think they will be away most of the month. He was near exhaustion after the holidays and Beth insisted he take a good long rest. They love the area he's from, you know, like to go in the winter to ski."

Cocheta felt her stomach lurch in surprise and dismay. "But he's leaving the restaurant a long time with only the chef in charge, isn't he?"

"Yes, I know. Bernard seems a little nutty, but he's a good chef. I think Mr. Perrault believes he needs time in January, a slow period, to prove he can work well without interference. We'll see."

To mask her disappointment, Cocheta aimlessly pushed a broom around the shop. He would forget her, gone so long. She was nothing to him.

"When do your classes start again, Cocheta? You seem bored. It's a quiet time after the frenzy of the holidays, not much for you to do here, I know. Mr. Perrault will come back with wonderful new purchases and ideas from France and then things will perk up again." He smiled and handed her the dustpan.

"Yes, when he's back."

Cocheta decided she'd look for a special hideaway anyway, just in case, and spent the afternoons after finishing at the farm store, driving the Jeep into the back roads and hollows of Wayne County. Snow came soon after New Year's and she relished the beauty of the woods under its fresh, white blanket, its trails unblemished but for the light tracks of rabbit or fox, the silence absolute. She had her eye on an old log cabin about a mile into Prattle Hollow from the main road, nestled into the woods where a little brook, now partially frozen, glittered. Her friend Tracy once told her she used to go there to drink with her boyfriend and no one ever came by or noticed anything. She'd described it as pretty clean, solidly built, no leaks or drafts, with a big fireplace.

Cocheta pushed open the heavy wooden door, sagging a bit off its hinges, and looked around at the inside. Dark, an odor of ashes and moss, earthy but not unpleasant. A collection of dusty bottles and cans littered one corner, but no other sign of recent use was apparent. The two little windows were dingy, and the fireplace was filled with a heap of old, charred logs. The floor seemed clean enough and may have been swept not too long ago — no evidence of mouse droppings or other animals or insects. She'd check thoroughly with a flashlight later, though.

What to do? Should she prepare it for Daniel's return or wait and see what his frame of mind was? What if he laughed at her when she told him she'd found a secret spot where they could meet, or didn't even remember after weeks away he'd brought the idea up? Once the school semester started up, she wouldn't have much time to ready the cabin and make it welcoming, and even then, their moments together would be so brief! She needed to talk to somebody and decided she would tell Tracy what had happened.

"You are sworn to secrecy. No one hears about this!"

"I won't tell a soul, Cocheta, I promise. I can't believe it, though, a married man! A French guy!"

"Should I do this? I mean, what if he forgot about me while he was in France?"

"You'll have to find out, won't you? Just fix it up a little and see what happens."

"I guess I'll clean it at least, bring in some fresh wood for a fire. It could be such a cute place, snug and protected for Daniel and me to meet at." Cocheta sighed. "You're the only one I'm telling, Tracy. If my mom finds out or his wife, I'll be screwed forever. My uncles might actually kill him or something!"

"Lips are sealed."

Cocheta boxed up the bottles and cans and took them to the dump, then scrubbed the floor and windows. She swept out the fireplace and checked the flue with a lit piece of newspaper — it worked! She brought a big basket from her mother's root cellar and collected wood and kindling in the woods. When classes started again, she went to the Walmart in town and bought an egg crate foam pad and a cold weather sleeping bag, depleting her pay for most of the preceding month. She put a big, blue vase of red-berried holly branches inside next to the door and finally, as a homey touch, laid her gifts to Daniel on top of the sleeping bag. She liked the end result, rustic but cheerful. When the afternoon sun sparkled through the trees casting shafts of light across the wooden floor planks, it looked downright cozy.

Then she waited for his return.

Toward the end of January, Cocheta's heart jumped when she saw Daniel's red pickup in the farm store parking lot as she pulled into work. He was back! She checked her face in her rearview mirror. Her hair was in one long, thick braid down her back and she wore a pink turtle neck sweater under her winter coat, black leggings and knee-high, black boots. She took a moment to put on some pale pink lipstick and calm her beating heart, then leapt like a young colt from the Jeep, flushed and eager.

He was perusing the merchandise and making notes in a spiral notebook when she entered, bringing the freshness of a January morning inside with her — a cold, clean smell with a hint of wood smoke, maybe a faint sweetness, sap? He drank her in as she stood silhouetted in the open doorway, feeling his knees weaken beneath him. He let a soft moan escape his lips and slowly placed his notebook and pen on top of the display case. "Conchita." She closed the door and they came together in one long embrace.

"I wanted to get you out of my mind, but I fear I might not have," he mumbled into her hair. "What am I to do with you?"

For her part, Cocheta wept quietly onto his shoulder. "I thought you'd forgotten me, that you felt you'd made a terrible mistake being with me."

"I have!"

"My life these past weeks has been nothing but thinking about you, Daniel. I love you."

"I don't know how we can do this. It's reckless and insane for both of us."

Cocheta placed her forefinger to his lips. "Shh. I have a place for us, Daniel. When you're ready, I'll show it to you."

He looked at her, absorbing her flawless brown skin dappled with light freckles across her exquisite nose, the lush, coal-black lashes encircling those green pools of vast, almost surreal, enticement for him. He was lost again and could not explain why or how. He loved his wife! What spell had Conchita cast over him that he was incapable of resisting her?

"Where is this place?" He ran his hand along the loops of her braid and brought the ends to his nose and then his lips. She smelled of cinnamon, traces of warm bread, something from his childhood.

"Not far, about a mile off the main road up Prattle Hollow. It's a log cabin with a big fireplace. No other house is around."

"Whose place is this, Conchita? How do you know someone won't come around or notice something?

"I don't for sure, but it's the best place around. My friend Tracy told me the high school kids used to go there and drink, but they don't anymore."

"Wait, you told this Tracy about us?"

"No!"

"Let me think, Conchita, let me think." He backed away from her. "I have much to do, meetings, inventory, and Beth and I...we have things to do at the house. You understand." Cocheta nodded mutely, sad and disappointed. She slowly unbuttoned her coat and went into the stock room to hang it and collect the key for the cash register.

"Don't be unhappy! Here, I brought you a gift from France." He reached into his coat pocket and produced a small red leather box with 'Cartier' embossed in gold on the top, gold trim around the edges. "Open it." She took the box and thanked him with her eyes, then removed the top to uncover two pearl earrings and a silver bracelet nestled in soft, white cotton.

"Oh, these are *beautiful*!" she exclaimed.

"The real thing, Conchita, pearls and silver. For you, my country girl."

"Thank you, Daniel." She put on the bracelet and held one of the earrings to her ear lobe. "What do you think?"

"Perfect for the most beautiful girl in the world."

"Daniel, I have gifts for you too, but I don't have them here. They're at the cabin."

Daniel sighed. "I know you've done the right thing, Conchita. I told you it had to be so before I left. It's just, it's a big step. We need to be sure we want this. *Mon Dieu*, you're so young. I have a wife!" He tried not to look at her, her beautiful face radiantly juxtaposed against the soft pink of her sweater, the strong, slender thighs he'd spread to pleasure her, how she'd arched her back. She stood quietly before him, soft bangs framing her face, her comely braid curling across her breasts.

"You're afraid we'll be caught."

"No, I'm afraid for you."

"There's no reason. It's what I want, Daniel."

"I can't leave my wife."

"I know you can't. I don't ask this of you."

"You can live with sharing me?"

"Oh, yes!"

"But it will always be in secret."

"I don't care, as long as I can be with you an hour, a minute, a whole day. What does it matter?"

Daniel ran his hands through his hair. "Show me this place, then. Tonight."

"When, what time? I'll have to make an excuse to my mother."

"Ah, yes, your mother. What time are you done here, or at school?"

"I could skip class today."

"*Non!* I will never ask that of you."

"I'm done at four o'clock today."

"I suppose I could skip tonight's dinner service. Bernard's been doing well on his own and it's very quiet right now." He looked away from her. "My wife won't be back until late. She went into the city to check on the townhouse this morning." He couldn't tamp down the familiar pangs of remorse he always felt about what he might be doing to Beth. She often loomed painfully in his mind when he was with Conchita. And why not? He shouldn't be starting this up again. Beth didn't deserve this betrayal! But Conchita, Conchita. He had no defense against her! The heat she kindled in him had so far refused to sputter out.

"I'll walk from the restaurant and meet you at the little bridge over the river. You can pull up there, I think, without being seen. You know where I mean?" She nodded. "Five o'clock?" She nodded again.

He kissed her on both cheeks, her nose and finally her mouth, full, fleshy lips pressing into his, intense, fervent. Against his better judgement, Daniel was lost to her again.

The early evening was clear but brisk and patches of an earlier snowfall, crusty and mud-spattered, dotted the roads and countryside. Dusk was imminent and there was no moon. Daniel paused, coatless, on the front porch of the restaurant looking up at the sky. He began to pace, torn between the allure of an hour of bliss with Conchita and his awareness of how wrong, wrong, wrong it was for her, for Beth, for him. He'd almost confessed the temptation he faced to his father while in Périgord, his father who'd had a brief affair many years ago but who'd always put Daniel's mother on a pedestal, declaring her the only one he'd ever loved. His dalliance did no damage to the marriage as far as Daniel knew.

So why would making occasional love to Conchita be so sinful? He loved Beth even though the early excitement of their marriage had faded into the mundane, their interests diverging. He knew she wanted a child and he didn't, at least not yet. In Périgord, as he tried to put Conchita out of his thoughts, he spent every moment with Beth and they'd been companionable enough, skiing, eating out with friends, shopping. He bought her lavish gifts: a gold choker of a red-eyed lizard with a small jade clasp, expensive perfumes, a Dior purse. He was glad he'd bought something for Conchita too, hiding the box in the back of a file cabinet at the restaurant so Beth wouldn't find it. *Why shouldn't he buy her expensive presents? She'd never see anything like this back in Wayne County! She could sell them someday if she needed the money.*

His parents loved Beth, always had. She was an engaging conversationalist, even in French, and enjoyed discussing politics and Franco-American relations with them, subjects Daniel hated to involve himself in. Her intelligence had been a major reason he was attracted to her in the first place, and he knew living in Scarcity deprived her of the stimulation she'd been used to through work and city life to a certain extent. He should pay more attention! She deserved it! The early success of Perigeaux, as well as the artists' atelier, was at least partially due to her; she'd never wavered in her support of him. He'd been unfair and negligent, accusing her of fooling around with Marcus, demeaning her photography. What a *malotru* he was! A cad, plain and simple! He paced.

He thought of Fleur, a depraved but minor transgression on his part, never to be repeated and he would halt the obsession with Conchita! He would! And yet, making love to Beth was merely adequate and at their most passionate moments, it was Conchita's face he saw.

Should he go to this secret place with Conchita? Where would it end if he did? *Maybe once.* Beth would sense something, surely, smell her on him. *She's seventeen! What's wrong with him? He doesn't even know if she'd turned eighteen yet, what she was studying, who she was, really. Why this strange hold on him? Why, why, why?* He closed his eyes and thought of the little gap between her front teeth, the taste on her tongue, the way she purred with pleasure when they'd been together in his pickup.

He rushed back into the restaurant and grabbed his coat, telling Bernard he had some things to take care of and would stop in later to see how the dinner service went.

He moved his pickup further over in the parking area where he thought it wouldn't be noticed and sprinted, hands in the pockets of his pea-coat, head down like a criminal on the lam, crossing the street in front of the restaurant then taking a path along an open field to the little wooden bridge over the Spendthrift River just out-side of town. He waited, pressed against the railing, until he saw the green Jeep come down the road and pull over opposite the bridge.

Daniel jumped in the passenger side and settled in, slouching down in case there might be eyes around. Cocheta pulled carefully back onto the road and then out onto the highway.

"It's not very far. I drove up there a couple of days ago and there's very little ice left on the road. Just a couple of spots where the sun can't reach."

"Conchita, I almost didn't come. But I'm here. I don't know if we should do this again." He rubbed his hands together to warm them then put them over his ears, which were red with cold. His coat wasn't nearly thick enough and he shivered. She said nothing. "It doesn't mean I don't want to, I do. But I don't want to hurt you or anybody."

She turned onto the gravel road known as Prattle Hollow, and with the sky darkening, put on the high beams. "It's up here about a mile on the right, hard to see, I'm guessing, in the nighttime so we need to look for an old rusty mailbox, bent over. That's the turnoff."

"Are you listening? I don't want this to be a bad experience for you or for me."

"I'm listening."

"This is very dangerous for many people: you, me, my wife, your mother even."

"I won't press you if you never want to come here again."

"That's fair. And I would never ask you to do anything that inter-feres with school, work or others."

"Here we are." She turned into a driveway and rolled over a wooden bridge barely wide enough for the Jeep. The cabin was in a small clearing but protected from view by a swath of pines in front.

She led the way, pushing the door open. They went in and Daniel saw how she'd prepared the space for their... what else could he call it but a tryst? She strode in, drew a box of matches from her pocket and lit two candles in holders next to the sleeping bag, then put a match to the wood she'd prepared for a fire. Soon, the little one-room cabin was warming up in a honey-colored glow.

"Won't someone notice the smoke from the chimney?" Daniel peered out the window but saw no sign of the lights of another house.

"We're far enough from the road, I think, and with the trees, it won't be seen."

"What about smelling the smoke?"

"There're enough people who heat with firewood up in the hollows. It wouldn't be unusual."

"Conchita, how old are you? Are you eighteen yet?" He paced again, hands back in his pockets.

"In April."

"Not until April?"

"Look, Daniel, I bought you two gifts." She bent to gather the two small presents she'd placed on the sleeping bag, wrapped in crimson Christmas paper decorated with prancing reindeer pulling sleighs and knotted with little white bows.

He unwrapped the wallet where she'd tucked a lock of her ribbon-tied hair and then the picture frame with a photo of her inside. She was kneeling, facing the camera with her hands twisting her long hair in front of her, the hint of a smile on her lips. She wore a white bikini. It was a very sensual picture.

"Thank you, very nice. I will leave them here on the mantel for now." He turned to face her. "Conchita, tell me about you. I don't know anything about you. What are you studying? Do you like working for Mr. Pantoja at the farm store?" It bothered him they'd rarely talked about anything. He was interested, this was not just about wanting her!

"There's not much to tell. I live with my mother. My father was never part of my life. My mother was disowned by her father when she got pregnant with me, and she earned money by sewing and selling her dresses at flea markets and by cleaning houses. I love working at the store and Mr. Pantoja is very kind to me. I open it at seven and he comes by in the late morning so I can get to school on time. I'm studying to be a nurse at the community college. I have one friend, Tracy. That's it, really"

Daniel thought of his life, the opulent childhood home on the hillsides of Périgord with limitless views of the Dordogne, the river and valley, ski trips, summering on the Mediterranean on friends' yachts, his happy extended family, and he was sad for Conchita.

"I wish I could help you. A nurse! That is wonderful. Is the work difficult?"

"It can be challenging. I'll have to study later than usual tonight." She smiled. "Don't feel sorry for me, Daniel. I'm happy knowing you, even if it's this way."

"But you are too special to live this *insulaire* life. I will help you."

"You *are* helping me. I feel special when I'm with you."

"I'd like to do more someday, make sure you have a happy life, Conchita."

Daniel was finally warm enough to remove his coat and stood facing the fire. He knew he shouldn't be here. Conchita was so young, nearly twenty years his junior, trusting and inexperienced in the ways of the world. *Was his attraction to her fair?* She would need more than a love affair with a married man to escape life in the hollows and make something of herself. If she was worth him risking everything, he would find a way to help her.

For now, though, his interest was in making love to her.

She began by breathing gently into his ear, sending a tingle down his spine and into his groin. Then she slipped her tongue inside, deep, and gently thrust in and out for several moments, switching from one ear to the other. "I want to touch every part of you with my tongue first," she said. She nibbled one ear lobe and traced his jaw line with her tongue to the other. Daniel was in agony but wanted to suffer as long as she wanted him to. He removed his clothes and watched as she removed hers. Her body, so young, so nubile! The curve of her neck and shoulders, the flat belly and slender legs. A vision of loveliness he couldn't believe was being offered to him now, at this moment, in this place.

By the time she was on her knees kissing his inner thighs, he could bear it no longer. He scooped her into his arms and brought her into the sleeping bag where they feasted on each other, oblivious to the passage of time, first he on top then she, driving him to the brink, teasing him, her juicy breasts hanging over his mouth, her long hair covering him like an enchanted curtain. He could not stop, he could not get enough of her, her smells, her taste, nor she of him. She was as tireless as she was enchanting. Daniel lay exhausted when she began again, sucking on each toe, spreading his legs wide so she could fill her mouth with him and then bring him into her again, heaving and panting until she cried out. At last they were both spent.

After making love to Conchita the first time that late winter afternoon in the cabin, the mere scent of her whenever he entered L'Esprit du Pays drove him into vigorous longing for her. His name for her, Conchita, rolled around in his brain during the slightest lull in his day, and excruciatingly at night as he lay awake and imagined her with him. She became the goddess of his most ardent desires and cravings. He hungered for her constantly, consumed by passion and sexual eroticism. She would do anything for and with him, she was a minx and a dominatrix without even knowing. A girl of seventeen with a voice as seductive as any grown woman. What she could do with her hands and her tongue! She was his Lolita, his muse, his vessel, his bottomless pit of gluttony and debauchery, leaving him always insatiate.

But like most white-hot passions, it was inevitably destined to ebb and, finally, burn out.

● ● ●

Sheriff Stryker exited the interview room leaving Deputy Crawford sitting with Cocheta and her mother. Detective Koons had arrived with a warrant to search the Shanahan house and property. He skimmed it hurriedly until he saw Ronnie Swiggert's patrol car swing into the station parking lot. He strode over to the front door to hold it open for him.

"Glad to see you finally decided to join the department again, Deputy Swiggert. We got a humdinger of a case goin' on here and I've needed your help. I gotta get you up to speed and get you investigatin' with me. We still haven't got a rock-hard suspect, godammit!"

"I'm real sorry 'bout bein' ill the last coupla days, Sheriff. Real sorry 'bout it."

"Well, never mind. I want you to read up on the reports we got so far, but first you and Bodie is gonna go up Prattle Hollow and find the little love nest this Miss Shanahan and the deceased apparently shared. She said it's 'bout a mile up on the right, an abandoned log cabin."

"Sheriff, I don't need the Chief Deputy with me. I know Prattle Hollow like the back of my hand. I know the cabin. My place is in that hollow, you know."

"Ronnie, I know, but I want Bodie with you. I don't want anything touched. You and Bodie get pictures of every square inch inside and out, you got that? Forensics will be up there soon's they can be."

"Yes, sir, but…"

"Bodie is goin' and that's an order!"

"Yes, sir." He caught sight of Cocheta in the interview room as Spike held open the door to let Cody take a break before Spike went in to resume his questioning. She saw him, too, and gave him a frosty glance.

With Chief Deputy Talon in the passenger seat, Deputy Swiggert steered his patrol car slowly up the gravel road toward the turnoff for the cabin. He was peeved at the sheriff for sending him back up Prattle Hollow, passing his own place in the process. He'd much rather be present in the interview room and hear what Cocheta had to say for herself.

"The sheriff is thinking Daniel Perrault was killed up here, Ronnie. He must have been up here Monday night; I guess the girl will confirm that sometime today," Bodie mused.

"Yeah, sounding like it."

"Sure is something, carrying on like that with someone half his age. But she loved him, I guess."

"Yeah, I guess."

"So what was wrong with you? Had the flu or what?"

"Don't know, musta caught something over last weekend."

"Sheriff was pretty mad you weren't in. He wanted you at the autopsy. I almost had to go but luckily he got Deputy Overstreet. I hate going to those things."

"Yeah, me too."

Swiggert parked before crossing the little wooden bridge. They'd need pictures of any tire tracks near the cabin and didn't want to compromise the area.

"Do you want me to start taking pictures out here, Bodie, while you go inside?"

"Sure thing."

Bodie carefully pushed open the door and turned on his flashlight. Even in the early afternoon light, the cabin was pretty dark. He shone it in all the corners and took pictures before stepping inside. There was an empty flower vase inside by the door, an egg crate foam pad pushed against the wall under one of the windows, a couple of candlesticks melted down to the nubs. The fireplace had ash and a few charred logs, and on the mantel was a framed picture of the girl Sheriff Stryker was interviewing, Miss Cocheta Shanahan.

Meanwhile, Ronnie Swiggert walked the perimeter of the cabin, then out the dirt driveway to the road searching left and right along the roadside ditch. He spotted the missing yellow flip-flop tangled up in some briars further down the slope. He glanced back at the cabin to see if Bodie'd come back out, then jumped down to retrieve it, holding it by the heel. He'd heard this was missing from the deceased, as well as his shirt. He went back to his cruiser and put it in a sterile bag in the cruiser trunk to give to forensics.

Bodie emerged, shaking his head. "Guessing this is where our man was attacked. Whoever did this must have known they were meeting here pretty regular."

"Probably right. Seems pretty clear whatever happened, it happened up here."

"So, Miss Shanahan, how long and how often did you and Mr. Perrault use the cabin?" Spike looked at her mother's distraught face. "And ma'am, if you'd like to be excused and wait in another room, that'd be fine." Skye nodded silently and rose to leave the room. She hugged Cocheta, both of them tearful and upset.

"We met a couple of times a month from February on. Sometime in June, mid-June, Daniel told me it was over, he couldn't do it anymore. His wife had seen us together once at the farm store, in April and she made him fire me the next day." Cocheta stopped, unable to continue as she choked back a sob. "But we couldn't stop and still met whenever we could."

Spike was silent for a few minutes until she recovered. "All right, so he tried unsuccessfully to end it in June. What was the contact after that?"

"Well, if he could meet me, he'd leave word in an envelope under a flower pot on the farm store porch."

"How often was that?"

Probably four or five times. He didn't want to risk meeting if Beth was around, so he'd wait until she went to the city

"And then you called his house on Monday past. Why?"

"I saw Mr. Pantoja last Saturday and he told me Daniel was selling everything, even his house and farm. He'd closed the restaurant on Labor Day weekend and Mr. Pantoja was going to buy the farm store from him. He told me Daniel was returning to France with his wife. Permanently! You can imagine how I felt, I loved him, after all." She stopped again to compose herself. "Daniel didn't tell me himself. I think he didn't want to hurt me. But I was frantic.

"I called to ask if he would meet me that night at our place to say goodbye and he agreed. I thought it would be a special way to remember each other by going back to where we were happy together."

"You called his landline, why?"

"I never knew his cell phone number and he'd always said to never contact him at all. His wife. He didn't want her to know we were still seeing each other, obviously."

"His wife Beth happened to be away. Did you know that when you took the risk of calling?"

"Mr. Pantoja told me she was going to visit her mother and was away for a few days."

"Mr. Pantoja seems to be giving you quite a bit of information."

"He was involved with Daniel's business and was helping to wind things down, I think. That's when he told me he was buying the farm store from him."

"You called him at 7:19 p.m. Why so late? What did you tell your mother?"

"I was afraid. I sat by the phone from the time I got home from class and stared at it."

"Then what happened?"

"We agreed to meet around ten o'clock at the cabin. I'd already told my mother I was going to spend the night at my friend Tracy's. She didn't know anything about this."

"Were you planning on spending the night with Mr. Perrault there?"

"Yes!"

"But that's not what happened, is it?"

"We...we were together for a while. He said it was the best goodbye and we should remember forever. He wanted to leave and said this would be the last time we would ever meet. I cried and asked him to stay, but in the end, I knew he was right. He told me he would watch me go, make sure I was on the road, then straighten up the cabin. The last thing I saw was him standing in the doorway of the cabin as I backed my car out. I drove over the little bridge to the road. I almost turned back, but I didn't. There didn't seem to be any point." Cocheta put her elbows on the table and rested her head on her fists. "Whoever hurt him must have already been there somewhere, but I never saw *anything*. It doesn't make any sense!" Two large tears rolled down her cheeks and she made no effort to wipe them away.

"What were you doing between the time you left him at the cabin Monday past and this morning when Deputy Crawford arrived at your mother's house? We're talkin' an entire day and night."

"I went to Tracy's and cried my eyes out for most of the rest of the night. She's my best, really only, friend and I went to her house many times for comfort. Her mother knew about me and Daniel, but I don't think she ever told anyone."

"So you spent the night at Tracy's — at least that was one truth you told your mother." Cocheta hung her head again. "What did you do after that?"

"I went with Tracy to her work on Tuesday so I wouldn't have to go home and be sad. I didn't have anything else to do since the farm store job was gone. I went to my classes that afternoon and stayed to do some studying at the library. Anything to not think about Daniel. After that, I went home pretty late, I hadn't eaten all day but I ran up to my room so my mother wouldn't start asking questions. I was ready to just be alone."

"When you and Mr. Perrault met at the cabin, did you drive separately other than the first time?"

"Yes. We always parked behind the cabin so no one could see the cars from the road."

"What time did you leave the cabin on Monday night?"

"I think it was around eleven."

"Was Tracy expecting you to come to her house?"

"No, I had to call her from my cell and wake her up. She let me in, I guess by then it was close to midnight."

"And you had no idea until this morning that Mr. Perrault was attacked and murdered very close to midnight according to the medical examiner? His pickup is missing, and his body was found along the main highway at two o'clock in the morning. Do you know how this could have happened?"

"It's really my fault this happened to him, isn't it?" she sobbed. "I asked him out and someone hurt him. I don't know who, I don't know why!" She put her head down on her arms on the table and wept.

"Miss Shanahan, someone had to know about your meeting place and that you met that night. We think he was attacked close to your hideaway. Who could have known you two rendez-vooed there? Mr. Pantoja? Your mother? Tracy or her mother? Beth? Who? You must think!"

"No one! I swear, Tracy and her mother are the only ones, but they couldn't have done anything like this, they knew how I loved him!"

"Did you kill Daniel Perrault? Or hire someone to?"

Cocheta looked in horror at Sheriff Stryker. "NO, *no, no, no!* Don't you see? I want to die now, too. I loved Daniel Perrault!"

"Did you lure him out to have him killed for leaving you?"

"NO! I wanted him to come back to me, it's true. And now I don't know…" she hiccupped and began to weep again. "…I don't know how I'll go on."

"Miss Shanahan, I'll have your mother come back in now. I'd like you both to stay for a while longer in case we've got more questions."

Rudy came into the interview room and whispered in Sheriff Stryker's ear. Spike immediately pushed himself up out of his chair and rushed out telling Rudy to get Miss Shanahan a glass of water and maybe a snack, saltine crackers or something.

Beth had been found and told of her husband's death.

CHAPTER TEN

ACCOMPANIED BY TWO female police officer escorts and her mother, Beth was on the next plane out of Portland to Wayne County and the medical examiner's office. Daniel's devastated parents would be arriving first thing in the morning. At the office, she was shepherded into a reception room where the medical examiner was waiting.

"Mrs. Perrault, I'm very, very sorry for your loss. If you would like to view your husband's body, I will accompany you into the morgue. If you prefer to identify by photo, which I have here, that is fine. Either way, we can then release the body to the funeral home per your instructions."

"This is real. This is happening to me," Beth wept, turning to her mother who pulled her head to her shoulder to comfort her. "Maybe there's been a terrible mistake, maybe it's not Daniel!" She looked at the photo the medical examiner held out to her and wanted to vomit. "I want to see him. I need to see him," she finally whispered.

"Very well."

She stared sadly at his once strong, sturdy body, now crisscrossed with incisions from the autopsy, stiff and bluish-white, his flaxen hair matted and dull. The beautiful, vibrant man she had always loved, now lifeless and exposed. How could this happen? How, how, how? She let out an anguished, guttural moan of anger and grief and the examiner gripped her arm to keep her from crumpling to the floor. She stroked Daniel's left cheek gently with the back of her fingers, tears trickling down her cheeks into the corners of her mouth and down her chin. "I love you. I forgave you, I forgive you. I will always love you, Daniel."

"Mrs. Perrault, I know this is a very difficult time, but I must ask for your help. We want to find out what happened to your husband

and I need to ask you a few questions, especially about the past few days." Sheriff Stryker and Chief Deputy Bodie Talon removed their hats and stood in the Perraults' kitchen where Beth, her mother and the police officers from Maine sat at the kitchen table. Both the sheriff and his deputy rotated their hats awkwardly by the brims and shifted their weight from one foot to the other. Neither had ever interrogated a murder victim's spouse before. It was late Wednesday afternoon, more than thirty-six hours after Daniel Perrault's death. Spike was hitting a brick wall everywhere he turned. The interview with Cocheta Shanahan had revealed nothing solid he could follow up on, other than Tracy and her mother, who were unlikely murderers, he figured. He'd send Deputy Swiggert to interview them after he drove Cocheta and her mother home. There wasn't any reason to hold them.

"I understand you've been told the circumstances surrounding your husband's death." Beth nodded numbly. Spike had asked the Maine police to tell her where Daniel Perrault was and who he was with the night he was killed.

The sky had darkened, even though sunset was an hour away, as a light rain began to fall, tapping gently against the kitchen windows. Spike looked around the elegant kitchen, noticing the professional-grade, sky-blue stove and oven the builder Marcus said Daniel had shipped from France. What would become of all this now?

He studied Beth for a few moments considering how to approach questioning her. *Sympathetically, but with resolve,* he decided. Christ, he'd never been in this kind of situation before! She didn't touch the cup of tea her mother had prepared, but rested, deflated and miserable, slumped against her mother's shoulder. *Seeing Beth like this with her mother mirrored Cocheta with her mother in the interview room,* Spike thought. *A weird twist to the situation to say the least.*

Even in her distress, Beth was a beautiful woman with thick dark hair brushed back from her face and large blue eyes. Though at least twenty years older than Cocheta, Beth was just as pretty in Spike's eyes. What possessed Daniel Perrault to betray his wife with a girl nearly half his age? What drives a man to risk everything like that? Both women loved him. It could never have ended well, even if he'd lived. Spike cleared his throat, and he and Deputy Talon sat in two chairs across from Beth. Spike took out his notepad and a pen.

"Mrs. Perrault, your neighbor, Thorne Tate, says he saw your car leave around ten o'clock on Saturday morning past. Is that when you left for Maine?"

"No, I was going to my townhouse in the city. I wanted to collect some items there to take to my mother's in Maine."

"When did you leave the townhouse for your mother's?"

"I left around noon."

"Did you stop for the night? It's a long drive to your mother's."

"Yes, I stopped at a place I have stayed at before when I make that drive."

"Could I have the name of that place to confirm?"

"The Blue Mango. It's a spa."

"You, Mrs. Lambert, called the house Saturday morning, but you knew your daughter should have been on her way to either the townhouse or you. Why did you call the home phone?"

"She didn't answer her cell phone. She'd forgotten to charge it. I thought I could reach Daniel to find out when she'd left the house in Scarcity."

"Did Mr. Perrault answer the phone?"

"No. I left a message I'd called." Sophia Lambert mouth was set in a grim line. The past few hours had taken a heavy toll on her too; gray hair messily pinned up, worry bands across her brow, red-rimmed eyes.

"All right, Mrs. Perrault. Why did you choose go to Maine this particular weekend?"

"Daniel and I were going to move to Périgord as soon as we could get our affairs in order and finalize things. You may know the store and this property have been sold and the restaurant is closed and on the market. I'd been very busy trying to figure out what to store or ship and I wanted to spend some time with my mother before we left. I also wanted to tell her I was pregnant, she was going to be a grandmother." Beth began to cry quietly, and Spike put his notepad away. He looked down towards the floorboards as he blinked back moisture in his own eyes.

"The department tried to reach you, Mrs. Perrault, from yesterday morning on, but your cell phone was off. Why is that?" Deputy Talon asked as gently as he could.

"My mother and I went to a yoga retreat. She insisted I leave my phone at the house. I didn't know anything until we returned to her house this morning, with the police waiting."

"Did you try to contact your husband during the time period Saturday to Wednesday?"

"Yes, I called his cell when I got to my mother's Sunday evening, and told him I'd call him after my mother and I got home from the yoga place to let him know when I would be driving back."

"When you left on Saturday, where was your husband?"

"He was in his office downstairs on the computer. He accompanied me out to the drive as I got in the car to leave. That's the last time I saw him. Oh, God, I never should have gone away! None of this would have happened!"

"Mrs. Perrault, the next questions are going to be difficult, but they must be asked. You knew about your husband's affair with Miss Shanahan, is that correct?" Sheriff Stryker asked.

"Yes."

"In an interview yesterday with your former builder, Marcus McGrath, he indicated that at one time he had feelings for you. Did you have a romantic relationship with him at any point?"

"Officers, don't you think that's enough for today? My daughter is exhausted, in shock, and she needs to rest." Sophia Lambert stared angrily at the sheriff. "It's clearly the fault of that little tart, chasing after Daniel after he'd cut it off. She knows something she's not telling!"

"Mrs. Lambert, we still have questions for Miss Cocheta Shanahan. I promise we'll get to the bottom of this very, very soon."

• • •

From the beginning, Beth wasn't sure she could adjust to rural life. She'd traveled all over the world for work and had always lived in cities — New York, Geneva, Riyadh and Washington D.C. — thriving on her work in the energy sector. But once Daniel's heart was set on the restaurant idea in tiny Nickel, what choice did she have? It was her own fault for insisting they needed a weekend in the country to perk him up. Constantly complaining and bored as one venture after another collapsed, he spent his days staring at his stock portfolio on the computer and grousing about life's unfairness. She couldn't deny his excitement and happiness as his plans took shape for Scarcity brightened her own mood, but she found the whole scheme daunting, and preferred to hang on as long as possible to her old life, the townhouse, and her work.

Happily, Daniel agreed Marcus was the best choice for a builder. He'd just completed a beautiful renovation of her three-story townhouse and his even-tempered personality kept her sane through even the most nerve-racking early morning days of noise and dust. He'd become a close friend and having him on the Scarcity project was a comfort, a strong link to her city life and support during her long transition to life in the sticks.

Often, Beth and Marcus discussed Daniel's mood swings, his edginess and irritability, how short his fuse could be. Marcus complained Daniel never took the time to understand the intricacies of the permitting process, how sometimes it came down to a bit of cajolery to win the good favor of someone from historic preservation or building inspection, which took time and effort. Marcus resented, too, how his attempts to explain the complexities of turning dilapidated infrastructures of nineteenth-century buildings into state-of-the-art, twenty-first century showpieces were dismissed by Daniel as tedious and dull information.

"I mean, the guy wants perfection, but he doesn't need or care to understand how interwoven everything is, how renovations of this kind are multifaceted and entangled, and sometimes one thing can't happen until a whole slew of other things come first."

"I know, he's a spirited horse at the starting gate, just wants to zip to the finish line."

Beth was more concerned about Daniel's petulance than she let on, even to Marcus. She never knew what frame of mind he'd be in when he woke up. He often rushed out to Scarcity from the city in those early months after he bought the building for his restaurant, leaving her alone for days at a time. Eventually, she knew there was no going back — she'd have to make her life in Scarcity if she wanted to be with Daniel. She couldn't help feeling annoyed at the fast pace at which he was moving, though. It was as if everything that mattered to her — friends, routines, and work — should be abandoned immediately, an inferior life easily jettisoned in favor of Daniel's interests.

But adapt she did, finding fulfillment as the months progressed, working with Marcus on her office remodel, designing and decorating their future home and the restaurant. She left her job but continued to consult, bought a fancy camera to pursue a life-long interest in photography, and escaped to the townhouse if she needed a respite from Daniel's exhausting drive. She loved observing and photographing the farm animals, especially the lambs in springtime, following their mamas on wobbly little legs. Maybe this rural thing wouldn't be so bad after all.

Except Daniel began to change, and not for the better. His occasional explosive jealousy over Beth's friendship with Marcus alarmed and perplexed her. When he fired Marcus at the tail end of the projects, she marched into his office where he'd gone to cool down after the ugly confrontation with Marcus on the road. She was fuming at his lack of grace and asinine behavior.

"You're a fool to let Marcus go! Look at this place! Look at the work this man has done, everything you wanted!"

"He has dragged his feet along for so long, I've lost count of how many months we've waited for him to finish. Look at the yard, still a mess! The things he did wrong are too numerous to count, Beth."

"He did everything you wanted him to do! He *moved* out here for you, for Christ's sake. I know the geothermal wasn't well handled, but he's doing his best to wrap everything up for you. Your house, *our* house, is beautiful, the restaurant is glorious, the artists' atelier, even the farm store. He's done all this within the budget you set for him, with whatever local help he could find. What more do you want?"

"I want him out of my life and out of my wife's cunt!"

"Oh, you really *are* a fool, aren't you?" she fairly growled, glaring at Daniel with scorn and contempt. She ran from the house, grabbing her camera. What should she do? She strode up the lane towards Thorne's property, pausing to gaze at exquisite, puffy clusters of milk-white, cumulus clouds billowing above the verdant mountains surrounding her, a welcome antidote to Daniel's insufferable behavior. She snapped some photos, calmed as always by the beauty of nature.

She saw Thorne in the distance unloading grocery bags from his pickup and waved. He motioned for her to join him up on the porch.

"Daniel okay? What a scene! Thought your builder would've

killed him. Why'd Daniel act that way?" Thorne offered Beth a glass of lemonade and they sat side by side in the rockers.

"Thorne, I don't know what to do. Marcus is my friend, we've worked well together for years. Daniel's convinced we're having an affair, which of course isn't true. He just seems to have it in for Marcus, even after all his hard work." She paused and looked out over the vista she'd grown to love. "I adore Daniel, you of all people know that. I just don't understand these awful moods he gets into sometimes. I know he's under pressure. It's self-imposed, but still."

"He's lovable when he wants to be."

Beth chuckled. "Yes, he has charisma and charm, and he's hard on himself, too. He doesn't want to fail. He'd have a very hard time accepting failure, I'm afraid."

"I admire his ambition. But he's in a hurry. Nothing happens fast around here."

"I know, Thorne. You're such a good friend and neighbor. You'll come and see the restaurant before it opens, I hope. And of course, you're my guest to eat dinner there anytime, whether Daniel likes it or not!"

"Yeah, he's kinda had me on a roller coaster lately. Don't know if he still wants my help anymore, he seems to be avoiding me."

"Oh Thorne, I don't think so. He's grateful to you for your help even if he's incapable of showing it. He's pulled in so many directions, he forgets who and what truly matters. I'm trying really hard to understand him." She sighed. "I think I can confess to you I want to have a child. Daniel doesn't know what a good father he would be, and it would help him, change him, I know it!"

"Well, what's to stop you?" Thorne averted his eyes from Beth in discomfort as he remembered accidently seeing Daniel and Beth together on the office couch not that long ago.

"He says he doesn't want a child, at least not yet. It's been up and down with Daniel since we bought the property, honestly. Things can be so good and then he lashes out over nothing. I think a child would help center him."

"Yeah, well, I hope you get what you want, Beth. You of all people deserve it for puttin' up with a scoundrel like him." He laughed and patted Beth's hand.

Beth walked back to the house expecting Daniel to have gone out, but he had somehow strewn hundreds of rose petals up the stairway to their bedroom, put candles on each step and left her a note in his beautiful script on the first step: 'Forgive me'.

Daniel's mood was ebullient and triumphant at the success of his Bastille Day event, with accolades all around from his parents and friends and admiration from the invited guests. Beth felt validated as well, her design and decorating soon to be written up in the magazine *La Bonne Cuisine* and her promotional events for the artists on solid footing with Sally's help. Her efforts were well received by the local community, and a mention in a survey of regional art happenings in one of the city papers put the atelier on the map.

From being on cloud nine, Daniel sank to the depths of despair as everything came crashing down and he ultimately had to turn to Beth for help. The rest of the summer until the restaurant reopened in October was hellish. When Daniel wasn't yelling into the phone, he was carping at Beth about one thing or another. The weather those summer months was abysmal. Days were brutally hot with barely a rustling of leaves, and nights were heavy with humidity with slashes of lightening across the ink-black sky, but little rain or relief. Beth spent two weeks with her mother in Maine to get away.

When Restaurant Perigeaux reopened to great fanfare, the stars at last seemed aligned. Daniel finally accepted the blow to his ego of having Beth as the legal owner of the restaurant after the ABC debacle. The publicity was mostly positive and everyone, from the artists to the kitchen staff, seemed happy.

Beth never rubbed in her nominal ownership at Daniel's expense and he was grateful for her decency. He'd been stung by the disrespect of so many as he tried to launch a world-class, French restaurant, and her quiet support became a tonic for his moments of insecurity. For a brief few weeks, he pushed thoughts of the delicious creature over at L'Esprit du Pays aside and enjoyed watching the restaurant flourish and Beth and Sally running the artists' cooperative.

As she and Sally toasted Daniel with congratulatory glasses of wine at the bar on an October afternoon, Beth was happier than she'd been since the Bastille Day fête. Seeing Daniel relish the fruition of his dream meant the rough patches were surely over for them! He would settle down a bit, relax more, maybe take more time with the farm. She in turn wanted to expand the garden, adding raised vegetable beds and an orchard, and she cut her consulting work back almost completely. Photography was a passion though she insisted it was only a hobby.

Daniel was particularly amorous towards her during those early autumn days, unabashedly kissing her in front of others and making love to her in the slow, sensual way she'd always savored from their early days, his lightest touch sending shivers down her spine. Under their bedroom skylights as the stars twinkled or a full moon illuminated their bodies like a spotlight, he would seduce her with abandon. She thought she'd never been more in love with him, or happier.

"We should go to Périgord after the holidays, Daniel. You'll need a break by then. We could see our friends and your family, do some shopping, get ideas for the farm store." Beth mentioned several times they both needed a change of scenery, but Daniel remained uncommitted. As the holidays loomed, he became testier and more distracted.

"*Oui, peut être, on verra*," was his usual wishy-washy reply.

Beth planned to insist on a good long break for them in Périgord for them in January; she didn't want to lose to the blissful relations they'd nurtured through the fall to a dreary post-holiday spell in Scarcity. Daniel always turned into the high- spirited, lovable Daniel she'd married when he was with his parents and friends. He and Beth would eat and drink with friends at their favorite haunts, and hike Daniel's preferred Dordogne trails or ski. She longed to go to Geneva, where they'd met to remind him of their happy, early days. She thought there she could persuade him to have a child with her.

Nothing seemed right with Daniel when Beth returned from a pre-Christmas outing in the city. The townhouse had needed a good cleaning, and she had shopped for gifts for Sally and Fleur and a couple of the other artists she'd become close to. She wanted to pick up little gifts for the restaurant workers, too. She bought a luxurious leather jacket and an exquisite Pierre Cardin luggage set for Daniel knowing he'd want to be stylish for Périgord now that he'd finally agreed they should go.

When she returned, Beth knew Daniel would be in an extreme

state of turmoil. First Bernard, then Daniel, called her cell phone after the melee and each told their side of the story.

"He was messing up orders, so I called him out on it. And the worst is, I'm completely stuck with him! This may be our busiest time and I'll never be able to keep up if I fire him."

"Bernard said you arrived in the middle of dinner service and yelled at him in front of both diners and kitchen staff. He felt mistreated by you, and I agree it was an aggressive tack. What in the world drove you to do such a thing, Daniel?" Beth listened to Daniel's rant. "I'm not excusing Bernard's nuttiness, but the lights will get fixed, Daniel. I persuaded Bernard to stay and promised him you'd back off a bit."

"That's not the point! The stupid deputy *mec* said something about a court hearing and I'll have to pay for my own repairs and I don't know what all. *C'est injuste!*"

"The important thing is to get back to normal and hope the bad publicity doesn't affect people's desire to come back. God, Daniel, why can't you calm down? Périgord isn't coming a moment too soon!"

But Daniel only got more morose and Beth worried he didn't want to go to France after all. Possibly he was worried about Bernard's ability in his absence. He assured her he was anxious to go, wanted to be with her and desperately needed to get away. But even in Europe amongst everything he loved, he was brooding and detached. Beth was unsure how to approach him and gave him a wide berth. His mother questioned if something was wrong between them.

From their return at the end of January until the second Bastille Day gala Daniel planned, things collapsed like a house of cards in slow motion. After the holidays, reservations were sluggish until the special Valentine's Day dinner. Bernard had concocted an elaborate tasting menu with wine pairings: scallops, *foie gras* with date and pomegranate puree, venison with a lentil ragout, *langoustine* with garlic butter, duck with cauliflower parmesan and his tour de force, pink-iced, heart-shaped brownie cupcakes with a molten chocolate walnut inside. While Daniel worried about the cost and whether the numbers would be good enough to defray January's losses, Beth asked one of the artists to design special, colorful menus and posted them at the farm store and various other outlets. She talked it up with people she ran into and called on her city contacts to come out. Happily, Restaurant Perigeaux was booked solid for the evening, which boded well for moving into spring.

Dinner service was uneven at best. Short-handed in both the kitchen and wait-staff since Daniel had let several workers go temporarily to save money, Bernard struggled to get food out in a timely manner and some items were lukewarm by the time they were set in front of diners. The *langoustines* were overcooked and the duck was tougher than it should have been. Beth could see Daniel was boiling and she, too, was upset as she watched plates go back half-eaten.

It didn't take long for word of mouth to get around that Restaurant Perigeaux was not as good as last fall or during the holidays, that its glory days may already be behind it. Daniel blamed Bernard, who blamed Daniel. The wasted food and money sent Daniel over the edge yet again.

The next morning in a meeting Daniel insisted on, he vented his frustration to both Bernard and Beth.

"I thought I could hand the reins to you, but you have failed!"

"You're the one who cut staff! How can I do it all? I cannot! Besides, I work for Beth, not for you."

Daniel turned to Beth. "*You* take charge then! We'll see if you can do a better job than I'm doing with this guy. I'll back off. You two deserve each other!" He stomped out of the office and out of the restaurant to march around the parking lot, seething.

Beth watched him from a restaurant window, realizing sadly that Daniel's mood was back to the uncertain days when Restaurant Perigeaux closed after the ABC trouble. He was testy and often bad-tempered. She would do the best she could to set things right with the restaurant's reputation, but his ego had been dealt a blow and she still wanted this to be *his* success. She decided she would work with Bernard on simplifying the menus and doing special events to draw customers while Daniel would still oversee the purchasing and the numbers and be a presence at the dinner service. It was the best way. He had to stay involved.

Spring meant much work to be done at the farm, repairing fences and selling off some of the livestock. Beth liked to meet with Bernard in the mornings and then have the day to wander the property, work with Garret or Quinn in the flower and vegetable gardens and do paperwork in her office. She carried her camera everywhere, snapping pictures of Daniel, the countryside and often, Bernard's most elegantly prepared dishes. Daniel's mood seemed to improve as well. He took pleasure again in being outdoors, working on chores from early morning until lunchtime. Beth hoped the post-holiday turmoil was put to rest and things were on an even keel once again.

Occasionally, Daniel took off in his pickup, leaving mid-afternoon before dinner service was underway, the time of day Beth liked to sit with him on her office veranda, be close with him, wordless or talkative. He wanted to make the rounds of the farms, he said, see what new produce they could introduce. Beth sensed he wanted to avoid her and more than once she'd broached the subject of his standoffishness, thinking he was still piqued about her taking on a larger role at the restaurant. Their sex life, though passionate, was infrequent. He assured her he was usually just tired and blamed it on the manual labor and all.

Beth's attachment to the farm as well as to Wayne County had deepened since the previous autumn, and she started to give serious consideration to selling the townhouse in the city. She was busy most days with household tasks, cleaning their house herself, and with the restaurant and the artists' ateliers. She'd allowed her ties to city friends and former colleagues to dwindle to occasional phone calls. Watching seeds she'd planted herself start to sprout gave her the most joy of all now: carrots, lettuce, snap peas, cucumbers, beans and squash. The kitchen garden provided her favorite herbs for cooking, and last year she'd canned tomatoes and peaches and made her own blueberry preserves! This summer, she planned to plant various types of melons, maybe even watermelon and to make peach jelly. Nothing gave her greater pleasure than seeing the first pale pink hues of peach tree blossoms in the orchard from her office window. Why give this up to fight traffic and scour the street for a parking spot? It just wasn't worth it anymore.

Opening the kitchen door and brandishing a basket full of early baby spinach, she found Daniel gulping down a glass of water after his morning workout.

"I'm a country girl at last, Daniel!" she laughed indicating her muddy boots and holding up her dirt-encrusted gloves. "Just look at this spinach! If we had a greenhouse, we'd have even more veggies up by now. What do you think about Garret and Quinn building a small one? I think it'd be a good investment."

Daniel toasted her with his water glass. "Great idea, but do those two know anything about how to build something like that?"

"Probably not. But who else could I ask?" Beth thought she might have Marcus build it and somehow settle the silly lawsuit and animus between him and Daniel. "Which reminds me, speaking of building, I think it's time to get rid of the townhouse."

"But that's crazy, Beth! You still love your city escapes. You'd regret selling the house."

"You haven't been in months! Why should I keep it, just to go in and make sure it's still there? I loved living there but now it's become a burden, honestly. With the beautiful renovation work Marcus did, I could get a fantastic price for it."

"Yes, well why don't you take Marcus with you to see what else you two could do?" Daniel noisily slapped his glass onto the kitchen counter.

"This is a very unappealing side of you, Daniel. Why do you always come back to that train of thought?"

"Because I do. He's a crook who stole from me. Tried to steal you from me, I guarantee it!"

"You always talk nonsense when it comes to Marcus. The only one who's stealing from you is the lawyer, racking up fees for keeping this ridiculous lawsuit going."

Beth set down the basket and went to the sink to wash. Daniel came up behind her and put his arms around her. "Don't sell the townhouse. I still think you need to get away sometimes."

Easter was the following Sunday and she and Bernard planned a special mid-day *prix fixe* menu — onion soup, tender roasted leg of lamb, *gratin Dauphinois*, Brussel sprouts and strawberry sorbet with orange *tartelettes*. This would be a crowd pleaser! Beth hurried to have the menu printed so she could post it in the artists' atelier and at the farm store as well as get it into the local newspaper before its deadline. Since it was a perfect spring morning, she took Daniel's Aston Martin and put the top down to savor the special weather.

He'd already taken off in the pickup to collect some extra cases of wine he thought they'd need, he said.

The country air smelled of cow and damp earth after an earlier light rain while the redbuds washed the roadsides in crimson clouds of bloom. She headed to L'Esprit du Pays, usually opened by Cocheta at seven in the morning, and parked on the street. The front door still had the "closed" sign on, and the door was locked, so she went around to see if the back door was open yet. Right away, she noticed Daniel's pickup parked in the lot. Why would he be here? Heart pounding, she quietly entered the store and looked around. No one. She stood still, unmoving. Behind the closed stockroom door, she started to hear noises.

"Hello?" Slowly, she approached the door, turned the knob and threw the door open. Daniel and Cocheta abruptly broke apart, Daniel's face flushed and sweaty. Cocheta, her lipstick smeared, and her cream-colored blouse unbuttoned, let out a small scream and ran to the back of the stock room crying. Beth stood completely thunderstruck; she felt as though she were viewing a movie reel that had gotten snagged, audio and visual whirling in slow motion to a stop, an eddy of water sucked into a drain. She dropped the menu flyer, flung open the front door and sprinted for her car.

Daniel ran after her. "Beth, please, stop. Let me explain!" She wrested his arm from hers and took off at full speed.

Back at the house, Beth was in the bedroom angrily packing a suitcase when Daniel ran in, white-faced and agitated.

"Let me explain, Beth!"

"I don't think you need to explain! I think it's pretty clear what's going on. No wonder you want me to keep the townhouse, so you can encourage me to — how did you put it? — 'get away sometimes.' Then you and that little shit can do whatever you want together, when I'm away." Tears of anger were streaming down Beth's face as she mindlessly threw things in her bag.

"This is nothing. She's been trying to seduce me for some time. I kept telling her how much I loved my wife, but she pursued and grabbed me this morning. That's all, I swear!"

"You are such a fucking liar! I suppose you tell me you're picking up wine and then dash to see your little sweetie, thinking I'm none the wiser. I've been trying to save your bloody restaurant and this is how you repay me? Having little trysts with a teenage girl? You are sick, my friend."

Daniel sat down heavily on the bed and held his head in his hands. "You've got it all wrong. It was just a little kiss. I don't love her. I love and want you. Forgive me, Beth!"

"I want that girl fired as of today. Go fuck her one more time if you want! I AM going to the city. When you figure out who you are and what you want, maybe you can give me a call. I'm done with you, Daniel! Now I know why you're so 'tired' all the time. You are a pathetic human being!" Beth marched downstairs with her small suitcase, slammed the door and jumped into the Mercedes without a backward glance. Daniel watched from the upstairs window as clouds of dust billowed behind the car. Then she was gone.

For the first time in his life, Daniel wept.

CHAPTER ELEVEN

BETH WOULDN'T answer her cell phone. Daniel got out a bottle of whiskey and drank himself into a stupor, spending the next two days in bed. On Easter Sunday, he drove his tractor to Garret and Quinn's and told them to figure out how to build a greenhouse for his wife.

"The best greenhouse there is, *nom de Dieu*. I don't care what it costs." He stumbled around Beth's vegetable patches and back into the house, collapsing onto their bed in misery. Bernard called several times on Daniel's cell, wondering where he and Beth were, but Daniel never answered. At the moment, he didn't care one whit for Restaurant Perigeaux or Conchita or the farm store or anything other than Beth. How could he fix this? He'd never considered leaving Beth for Conchita who was, while beguiling, nothing more than a country girl, she'd said it herself! As good as sex with her was, he could never truly be with her, she'd known that from the beginning. He didn't love her.

The next morning, Daniel decided to walk over to the farm store from the restaurant giving him time to gather his courage and think about how to approach firing Conchita. It was going to be disagreeable for them both, but he must do it. He wanted a clean break with her anyway. This might be the best way to bring their affair to a peaceful close. He wanted to arrive as soon as she opened. Surely she would know as soon as she saw him, why he was there.

"There's no other way. I'll tell Mr. Pantoja you want to take more classes or something and he'll find a new person. I'm sorry, Conchita, but I have to do this." He stood in the doorway and Cocheta stood stiffly behind the counter. *Don't go to her*, he told himself. She wore an off-the-shoulder, deep-blue floral blouse and her hair was piled prettily on her head with strands hugging the nape of her neck. The perfect curvature of her shoulders and soft swelling of the breasts beneath were painful for him to look at, and he averted his eyes. Cocheta steadied herself with two hands on the counter and began weeping.

"You'll stay until a replacement can be found, of course. I'll give you enough money to tide you over for a couple of months, Conchita. I don't want to give you up, but I must if I want to save my marriage."

"I am only guilty of loving you. I'm sorry."

"Well, that's the end then." He turned and left, stopping at Conchita's jeep as an unpleasant and unwelcome tightness in his chest overcame him. He put his hands on her car and let his head drop, taking a few deep breaths. *Never touching Conchita again, was he strong enough? Non!* He was a flawed man, unable to resist, he feared.

He heard the crunch of gravel as a car pulled into the lot. Straightening, he saw it was a deputy's. Sure enough, a deputy stepped out, tossed his hat onto the driver's seat and headed toward the farm store, the same deputy who'd been so annoying after Bernard bashed out the lights. Daniel had written to the newspaper, complaining about him and the other deputy without identifying them by name. Everyone probably knew who he meant, though. Bernard never did pay for the reparations — why go through the idiocy of a country court procedure? He'd simply docked Bernard's pay to cover his costs, but the deputy, Swiggert was his name, had kept calling him, harassing him really, to deal with the paperwork and close the case.

Ronnie Swiggert noticed Daniel right away and stared stonily at him. "Well, if it isn't the restaurant guy. How's things going there? Your chef bashed anything to bits lately?" He snickered.

Daniel eyed the deputy smugly. "I own this store you seem to be patronizing."

"It's only got one thing in there I want. Coffee from that pretty little thing that works here. Most of the stuff in there is fluff, nothing the locals want."

"What would you know about that? Most of the items are high-end or imported. You wouldn't be a targeted customer."

Deputy Swiggert mumbled something Daniel didn't hear. He'd have to walk right by him to leave the parking area, so he waited for the deputy to move on and go into the store. He turned away to look at Conchita's car. "That girl is my employee and I just fired her. She displeased me."

"That so? Well now that's a mighty big shame. She's the reason I like to stop here first thing for coffee, she makes a good pot. What'd she do wrong?"

Daniel had a pounding headache and the sun climbing over the tree tops hurt his eyes. "Just about everything," he growled.

"Hard to believe, she's just about the best thing in this county." Swiggert ran his hands across his close-cropped hair, straightened his tie and pulled at his cuffs. "I'll see if I can't cheer her up." He smirked and strode into the store. Daniel bristled at the thought that somebody like Swiggert would most likely end up with his beautiful Conchita.

Daniel jogged back to his pickup, then drove aimlessly around back country roads, including up and down Prattle Hollow, trying to catch a glimpse of Conchita's and his little cabin meeting place through the trees. Later, he stewed in his office at the restaurant for a couple of hours going over accounts and purchasing orders, noticing that a couple of cases of wine he'd ordered were missing. Bernard's signature was on a delivery confirmation receipt he found buried in the filed cabinet. Storming into the kitchen, waving the receipt and bills of ladling, he confronted Bernard and accused him of stealing.

Silence. One week and Beth still had not answered Daniel's entreaties to come back, maybe not even listened to his messages. The girl was fired and would be gone as soon as a new person was hired. He'd fired Bernard, too, after he went crazy and killed his own cat. What a nightmare in the restaurant that night, with Bernard crying like a lunatic and that homely, country-born, hick deputy back again, making matters worse. It was all over the local paper and people were talking. He had to rely on Eddy now, the backup cook who isn't the best. He really needed Beth to come back and help him. Silence.

Two weeks, then three without word from Beth. Not the slightest sign of her mood or thoughts. How could she ignore him this way? Should he drive to the townhouse and woo her back? Confront her hard-heartedness? Damn her! With each passing day, his bitterness grew. If she deserted him, she abandoned her own restaurant to ruin, too! He was tempted to surprise her at the townhouse and see if that shit Marcus was with her, and imagined Beth drowning her sorrows with his fat, wet dick.

After firing Bernard with a letter telling him to never show his face at the door again, Daniel considered his options. He knew the uproar and bad publicity would bring in curious diners for a few days, but after that? Eddy was just a local kid who couldn't possibly cook on Bernard's level; he didn't have enough skills or know-how to create on his own. Daniel would have to cut staff and reduce prices to make ends meet until he could find a new chef. He knew with the quality down, bookings would go down. A few artists made a point of coming for dinner; Sally and Fleur came every night, as a show of both solidarity and unease. If the restaurant failed, what would happen to the studios? They wondered where Beth was but could tell from Daniel's demeanor he was in no mood to talk about anything with them.

Daniel, alone day after day, seethed at Beth and her tortuous snub of his loving overtures. What more did she want from him? He'd begged long enough! If she wouldn't come back to him, she'd force him to return to Conchita for comfort. It would be all her fault! The daily drudge of keeping the restaurant afloat was making him sick. He was eating every meal except breakfast there and gaining weight. The food was banal, and the wait staff's morale was low. No one responded to his ads for a new chef.

Mr. Pantoja called early one morning to tell Daniel he had found a replacement for Cocheta, one of the elementary school special-ed teachers, but she couldn't start until late May. Cocheta would still open the store for a few more days and work until noon. Daniel thanked him and lay in bed as a hollow feeling pulsed through his gut. When she was gone, how would he see her? Should he see her? She would vanish into memory. It had been one long month and his ardor hadn't cooled as he had hoped. He must stay away or all would be lost! Beth would divorce him, take half his money, maybe the house and restaurant too. What would he do, move into the cabin with Conchita? What folly! He staggered into the bathroom — no more whiskey! Staring at his face in the bathroom mirror, eyes bloodshot, he rubbed them until they teared and stung. *Conchita gone! She was so delicious, a succulent nymph at the height of her sexuality.* He had to have her one more time!

Daniel went to the farm store early and waited for Cocheta to arrive. When she walked in, aware of his presence from his pickup in the lot, he took her into his arms. She wore a yellow, summer sundress with a fitted bodice and her black hair was loose, flowing down her back like a rushing river in the deepest night. She babbled in happiness through her tears. "You've come! I knew you would!" He twisted her long, luscious hair into a knot with one hand and pulled her face to his with his other hand on the nape of her swan-like neck. He kissed her with a ferocity he'd never known, ultimately pushing her against the door in his excitement, surely bruising her delectable lips with his own. He had a plan.

"Beth is gone. She might divorce me. I hope she doesn't because, and I know this is hard, Conchita, I still want her as my wife. I want her to come home. I love her. I'm probably going to go bring her back." Cocheta lowered her head and nodded.

"But here's what I know. I can't stay away from you, Conchita, not yet. When you leave this job at the store, we can still meet at our hideaway. Beth doesn't know anything about it. As long as you're gone from the store, she won't know I'm seeing you if we meet there." He nuzzled her neck just below her ear, breathing in the comforting smell of her, an undefinable earthiness, carnal and animal-like. "What do you think?"

"I think yes." She placed her head against his shoulder.

After all the pain he'd caused his wife, how could he still succumb to Conchita? What was wrong with him? He drove headlong up Prattle Hollow to the cabin in his pickup early the next evening to meet her, to hell with the dinner service! He slowed when he saw the telltale sign of a deputy's vehicle coming from the opposite direction; he could barely make out the face of who was driving from behind the tinted window as he cruised by leaving a swirl of dust in his wake.

Conchita was waiting, looking comely as always in a crisp, white, sleeveless shirt, ripped and frayed denim shorts. They stood together for a few minutes at the open doorway, listening to spring peepers chirp their mating calls and watching fresh, green leaves shimmer on the trees in a light, mesmerizing breeze. Daniel's hand inched into the back of her shorts to grasp a perfectly rounded buttock, his breath quickening in anticipation of the pleasures to come. He fingered her, and she swayed with bliss, dampening him with her arousal. Slowly, she undid the tiny, pearl-white buttons of her shirt and dropped her shorts, her lacey, pink underwear a blur as Daniel drank in her flawless body from head to toe. How many times had her ravished her, ten? Twenty? Always needing more and more of her. It was debauchery, plain and simple, and he was beyond redemption.

Conchita had new tricks, massaging, nibbling, sucking. Only she could satiate his craving, apparently unquenchable any other way. He'd become an addict and Conchita was his drug. They rarely talked, lost as they were in a frenzy of feral lust. She was his siren song and he was drowning. He came in her mouth then fucked her hard while his finger pushed into her anus. He let out a primal cry of remorse and contrition over his errant ways, hating himself, unable to stop.

As they lay side by side, depleted, they heard the snap of a twig not too far from the open cabin window.

"Could it be a bear?" Daniel whispered. The rough sex had left him feeling uneasy, angst-ridden. What was he doing? To her, to Beth? He wanted to flee. He didn't even know himself anymore.

"Probably. We've had them nosing around our house lately. They're just coming out of hibernation. We can't even fill our bird feeders, or they'd be destroyed."

"It wouldn't be one of the neighbors out investigating, would it? It's still light enough to see the cars, or us."

"Neighbors? I doubt that. There's no house around until you get further up the hollow. It would be a long walk and we would have heard a car."

"I'll make some noise at the door to scare whatever it is off, so it is safe to leave." Daniel took a stick from the unused fireplace and rapped it on the door, then opened it and scraped the stick back and forth along the door jamb. He heard something crash away through the woods until all was quiet again. "Let's get out of here, I don't like the sound of this."

"When will I see you again, Daniel?" Cocheta pulled on her clothes with an anxious look.

"Conchita, I don't know, I don't know. I'll leave word at the store."

"My last day is next week. I haven't found another job yet."

"I'll leave you a note on the farm store front porch. Look under the flower pot nearest the driveway to the parking lot. Look every day, Conchita."

Daniel didn't bother going to the restaurant to check on the dinner service but went straight home. He took a shower under the hottest water he could stand and scrubbed for a full twenty minutes. Who could he call? He needed a friend, but he truly had none here. Thorne? Garret? Someone from the restaurant? Sally? Any offhand acquaintance? No one!

He called his parents even though it was the wee hours of the morning in Périgord and asked them to come; he needed help, advice. Then he got into his Aston Martin and drove to the townhouse, banging on the door at midnight, begging Beth to open and be his wife again.

The plight of Restaurant Perigeaux was worse than Beth expected. She'd read the ugly story of Bernard's breakdown in the local paper online and the subsequent article criticizing both the food and service as well as two or three letters to the editor questioning Daniel's treatment of staff. He'd been unable to pay either his suppliers or staff for at least two weeks and no reputable chef would touch the place with a ten-foot pole. Other bills and taxes loomed, and she had no idea where the money would come from if they couldn't drum up business soon.

"Daniel, I think you need to face facts. The restaurant's reputation is in shambles right now. Unless a good chef is willing to come on board, I think we'll be obliged to close by Labor Day if not before. Permanently."

He stood with his back to Beth, gazing out the restaurant window at the distant mountains he'd grown to love. "Everyone's had it in for me from the beginning except you, Beth. This place, these people, didn't want me to succeed, to bring life to this no-man's land my way."

"Some of it is your fault, Daniel," she said gently. His state of mind was unpredictable; he would rant about the injustice of it all, then fall into a sentimental mood, proclaiming his affection for the region. "Those two cases of wine you accused Bernard of stealing? Eddy had put them in one of the unused studios, out of the way. Bernard didn't know, and rightly felt you attacked his honesty. I'm not excusing him, but you set this in motion, Daniel."

He scowled. "Bernard was a madman. I should have fired him after he broke my lights! If we can't find a good enough chef to replace him, it's not because of me but because of the idiocy of this town, this county, this rural backwater!"

"Well you're not going to win any hearts and minds that way." Beth saw how on edge he continued to be but resisted the urge to soothe him. She hadn't shaken his betrayal but believed his heartfelt regret about the girl. He'd roused her from sleep, shouting at the townhouse door to forgive him, and she'd let him in to blubber his remorse and shame into her breasts. He couldn't survive without her, he needed her advice and steady hand, the girl was nothing to him, without Beth life was an empty shell, on and on for an hour until, exhausted, he fell asleep fully clothed beside her.

"The first thing is to sell the farm store to Neeraj, if he's interested. He and his wife already supply half your merchandise. The money could buy us some time."

Daniel reluctantly agreed, ruing the effort they'd put into creating a little bit of France in the tiny town of Nickel, the chocolates, wines, sandwiches and the delicacies in tins from Périgord: mushrooms, chestnuts, duck terrines, foie gras, walnuts, black truffles, honey! The interior was cozy and charming, the exterior colorful, with planters brimming with seasonal flowers and a country touch of two rockers on the front porch. None of this existed anywhere else in the county! Pantoja would turn it into a wine and sundries place, maybe a sandwich shop. *Dieu!* What a loss! Well, the locals deserved it! They never shopped there anyway, or sat in the rockers, preferring the ordinariness of Farrin's.

He drove his tractor around the property, following well-worn ruts in the dirt roads and parking at his favorite spot, a hill where he could see his entire spread: fence lines, his cattle and sheep, the barn he'd rebuilt with Garret and Quinn, the house with its annexes and bridges looking like little ships on a sea of green. It was time; this place wasn't ready for his vision and would never be. He felt a new but unmitigated tug toward Périgord. He wanted to go home,

with Beth at his side. Wayne County would never understand someone like him, a worldly visionary. It would go back to what it was
before his arrival, completely unaware of the once-in-a-lifetime
chance he'd offered!

He saw Thorne in the distance, checking on his cattle, but turned
away and moved down the opposite way toward the creek that
defined his property on the east.

And Conchita? He'd sworn to Beth it was nothing and he'd never
see her again. Her last days at the farm store had come and gone.
Such a young girl, he must tell her face to face their affair was over.
He'd leave her word to meet him one last time, no sex, just talk.
He'd give her money. Did that mean he'd paid for her attentions?
Did it matter now?

They met a week later on a languid June afternoon with no breeze.
Daniel sweated through his T-shirt before he even reached the door
and the cabin was stifling. He had six hundred dollars in cash to give
her, which she swatted to the floor.

"I'm not for sale! I love you. I don't know why I thought you
might leave your wife for me. I always hoped, Daniel, you would
choose me." She wiped her eyes with the backs of her wrists and
stared sadly at the bills scattered across the floor.

"Conchita.."

"Stop calling me that! I am Cocheta!"

"I never told you I would leave my wife for you, never. It's been
fantastique with you, I'll never forget you, but you need to study,
become a nurse, find a nice local boy for a lover or husband. You
are special, Con… and you deserve a good life. I want to help, please
take the money." Daniel stooped and gathered up the bills. Cocheta
kicked him in the buttock and pounced on his back, biting the back
of his neck. "*Mais tu es folle!* he cried, pushing her to the floor and
rubbing his neck to check for blood. She started to wail and beat
her fists against the wall of the cabin. Daniel grabbed her hands
and pulled them behind her back, whispering "*du calme, s'il te plaît,
du calme.*" Eventually she sat passively, Indian-style, back against
the wall, sniffling. She took the wad of bills he held out. "You're
a beautiful woman and a great life awaits you. You're smart, and
someone will be very lucky to be your husband. You will succeed.
I will always be your friend and will help you if I can." He patted

her head, smiled sweetly, and made for the door where he turned, jingling his car keys. He said, "I can't see you anymore, much as I want to."

He felt sad as he drove slowly back down Prattle Hollow. She'd probably go home and cry a little more and that would be that. The sleeping bag, the candles, her photograph on the mantel would gather the dust of time and rot away, a mystery someone many years hence might try to unravel in that long-abandoned cabin.

Another cop car coming his way! Why, on this dinky little dirt road? He rolled his up window and angled his face down, trying to see through the tinted window out of the corner of his eye. Swiggert? In the rearview mirror, he saw Cocheta stopped at the mailboxes, preparing to turn, and the deputy slowing. Daniel pressed on the accelerator and bolted down the road.

His parents arrived and, in spite of a heads-up from Beth over the phone, were shocked at Daniel's weight gain and untidy appearance, his unruly hair and scruffy stubble. His father, François, dug into Daniel's files at the restaurant, going over the accounts with him in detail and agreed with Beth: close on Labor Day and let Pantoja purchase the store.

"You're too far in debt to continue unless a miracle happens. In my opinion, the sooner you can close and put the building on the market, the better."

"And the kitchen equipment? The silver, crystal, all Beth's beautiful work?"

"Sell everything, unless a buyer wants it to continue as a restaurant. Auction it off if you have to."

Daniel frowned but nodded in agreement. "My vision was too sophisticated for this place. Everything I did here was in the best taste but misunderstood and unappreciated! Stymied at every turn!" He slammed the file cabinet drawer shut.

"Take some blame, Daniel. You made mistakes."

Daniel sat with his father at the bar before the dinner service — only three bookings. Monty, the bartender, wouldn't understand French and Daniel needed to unburden himself. His father's advice had always helped him in the past and though he hated to appear weak, he felt he was walking a tightrope looking down into disaster.

"Papa, I've been cheating on Beth. She knows a little but doesn't know how often or where. I've broken it off but I'm not sure I can stay away from her. I think about her constantly." He studied his father's reaction, his handsome face youthful and healthy looking despite his age. Perched on the barstool wearing white trousers, off-white, slip-on Calsins and a blue, button-down shirt, he looked elegant and at ease, more at the helm of a sailboat than sitting in rural Wayne County.

"You don't need such a problem on top of everything else. How long?"

"Six months. She's eighteen."

"*Mon Dieu*, Daniel! Local girl? She's not pregnant, I hope?"

"No! Don't tell Maman. I want to talk to Beth about leaving here completely and returning to Périgord. I love the farm, but I can't live with closing the restaurant and the constant desire to be with the girl."

François took a sip of his Campari. "Then you must follow through with that decision. Eighteen. Daniel, you're twice her age. I know the temptation, the beauty of youth, but these types of obsessions rarely last. She's a child!"

"I long for her, Papa, I can't lie. I hate betraying Beth."

"Then don't. It can't be more than a sexual affair. How would that sustain you in ten, twenty years? What do you even talk about? Facebook?" Daniel grimaced, knowing they rarely talked at all. "Beth has forgiven you, what you've told her at least?"

"I think so, yes."

"She's your wife. Do you want her to divorce you over this, then take up with... what is her name?"

"Cocheta." He wouldn't call her Conchita ever again.

"Odd name. Where could this lead? Beth would take everything from you and then what a joke you would truly be here in this little town."

"That's harsh, Papa. I don't want to lose Beth. I love her."

"Then your plan is a good one, to leave this place lock, stock and barrel. You did the best you could. This 'affair'? There's a reason it's found with 'tryst,' 'liaison,' and 'intrigue' in the thesaurus. Trust me, I've looked it up." He took another sip of his drink. "Think about what truly matters to you, Daniel, not for ego or easy gratification but for a lifetime of happiness and purpose. You've got assets and will have plenty of money again. Start afresh. However your mother and I can help, we will."

Relieved at confiding his darkest secret, Daniel smiled, held his drink glass up to clink with his father's, and resolved to talk to Beth about leaving this place behind forever.

For the next few days, while his parents were staying with them, Daniel was in better spirits than he'd been in months and Beth was cautiously relieved. She wasn't surprised when Daniel brought up what she'd suspected was on his mind for a while; it was time to move on, sell everything and return to France. His ego, she knew, couldn't withstand driving through Nickel and seeing his beautiful Restaurant Perigeaux boarded up with a "For Sale" sign stuck obscenely in front. She also knew the girl was out there, an irksome barb under the skin that might fester and ruin everything, as she already nearly had.

After hours of back and forth, Beth agreed they'd be happiest back in Europe. She wanted to retain the townhouse and rent it out until the dust settled; she'd find someone through one of her old colleagues. Keeping it gave her options. Selling the house complex and farm after they'd so lovingly restored everything was painful to contemplate but they had some time; it would be a long, affectionate goodbye.

"Of course, you'll let Sally know she's still under contract with me. I've already told her ten times, but she keeps haranguing me about it. I'll have my lawyer send her a letter stating her obligations."

"She isn't happy, and she'll probably just stop paying. I know you need that money, Daniel, but you might be trying to get it from a stone."

"I don't care! I never liked her anyway."

His parents were leaving the morning after Bastille Day. There would be no special event at the restaurant after all. Daniel decided to close and give the staff the night off, without pay. Eddy was the only employee Daniel had continued to pay regularly — food had to come out of that kitchen somehow. His assistant Diego was server, busboy, dishwasher and bartender, and Daniel paid him too. But some of the wait-staff hadn't been paid since early June, and many had already quit. They weren't professionals anyway, just local kids, one of the many problems.

Daniel appeared in their kitchen at home brandishing two chilled bottles of Veuve Clicquot Yellow Label Brut champagne. "Eight hundred dollars each," he gushed with pleasure. "Only the best for the three people I love most in the world!" François did the honors and they clinked glasses, toasting to a better year ahead.

Beth thought finally she might have the old Daniel back, the devil-may-care, effusive and exuberant man she loved. He'd lost a couple of pounds working out again and doing chores with his father, gotten his hair cut, and his demeanor was alert rather than clouded with worry. As she tended to her dinner preparations for 'vegetable tian,' a baked dish of squash, peppers, potatoes, onions and eggplant, much of which came from her garden, he embraced her from behind and planted a gentle kiss on her cheek. "You my woman and I sweep you away to my France. Mmm, you are a superb cook. I should have had you in the kitchen and none of the others!" Deciding to leave was definitely the right thing to do. It had lifted Daniel's spirits even beyond what she'd hoped.

After his parents departed, his self-imposed exile from Cocheta lasted a mere two weeks. He left her a disorderly note of guilt and desire and asked her to meet him the following night. She wasn't there! He paced and fumed in the empty cabin knowing he couldn't very well drive up to her mother's house looking for her. He left her another note the following week and she was at the cabin waiting when he pulled around the back in his pickup. "I think I looked under the wrong flower pot! I never would have missed meeting you here, Daniel."

With Beth back and forth arranging storage or shipment for the townhouse furnishings, Daniel planned on stealing a few hours here and there to meet Cocheta, no matter the risks. He hadn't forgotten his father's comment that Cocheta was undoubtedly nothing more than a sexual obsession. It was true he had little in common with her, but she was still irresistible to him, a delectable concoction he needed to suck the last drops from before leaving her forever. Even the treachery he committed against his own wife, whom he truly did love, didn't matter whenever he drove in ecstatic anticipation up Prattle Hollow to meet Cocheta.

Shrubs and trees around the cabin began to show the fatigue of a long season of growth in the waning days of summer. Leaves started to droop and lose their vibrant colors. Even the little brook next to the cabin slowed to a trickle. It was the height of summer's sultry mixture of heat and humidity, cicadas drumming nonstop and bird-song nearly silent.

Daniel knew they were near the end, and Cocheta sensed there was an urgency to their secret trysts. Their coupling became rough, almost violent, as he tried to wrest his psyche from her. The last time, just after Labor Day when Restaurant Perigeaux closed forever, he took a risk and left Beth tending to her garden, harvesting the last of her lettuces and leeks. He fucked Cocheta brutally from behind, his body slippery and smelly, grasping at her breasts then pulling her head back by her hair so he could devour her lips. She cried but writhed with him. It was debasing for them both. This was it, he would stop this for her, for him. He didn't want this anymore. The obsession would end now.

Once the restaurant officially shut down, they got an attractive offer for the house and property including the livestock and Neeraj bought the farm store from them, paying cash. Things were going their way at last. Daniel spent his days winding down the numbers from the restaurant and store and searching online for opportunities in Dordogne and beyond. Often, he made the rounds of the property on his tractor knowing it was the land he would miss the most, its ever-changing beauty, its seclusion and promise, the one part of him that was honest through and through.

August was pitilessly hot and humid, and when the heat broke in early September, Beth threw open all the windows and freshened every room from top to bottom. Autumn was Beth's favorite season, too short in Maine, and she reveled in the early morning crispness, the faint change in nature's colors heralding October's rich display. She spent many hours in her office sorting papers and organizing her photographs, and often relaxed on the veranda with a late afternoon glass of wine, Daniel beside her. It was paradise, no doubt about it, and difficult to give up. But it was for Daniel's health and that of their marriage.

"We haven't seen Thorne in a while or had him over, and I feel really negligent about it, Daniel. He was a really good neighbor and friend. I'm taking him some of my photographs to keep, those of his property and cows, a couple of him with you. I think you should come with me and visit a little. We need to let him know what's going on."

"You're right, I will. I was thinking of giving him my tractor, a gift. He was pretty decent, and I've not been." He looked out over his pastures and livestock, the barn, so much Thorne had helped him with.

"I'll let him know you'll be by soon, then."

Beth ambled up the road toward Thorne's and found him dozing in his backyard hammock. His house was simple, a brick rambler, but he'd created a pleasant little garden in the back shaded by two enormous poplar trees. He wasn't much for flowers, but his wife years ago had a decent-sized pond dug and Thorne delighted in the waterlilies, stocked it with colorful fish, and spent many an afternoon watching dragonflies flit. He liked listening to the nightly serenade of frogs while he ate his dinner.

She accepted his offer of lemonade and they sat on his back porch with a view as exquisite as the one from his front porch.

"Real sorry about you leavin', closing the restaurant and all."

"I know, Thorne. It's not at all what I, we, wanted, but it just wasn't the right fit for this place. The new owners of the property are buying everything, and I know you'll like them. They say they'll stop by to introduce themselves soon. We should be gone before the end of November, but we've got lots to wrap up before then. You want to buy a restaurant?" She laughed and squinted at Thorne's hummingbird feeder. "Look! Four of those little guys going at it at once!"

"Beth, if there's anything I can do before you go, just let me know."

"Well, you'll come for dinner soon. Maybe you could visit us in France, Thorne, why not? You've never been out of Wayne County, have you?" she smiled.

"Yes, I have!" He puffed up his chest with feigned indignity. "Been to Amherst County and Floyd County, and a few others I don't remember." Thorne leafed through the photos she'd brought. "Thank you for these, they're all beautiful." He peered at one, a long view from one of his hills toward Daniel's barn. "Ha, look at this, po-lice car tucked behind the barn, probably lookin' to catch a tractor speedin' down our lane. Huh, can't get away from 'em."

"Probably not." She gave Thorne a hug and a peck on the cheek which made him blush. "We'll have you over before we go. You've been a wonderful friend, Thorne. If you ever do come to France..."

"Not likely, but thanks." He watched her walk back down the road, wondering if moving to France was an end or a beginning for them. He was not a church-going man, but he thought he might go just once so he could offer up a little prayer for Beth. She deserved to be happy.

Beth, always super organized, had to-do lists a mile long for the move to France. Everything from Scarcity would ship to Europe and she would do an inventory of the townhouse: what to ship, store, or pack up and drive to her mother's in Maine. She was looking forward to spending a week away, a reprieve from the trauma of the last couple of months. Daniel's so-called affair had wounded the marriage but not broken it. The girl had been a little plaything he would forget about soon enough. It will be far harder to help Daniel acknowledge failure in Wayne County and assuage his fragile ego. While he'd never admit it, his lack of success was mostly due to an inability to understand the locals, to relate to them instead of disdaining them. He couldn't let go of an attitude of superiority, that he was offering sophistication and refinement to an uncultured populace.

Saturday morning, she was ready to depart. "Daniel, I'm off to the city, then to Maine and mother's. I'm sure I'll get back before next Saturday."

Daniel was on his computer in his study scrutinizing small farms for sale in the Dordogne region, looking excited and happy. He let Beth nuzzle his neck, not taking his eyes from the computer screen. "Give my love to your mother."

"Yeah, no love lost there for you, I know. I want her to come to France for a visit soon, though, so you'll need to bite the bullet. She doesn't understand what in the world we're doing with our lives."

"Better that way," he said getting up and accompanying her outside. He hugged her, gave her cheek a light pinch, and touched her belly lightly. "Drive carefully, I need you two back safe and sound."

"Daniel, I love you. Be true to me, to yourself." With that she was gone.

CHAPTER TWELVE

DEPUTIES SWIGGERT and Jenks inched their way up the mountain lane to the Shanahan's residence in the gathering dusk. Sheriff Stryker had said Cocheta and her mother could go, reserving the right to call them back in for questioning in the morning. Cocheta and her mother sat gloomily in the back, Cocheta resting her head against the window with eyes closed, her mother staring silently out the opposite window, her hand reaching to squeeze her daughter's limp one resting in her lap. She'd clutched the warrant tightly in her hand when Sheriff Stryker handed it to her and now it lay crumpled on the cruiser floor at her feet, both feet on top, crushing and unmoving as though the papers were a wasp that could still escape and sting her. Deputies in her house right now! Going through their things! Skye was both perplexed and worried. What kind of trouble would she be in for not leveling with the first deputy about Cocheta? While it was true she didn't know the Perraults, she knew he owned the store where her daughter worked and she'd long suspected Cocheta had a crush on the man. She talked about him nearly every day. She'd just wanted to protect her daughter if she'd caused trouble by calling the man at home. And now, this horrible mess. And her daughter sneaking away for sex with him like this. And him dead. How could she do this under her very nose? What's going to happen with her?

"Is my daughter a suspect, officer?"

"Not for me to say, ma'am," Swiggert replied. "Sheriff says she's a person of interest, but there's others too, even the wife. Miss Shanahan was the last to see him alive, though."

"I wasn't. His killer was," Cocheta whispered.

"Whatever you say."

The deputies walked Cocheta and her mother up to the front door.

"Sheriff Stryker says not to discuss this with anyone or leave the county until the investigation is complete. Until the deputies complete their search inside, you're respectfully asked to stay out of the way and let them finish. And as the sheriff said, he may need to have you, Miss Shanahan, come in for further interrogation, and take the authorities through the cabin you and the deceased used." Swiggert placed his hands on his hips. "I live up Prattle Hollow, you know. I used to go to that cabin in high school. Us guys would drink and talk about girls, nothing bad."

"Can I go in the house now?" Cocheta didn't want to hear any more. She didn't want to envision boys drinking and probably thinking dirty thoughts, even if it was years ago, in the cabin where she and Daniel had spent so many blissful hours. She knew Deputy Swiggert from middle school and high school; he had been a senior when she was a freshman, an awkward, pimply kid who played on the basketball team. Now as a deputy with the Sheriff's Department, he stopped occasionally at the farm store for morning coffee. He often lingered, perusing the shelves, commenting on how expensive everything was, things most local folks wouldn't be able to afford. He tried to flirt with her, even so far as trying to steal a kiss.

"Sure, sure, you go on in. Just make sure you remain where the deputies inside can see you and that you're available for further questioning in the a.m. if need be." Swiggert touched the rim of his hat and watched as Cocheta's mother pushed the door closed.

"Didn't realize what an attractive girl that one is. Seen her at the store and around, but never paid much attention," Rudy said as they walked back to their patrol car. "Shame it worked out this way for her."

"Yeah, yeah, it's a shame. She's a looker, all right. Why she got mixed up in all this, I'll never know."

"Love. Love and sex, I guess."

"Sex mostly, be my guess. A married man, French! I mean, c'mon! It's sick!"

• • •

Saturday morning, Beth came to see Daniel in his office to say goodbye. She was off to the city to pick up some boxes she'd packed to take to her mother's and then drive to Maine for the week. When she returned, things would start moving very quickly but for now everything was in good order. She found Daniel looking gallant, his beautiful, patrician face tanned and relaxed, his hair grown long but well-kept. He was viewing farms for sale in Périgord on his computer and looked so upbeat when he glanced brightly at Beth with a new sparkle in his eyes. He walked out to the driveway with her and watched her drive off after making her promise to keep in touch via cell phone.

Once the dust cloud from Beth's Mercedes dissipated, Daniel decided to head for the pool before returning to his office. The morning was warm for early October and cloudless, weather that wouldn't last much longer as a cold front steered toward the region. He stripped, as he and Beth always swam in the nude, and plunged in. He did a few dozen lazy laps, then backstrokes, enjoying the silky water rolling over his body. His brain flickered with memories of Cocheta, thoughts he struggled to push away even as an erection grew, thinking of her mouth on him, her long, black hair tickling his skin.

He returned to his office, saw a message flashing on the landline, and listened to an earlier message from Beth's mother making sure she got off all right. He didn't bother to delete it and didn't think there was any reason to call her back at this point. Beth had probably called her from the townhouse. His thoughts were jumbled and unhappy, and Sophia's voice in his ear was the last thing he wanted.

He spent the rest of the afternoon on the computer, trying to keep his dark mood at bay. He'd tried to keep his spirits up in for Beth's sake the past few weeks, but he was taking the collapse of his vision for Wayne County very hard, and then there was the hole Cocheta had left. While he was keen to leave this place forever and return to his roots, he couldn't help resenting the time he'd wasted, not to mention the money, on all he'd tried to accomplish. His plans had been flawless, impeccable! It was *les idiots* who live here who were to blame for this fiasco. And his father...he wouldn't be able to restrain himself from hinting that Daniel was returning from the bad old USA with his tail between his legs. *C'est injuste!*

The restaurant was pretty much shut up tight. He'd advertised all the equipment and furnishings for sale and of course the building was on the market, with no takers yet. Why would anyone want to start something in this place anyway? If he couldn't be successful, who could be? Even the bar he designed himself was for sale. *Perfidie*!

He walked around the property near dusk, checking on the animals, and the barn, admiring his compound from his favorite ridge.

He moped all day Sunday, thinking he'd go by Thorne's, thank him for all his help and tell him he wanted him to have his tractor. He planned to give Garret and Quinn a big bonus for their assistance with the farm and livestock over the past year. Instead, he stayed in the house all day, wandering the rooms, waiting for Beth to call from her mother's. In a way, he wished he'd gone with her. There was still that tiny itch, Cocheta, an itch he must not act on! He didn't plan on seeing her again, ever.

Monday evening, the landline rang in the pool house as he dried off from a pre-dinner swim, one of the last before he'd close the pool for good. There hadn't been even a trace of frost on the ground that morning, Indian summer was still in the air. Daniel especially enjoyed swimming laps in the dark as the stars came to life; tonight, a crescent moon was already low in the western sky. It was when he'd done his best thinking while planning for Restaurant Perigeaux. Now it was time for meditating, emptying his mind of all that weighed on him.

The caller ID said Shanahan, Cocheta's last name. He grabbed the receiver from its cradle on the second ring.

"You shouldn't be calling here," he barked.

"I know, I'm so sorry but, Daniel, Mr. Pantoja says you are moving back to France. Why didn't you tell me?" She was tearful and sniffling into the phone.

"I thought it best to fade out of your life. We must part, Cocheta."

"I know, but I need to see you one more time. Please, Daniel. Let's say goodbye in our secret place. Please meet me tonight."

Daniel hesitated. *This was definitely a bad idea. Very bad.* "What time?"

"I'll be there at ten. My mother thinks I am staying with my friend Tracy for the night."

"How did you know my wife wouldn't answer the phone? This was risky, Cocheta."

"Mr. Pantoja told me she was away."

"I'll meet you at ten." He hung up. This was lunacy, but did he really have anything to lose? He was lonely without Beth and wanted company. Cocheta loved him, that much was clear. She would never betray him to Beth, what could she gain from it? He didn't really want to see her. He'd finally shaken off the thought of her by substituting thoughts of his and Beth's future in France. No, he knew he owed Cocheta a proper farewell. She'd surely known it would come to this, with the restaurant closing and all.

On the other hand, there was no danger in seeing her one last time. Beth wouldn't be calling him since her nutty mother had dragged her off to some yoga retreat for a couple of nights where there was no cell service.

He pulled on a pair of gray sweatpants and a black T-shirt and eased his feet into his favorite yellow flip-flops.

He leisurely made himself dinner, humming as he moved smoothly around the kitchen with an aperitif of Pineau des Charentes in hand. Swimming always left him ravenous and he had a delectable meal planned. Garret had come by with some succulent pork chops from a hog they'd butchered. Daniel harvested a handful of Beth's Brussel sprouts and splurged on a slice of apple pie Beth had made before she left on Saturday. Surprised at how much he missed his wife, he toasted her framed picture on the sideboard and mouthed "I love you, Beth." He drank an entire bottle of wine with dinner, his favorite Cabernet Franc from Dordogne and topped it off with a glass of port, then another. Feeling a little bleary-eyed from the alcohol but confident, he hopped into his pickup and drove up Prattle Hollow, prepared to tell Cocheta *adieu*. He prayed she wouldn't make a scene.

"Were you going to tell me goodbye, Daniel? You wouldn't have left without saying goodbye, would you?"

"I thought it would be best if we just disappeared from each other's life, Cocheta. I've always told you our affair would hurt you as well as me."

"After all we have been to each other, can you just walk away like this?"

"It's for the best, Cocheta. You need to get on with your life as I do with mine. You deserve better than this," he spread his arms wide indicating the gloomy, dark cabin.

"But will you write to me?"

"No, Cocheta."

"Then I'll never see you again?"

"I will not come back here. You will fall in love and have a career and a wonderful life, you will!"

"This is horribly painful." She hid her face. "I want you to stay with me tonight, all night here. You owe me that!"

"No!"

"Then this. To remember me with." She made long, unhurried love to him, passionate and emotional while Daniel, muddled by alcohol, lay unmoving and melancholic. Afterwards, he insisted she leave first. He was shaky and unsteady on his feet. While she dressed, he sloppily nudged the embers of a small fire Cocheta had made to be certain it was out. He watched from the door as she got into her Jeep, wiping her eyes, her glorious, long hair mussed, framing her sad and beautiful face. She gave him one last, longing look, backed out of the grassy area behind the cabin and was gone.

Daniel's brain was swimming; the food and alcohol coupled with an hour with Cocheta, left him anxious to get home to bed. He spent a few minutes righting himself, examining the meager setting of their nearly ten-month affair and hoping he wouldn't be haunted by it for the rest of his life. For the last time, he looked at Cocheta's little framed photo on the mantel, picked it up and held it for a moment, then put it back. Let her image gaze out on this place where so much pleasure had been received and given. Maybe she'll come here to remember him. He closed the windows and gathered the sleeping bag. There was no need for anyone to find it.

He wobbled to his pickup and eased slowly around the cabin in the dark without his headlights on. He turned onto Prattle Hollow, still with his lights out. He'd put them on if a car appeared, but other than the deputy's car, he'd never come across anyone, thank God! Cocheta had done well, finding this little hideaway, unseen and for-gotten. The stretch was apparently sparsely populated, only a couple of inhabited houses toward the ridge. As he edged slowly down the road, a vehicle suddenly grazed his on the left, sending him into the roadside ditch. In shock and disoriented, he got out of the driver's seat as best he could and saw someone walking toward him from a dark pickup stopped a few yards ahead of his.

"What's the idea here? Where'd you come from and why'd you run me off the road?" Daniel cursed when he saw the long, ugly scratch on the driver's side of his truck. Before he could react, a fist hit him on the right side of his face. He recoiled and put both hands out to grab his attacker's shirt. "Why, you! I know you! What are you doing here? *Qu'est que tu veux?*" Another blow to his face sent him reeling and he lost his footing, one of his flip flops flying. He fell backwards into the ravine, hitting his head on a sharp rock.

He lay, head spinning, not even able to make out the starry sky above him. His eyes rolled back into darkness and he didn't hear a voice cry out, "Hey, hey! Oh, holy shit, what have I done?" The last image he had was Beth, skiing down a snowy slope and laughing into his arms. "Beth," he whispered.

• • •

Early Thursday morning before most of the other deputies got in, day three of the investigation, Sheriff Stryker sat in his office and puzzled over his list of possible suspects: Marcus, Thorne, Bernard, Sally, Cocheta, Beth. There was nothing — *nothing!* — he could find to link any of them to the attack on Daniel Perrault. Bernard's property had been searched and Daniel Perrault's pickup was nowhere on it. Sally's computer was searched and nothing incriminating was found on it, nor Fleur's. Beth had definitely been in Maine, and Cocheta's friend had confirmed her story. After further questioning yesterday afternoon, Cocheta had nothing new to offer. Could an uncle or her erstwhile father have been involved? There was no possible connection, they were all unaware of the affair. Tracy and her mother checked out, as did Neeraj Pantoja and his wife, the latter two shocked at the revelation that Daniel and Cocheta had been lovers. Marcus had an alibi, and Thorne hadn't been on Prattle Hollow in years and didn't budge from his house, according to Garret, who lived at the end of the right-of-way and was watching TV until midnight. He would've heard a truck go by. He'd stated he saw Daniel's truck go by a little before ten which fit the timeline. There was no evidence of a hired killer. So, it had to be wrong place, wrong time.

Someone on Prattle Hollow came across Daniel driving his pickup around 11 p.m. and somehow an altercation ensued. Who would have been out on Prattle Hollow at that hour? Deputies Swiggert and Talon had swept the mountain and found nothing unusual. At the top, the gravel road swung steeply down the other side toward the Spendthrift River skirting it then continuing over a one-lane bridge back toward Nickel and the main highway. That's the definition of a hollow: in backwoods, a gravel road, barely navigable, wrapping up, around and across a mountaintop, then spitting out somewhere on the other side, usually near the same spot it began. It's a long, meandering loop you wouldn't bother driving unless you were a tourist or realtor. It would be rare for anyone on the far side of the mountain to go the long way toward town.

Two houses clung to rocky bluffs up the road from the abandoned cabin. One was owned by an artist who'd initially rented one of the studios at Daniel Perrault's. She was overseas at the moment, according to the neighbor in the other house, Jim Buckley, Nickel's retired postmaster, who was taking care of her dog while she was away. He was elderly and not in robust health, incapable of attacking Daniel Perrault. Three smaller houses nestled deep in the woods were downward from the cabin toward the main road, including Deputy Swiggert's, which was difficult, if not impossible, to see while driving by on Prattle Hollow.

After checking the cabin and poking around the woods, Deputy Swiggert and Chief Deputy Talon reported back to Stryker there was still no trace of the missing red pickup. They ventured a theory that it had been stolen, after whoever did this brought his body down the mountain to be found roadside.

Spike paced around his office. If that pickup was stolen and out there somewhere, it would have been detected by now. Basic police work. It was hidden somewhere, maybe somewhere in this county. He grabbed his coffee mug and marched over to the coffee-maker. Passing Ronnie Swiggert's desk, he saw a note taped to his phone from yesterday evening's dispatcher. He picked it up and read it: "Tried to reach your cell, pickup's ready, had piece in shop, only took couple hours," dated 7 p.m. yesterday, Wednesday, from C.D. Murphy, owner of the local auto body shop. He felt a gut punch. Ronnie, out sick Tuesday and half of Wednesday, his pickup apparently damaged and repaired yesterday, lives in Prattle Hollow. *Shit, Ronnie's left-handed.* Spike's mind swirled as he put the pieces together. He decided to take a little trip up the hollow and have a chat with Deputy Ronnie Swiggert.

• • •

Cocheta Shanahan was the most beautiful girl in the whole school. All the boys were keen on her, but she was aloof. Ronnie Swiggert, four years ahead of her, had been smitten with her for years but his ardor intensified when he noticed her in the bleachers watching him play basketball his last year in high school. He called her on the phone a couple of times; she was polite but cool and when he finally got up the nerve to ask her out, she shook her head with a coy smile and said her mother didn't allow her to go out with older boys. Her mystery only made him love her more, but from a distance.

He wanted to go into police work after he graduated. His father had been a deputy, rising to chief deputy and then sergeant in another jurisdiction. Ronnie worked hard at his dream of joining the local force: he enlisted for a stint in the army and worked odd jobs to pay for his training. Sheriff Stryker, good friends with his father, took him under his wing and tutored him, told him he had the makings of a top-notch deputy. Once he became one, he hoped to climb the ladder and someday run for sheriff, should Spike step down. He knew from asking their mutual friend Tracy that Cocheta went to the community college to study nursing after graduating. When he had patrol duty, he occasionally saw her in her green Jeep as he made his rounds on the roads and hollows of Wayne County. He always opened his window to give her a friendly salute, but she never noticed, or, more likely, ignored the attention.

Gradually, she disappeared from his thoughts as he became busier at work, eventually making enough money to buy a small, brick rambler in Prattle Hollow with a few wooded acres. He'd had his eye on a stone cottage, a former mill on Sycamore Creek, but couldn't afford it plus the work he'd have to put in it. He fixed the rambler up as best he could and did some landscaping, as well as forging some paths through the woods behind the house, all the way up to park property.

It was inevitable he'd run into Cocheta again. 'Been heres' like them never truly leave the county or hollows, unless through luck or shear grit, they figure out a way to escape. When he walked into the farm store in Nickel on an early morning in late November to try the coffee, therefore, he wasn't surprised to find her there. If possible, she was even prettier now, and he made small talk as he sipped his coffee.

"So, when did you start working here?"

"I was hired when it opened in October. My mother knows the vintner who runs the place, Mr. Pantoja, and he hired me for the owner, Mr. Perrault. They needed someone who could open early and stay until around noon, which was perfect for me, being in school in the afternoon and all. We get the city papers and there're a few folks who come by early for them. One guy in particular, a retiree from the city, needs his *Wall Street Journal* right away every freaking day, no excuses!" She laughed.

She'd never said so many words to him and he was encouraged by her friendliness.

"What are you studying?" Of course he knew, but anything to keep her talking. She was so lovely, no one he could remember seeing compared to her.

"Nursing. I've been so lucky to be here at the store, though. Mr. Perrault is a wonderful boss and pays so well. He's French, you know, started Restaurant Perigeaux."

"That so?" A customer came in and Swiggert finished up his coffee and thanked Cocheta. *Well, Miss Shanahan, I think I'll be stepping in here from time to time.*

Little did Ronnie Swiggert know he would have the pleasure of meeting Mr. Perrault a few days later, when he called the sheriff's office to report destruction of property at his restaurant. While it was clear the chef who'd bashed out the lights with a hockey stick was a bit bonkers, Daniel Perrault was a complete fool: throwing his weight, making demands, trying to go around the way things are done out here. And the worst was his disrespect for law enforcement. Deputy Swiggert could have arrested him for that, then and there, and probably should have. That jerk had the gall to write a letter to the editor of the local paper complaining about his treatment at the hands of the deputies. *His* treatment? Everybody who overheard Perrault knew he'd stepped over the line, but Swiggert took the high road and wouldn't allow him any further limelight in the paper by responding. Fucking Frenchman!

After that, he popped into the farm store more regularly when he knew Cocheta'd be there, and hung around to have at least a few minutes of conversation with her. He'd definitely fallen for her all over again, but wanted to play his cards right and figure out how to ease in to asking her out. She seemed to enjoy his company, stopping to chat when there weren't any other customers. After Christmas, he brought her a box of chocolates from a little shop he'd come across while visiting his parents.

"Thanks, that's nice of you, Ronnie. Daniel, Mr. Perrault, is in Europe right now shopping for things that we'll be selling here, including chocolates. I can't wait to see what he brings back."

"That so? Anyone buy this European stuff?"

"Oh, yes! People love it, well the 'come heres' do. Of course, things are too expensive for most of us 'been heres,'" she laughed. "But they come and look anyway to see what Mr. Perrault selects. He has such excellent taste in everything."

It irritated Ronnie that Cocheta almost always seemed to steer the conversation back to Daniel Perrault, but if that's what it took to talk to her and gaze on her beautiful face, so be it.

Sometime in late February, Ronnie saw what he thought was Cocheta's green Jeep lumber by his house, going up Prattle Hollow. It was close to five o'clock, pitch black, but he'd been getting into his patrol car since he'd pulled the late shift at the station, and had turned his head lamps on. Trees were still bare of leaves, so he could make out a short stretch of road from his front window, and certainly could see a car passing his driveway. He wondered why she would come up this way, thinking maybe she was looking to see where he lived. That would be something! The highlight of his week was when he stopped in for coffee at the store. Maybe it wouldn't be too out of line to ask her out at this point. Maybe she thought deputies don't date! And now her mother wouldn't mind the difference in age: he was in law enforcement, owned a house, doin' pretty darn good for himself.

He went to the store on one of his days off to buy a sandwich for lunch, and saw her at the register finishing up with a customer. Her hair was in two long, thickly braided pigtails, cascading over her bulky, jade-green sweater. He bought the sandwich and stood around pretending to look at some of the other items in the display case until no one was left in the store.

"Say, listen, Cocheta, would you like to go to dinner with me in Bristow, maybe take in a movie? Maybe tonight? I'm off duty until Thursday."

"Um, that's nice of you, Ronnie, but I don't think so. I have to study." Cocheta couldn't imagine going anywhere with someone like Ronnie Swiggert. He was tall, lanky and ordinary looking. While she admired him for becoming a deputy, he was still the colorless, local boy she remembered from high school. Earnest and hard-working for sure, but not someone she'd want to spend any time with. Daniel had pretty much ruined her for any of the locals — he was so refined, so elegant. She wished *he* could take her to dinner and a movie!

Ronnie Swiggert didn't give up, though. He was sure Cocheta would eventually say *yes* to one of his invitations; he'd wear her down. There was no other girl in the county who could compare to Cocheta Shanahan. He knew she was part Negro, a mulatto they called her, but that only made her more exotic to him. He wasn't a racist, God knew!

He upped his visits to the farm store to twice a week in the spring. He felt they were getting close, and he confided his dream of running for sheriff if Sheriff Stryker stepped aside. He talked about some of the arrests he'd made. She listened when she didn't have something to do, told him about nursing school and the course load.

One thing continued to bother him: how she always gushed about Daniel Perrault, how smart and successful he was, how wonderful and generous he was as a boss. That really got under his skin. Ronnie found him easily the most dislikable person he'd ever met.

"Well he won't last here, I can tell you that," he told her.

"What do you mean by that? He likes it here, he has a beautiful house and property. The restaurant is going well."

"You've been to his house?"

"Well, no, but he's told me about it, described it."

"He doesn't fit here, that's all."

"He's so kind, remembered to bring me a present from France, earrings and a bracelet!" Cocheta looked toward the back door, willing Daniel to walk through it so Ronnie could see what a handsome and sophisticated man he was, a man she loved!

"That so?" Ronnie thought maybe he should bring Cocheta another gift sometime. *Why's that guy so great just 'cause he brought her some trinkets?* He needed to do something to get her attention. Couldn't she see he loved her?

He noticed her green Jeep going up Prattle Hollow again when he was out clearing up sticks strewn on his driveway from a particularly strong spring thunderstorm. Where could she be headed if she wasn't checking out his house? There wouldn't be any point in taking the long way back around to Nickel. A few minutes later, he saw a red pickup go by. This was a day's worth of traffic along his stretch of road. He thought he'd seen a red pickup a time or two in the farm store parking lot. Could it be Daniel Perrault's? Was there something going on here? He checked his watch, five o'clock.

A few days later, Ronnie was making his rounds and decided to drive along the right-of-way toward Thorne Tate's. It had been on his mind to go up ever since he saw the red pickup. He wanted to get a view of the Perrault property to satisfy his curiosity about the car. He pulled his patrol car behind the barn, Daniel Perrault's barn he presumed, and sat pretending to be on the radio. A woman out beyond the house was taking some photographs, Mrs. Perrault probably. He spotted a green Aston Martin parked in the driveway and, with his binoculars, saw a red pickup parked around the side of the house. He noted the license number and left.

He had to put in some overtime as it was getting close to Easter and a couple of the deputies were taking time off, so he wasn't home enough to see if those same two cars went by. Then, after months of having no contact with Daniel Perrault since the broken light mess, he had two unhappy encounters with him. Stopping for coffee in uniform right after Easter, he saw Daniel Perrault in the parking lot of the farm store, leaning on Cocheta's car looking upset. They acknowledged each other and traded mild insults. Everything about the man nagged at him like a splinter he couldn't pluck out.

Luckily no one was in the store yet, as Ronnie found Cocheta inside the store room, shaking and weeping. He resisted the urge to take her in his arms and comfort her. She turned away from him, embarrassed, but he could see her whole body heaving in grief.

"I saw the guy outside. I know he fired you, I'm sorry." Silence except for her sniffling. "Do you want me to help you get the coffee going?" he asked. She nodded. Once he'd got the contraption going, Cocheta emerged from the stockroom, red-eyed, and took up her position near the register.

"People will be coming in soon for the papers. Do you mind bringing them in from the front porch?"

"Be happy to," Ronnie smiled. She wore an off-the-shoulder, floral thing and it was impossible not to look at the cocoa-colored skin it revealed. "Pour you a cup?"

"No thanks. I don't drink coffee."

"Ah, I guess I should'a known that, never saw you with a cup."

Before he could stop himself, he leaned over the counter and kissed her full on the lips. Cocheta recoiled. "You shouldn't do that!" she cried. "I can't let anyone touch me ever again, only...!" She couldn't finish, looked to the door Daniel had left by and began to weep again. "You'd best go now, Ronnie."

Ronnie set down his coffee mug, a look of both shock and humiliation on his face. "I'm sorry, Cocheta. That was wrong of me. I respect you, want you to be happy and I see you're not."

"Please, just go now. Thank you for your help this morning." She turned away from him to busy herself with setting out the newspapers as Ronnie Swiggert strode briskly out the back door to his car.

The very next afternoon, Swiggert and Deputy Mabel Crone, his partner for the day, got a radio dispatch, something about a mad dog on the loose. Rudy had taken the call and said it came from the restaurant. They put on their siren and sped over while Mabel put in a call to Animal Control. When they arrived, they found the chef, the same one Swiggert interviewed at the last restaurant dust-up, crumpled on a bar-stool, his face flattened against the counter, weeping. Daniel Perrault was running around waving his hands in the air but stopped when he saw Swiggert and glowered.

Swiggert returned the hostile look, glaring with displeasure as Daniel made excuses and rudely pressed the deputies to leave, even going so far as to give Swiggert a little push on his back. The guy oughta be cited for contempt of an officer of the law, slapped with a misdemeanor, but he let it go. Later, he wished he hadn't.

He spent the next few days brooding over his rejected kiss with Cocheta and the mean-spiritedness of the guy she seemed to idolize. He decided he'd follow the whereabouts of Daniel Perrault's pickup whenever he could and find out what he was up to. He'd watch for Cocheta's green Jeep too. He began to park his cruiser partially hidden in a copse at the end of Daniel's right-of-way, using his radar gun, pretending to watch for speeders. No one at the station would know the difference. On his days off, he sat in his blue Ford pickup. He drifted up and down Prattle Hollow, peering through the trees and along old, disused tractor paths, looking for either car.

Then, bingo! He saw her car angling up the road as he was descending from the top of the hollow in his cruiser. He noted the time, five o'clock, and where she turned — that old abandoned cabin, of course! — then, whaddayaknow? Here came the red pickup. Swiggert casually passed Daniel, window rolled up, and slowed so Daniel wouldn't see him turn into his own driveway, a half mile farther down. Once he'd parked the cruiser, he ran around the back of his house and cut through the woods on one of the paths he'd forged until he had the back of the cabin in view. So, they meet here, him a married man and her barely of age! He could spit, it made him so angry. He loved her! He could give her a good life and here she's with this repulsive French guy. Ronnie crept slowly and quietly around to the side of the cabin where one window was cracked open. He sat to catch his breath, leaning against a pine tree. He could hear their voices and then all was quiet. He crawled stealthily on all fours like a panther ready to pounce on a kill, and pulled himself up to peek inside the window. It took a moment to adjust to the dimness of the room and make out anything, but soon he saw movement on the far side from where he stood. Daniel Perrault was on top of Cocheta, his dick in her mouth, and her with her legs spread wide. Jesus Christ! How could this be? He couldn't stop watching them as they panted and moaned for what seemed like an eternity, fucking each other like base animals. He'd never imagined anything like this before. She was a kid, what had that guy done to her? Drugged her? He couldn't prevent his own erection from pushing against his pants or his gut filling with desire. He carefully stepped away from his surveillance niche and moved to steal away, breaking into a sprint once he was far enough away to remain, he hoped, unheard and unseen.

Once Cocheta's job at the farm store ended, Swiggert stopped going by for coffee. Thinking about them together and how it had aroused him made him sick to his stomach. He wouldn't touch her with a ten-foot pole now that she'd been tainted by the likes of Daniel Perrault. That guy never should have come here, trying to bring his so-called European ways to Wayne County, supposedly dazzling a country girl like Cocheta but only using — and abusing! — her for sex. He longed to tell her mother or pry Tracy, her best friend, for information. Instead, Swiggert shadowed Daniel Perrault.

He heard the chef was fired after the bizarre episode he and Mabel had responded to, and the restaurant was in trouble. What could be better than Daniel Perrault closing and leaving for good? He was a toxin in their midst, violating in the most evil way the purity and sanctity of the girl he'd thought might one day be his. He made a point of being on or near Prattle Hollow every day around five o'clock, unless he absolutely had to be at the station or on a call.

Finally, on a humid June afternoon, they were at the cabin again. He caught sight of Daniel's pickup turning into the cabin right-of-way as he drove home from the station. As before, he parked then made a mad dash through the woods to the rear of the cabin, where he heard a shouting match going on and Cocheta howling in anger and distress. He peeked inside and saw her sitting on the floor while Daniel stood waving what looked like money in his hand. Ha! He's paying her like a prostitute, what further sin could he taint Cocheta with? He intended to get back to his patrol car quickly and make a show of cruising the hollow so when Daniel Perrault left the cabin, he might just wonder if his little secret was no longer a secret.

There wasn't any sign of either car for several weeks along Prattle Hollow, and Swiggert hoped Cocheta had ended it. After all, everything with Perrault's dirty thumbprint on it was doomed: the restaurant, farm store, artists' studio complex. Swiggert knew of his builder's lawsuit and breach of contract petitions from suppliers by poking into court docket sheets. *The guy was going down the tubes and rightfully so. The sooner the better.*

He kept his obsession to himself through the long, slow summer weeks, watching and waiting. He sensed they were still meeting and went into the cabin to look around every week or so to see if there were any tell-tale signs they'd been there. He noted the candles, whether they'd been lit, checked for used matches, sniffed at the rumpled sleeping bag. The only real adornment was Cocheta's framed picture on the mantel and Swiggert studied it carefully, his groin churning in desire and revulsion in equal measure. Did she think about him at all? Should he tell her he knew everything about the affair and threaten to expose them? The guy has a wife! There's no way this could have a happy ending for Cocheta.

Swiggert mulled over his options. He plotted to cross paths with those who might know Cocheta's frame of mind or what Daniel Perrault was up to, beginning with Neeraj Pantoja.

Striding casually into the farm store late one afternoon when he figured Pantoja would be minding the register, Swiggert found Mrs. Pantoja packing away the unsold sandwiches she'd made that morning.

"We feed uneaten ones to our pigs," she laughed, "not that they're not delicious, but day-old…"

"Well, I'll buy one. Us single guys need a little help with dinner sometimes," he chuckled. As she wrapped up his purchase along with some chips and a slice of her rhubarb pie, he asked how the new girl who opened the store in the morning was working out.

"Elaine? She's gone. She was a teacher and is back at the school. We're looking, but for now, I'm here all day."

"Could you rehire the one who was here before, Miss Shanahan? She sure made a good cup of coffee."

"Mr. Perrault said he didn't want her here anymore, never really understood why. We've bought the store from him, so we might take her back on. I don't have the time to be here all day, frankly."

"I didn't know that. I know the restaurant closed. No great loss, I guess."

Mrs. Pantoja glanced at Swiggert. "It *is* a loss. We are so sorry he's leaving the area. It will leave a big empty hole in our county."

"He's leaving the area?"

"Oh, yes. He and his wife are returning to Europe. Such a shame. They were real assets to our town. Mrs. Perrault is making all the arrangements going back and forth to their city place. I think I heard she's going to spend a few days in Maine with her mother before they go. Such a disappointment for them."

Leaving! That was the best news he'd had in a while. Daniel Perrault ruined, chased out of the county, crying 'uncle.' That was how it should be. Leaving us to our time-honored habits and age-old ways. And Cocheta? She'd realize she'd been used, cry to her mother maybe, or more likely her friend Tracy. He'd have to find a way to see what Tracy knew.

Positioning himself in his patrol car directly across from Tracy's and her mother's right-of-way, Swiggert waited an hour or so for a few mornings until he saw Tracy leave in her car. He followed her to the gas station and pulled in behind her.

As he pretended to fill his tank, he eyed her and gave her a wave.

"Hey, haven't seen you much lately. Whatcha been up to?" He replaced the gas pump and doffed his hat, coming around to give her a hug.

"Ronnie! Ugh, well work is boring." She hugged him back. "How're things with you?"

"Same old, same old. That French guy keeps us on our toes with his problems, though. You know, the one whose restaurant is closing, leaving the area?"

"Yeah, know about that. Know more than I'd like."

"Whatcha mean?"

"Well, Cocheta kinda had a crush on him and is over my house crying all the time that he's leaving. Told her to call the bastard and tell him he owed her at least a 'goodbye' gift, ya know what I mean?"

"I guess. Isn't that guy married?"

"Yeah, so she's getting up her nerve to call him once the wife's away, says she's away sometimes packing stuff up at another house they own or something. Wants to meet him one night while she's gone, this weekend, I think."

"I should arrest the guy for messing with Cocheta's head," Swiggert grinned. *What a bit of prime information this turned out to be!* They'd be meeting at the cabin soon, that much was certain. He'd make sure he was there to teach this intruder a lesson he'd never forget, big time!

● ● ●

Sheriff Stryker drove slowly up Prattle Hollow. Swiggert's place was about half a mile from the main cross-county road where Daniel Perrault's body had been found in a sleeping bag around 2 a.m. on Tuesday. The so-called "rendez-vous" cabin where Miss Shanahan and Mr. Perrault allegedly met was another half mile up from there. *What happened that night and was Ronnie involved somehow?*

Autumn had finally arrived in Wayne County after yesterday's cold front moved in. Spike had scraped a thin layer of silver frost from his windshield before heading to the station earlier in the morning and turned the heat on in his cruiser for the first time this season. The smell of wet leaves and the woodland silence after a summer of humming cicadas and birdsong signaled nature's long descent into winter's snow-swept depths. He sighed. He'd be up for re-election next year and wondered if he really wanted it enough to put in the effort. He and Pearl could retire comfortably, do a bit of travel. The peculiarity of Daniel Perrault's death had taken its toll on him. He was, if the truth be told, dog tired.

Swiggert opened the door before Spike even knocked, dressed in his freshly-pressed uniform.

"Hey, Sheriff. Bit of surprise to see ya here this early. Didya think I wasn't gonna make it in today, had to push me outta bed?" He eyed Spike nervously.

"No, Ronnie. I knew you'd be in early today. Right after you get someone to help you pick up the truck you left early Tuesday morning at C.D.'s for repairs."

Swiggert's eyebrows shot up.

"Message was left on your desk."

"Okay."

"Looks like we've got something to discuss here. You want to do it at the station or here?"

Swiggert's shoulders and head slumped and he stepped aside to let the sheriff in the house. He led him into his modest living room, the only notable item a grandfather clock in the corner polished to a lustrous sheen.

Seated stiffly across a coffee table from one another, both men looked at their hands. The ticking clock with the pendulum's parabolic movement was the only sound. It was deafening.

"What happened up here Monday night, Ronnie? You were sweet on that Shanahan girl, weren't you?"

Swiggert took a deep breath, leaned forward with his elbows on his knees, and hung his head. "Yeah, I used to care about her, but this was an accident, Spike, pure and simple, I swear. I didn't mean to hurt him, much less kill him. He reeked of alcohol. If he hadn't been drunk, he wouldn't have fallen. I covered it up because I didn't think anyone would believe that it wasn't my fault. He fell backwards and hit his head. I tried to help him, I did, but he was conked out."

"Tell me what the hell happened!"

• • •

After hearing from Tracy that Cocheta was planning on contacting Daniel Perrault while his wife was away, Ronnie Swiggert concocted his plan. He asked for desk duty over the weekend, claiming he had paperwork to catch up on, and even put in some overtime. But he made sure he was home just after dark, his senses on high alert, for as long as it took. Once Saturday had come and gone, he began to think Tracy was wrong, that Cocheta never intended to meet the guy again. He'd be gone and that would be that. But he'd keep at it a couple more nights, just in case.

He sat in his pickup, hidden in a small roadside pullout, a few hundred yards up from the cabin driveway. He wouldn't be noticed in the dark if they drove up, but he would have a clear view. He watched and waited Sunday, from dusk until after midnight. Then, lo and behold! Monday, a little after ten o'clock, Cocheta's green Jeep turned into the cabin access. Swiggert got out of his car and crept through the woods toward his usual viewing spot, screened by a swath of mountain laurel shrubs, and waited for the red pickup.

Perrault lurched from his pickup a few minutes later and staggered to the cabin doorway, clearly boozed up. Swiggert heard them talking but couldn't make out the words and pressed his ear closer to the closed door. Cocheta was crying. Swiggert moved to the window and watched as Cocheta, on top of him, made love to that lousy excuse for a husband, not just a two-timer and seducer, but a second-rate human who didn't know the meaning of courtesy or humility. All the years he'd fantasized about Cocheta, dreamed they might someday build a life together, were up in smoke. She'd never be honored with his attention ever again. He'd trash her name to anyone who would listen.

And Perrault! Swiggert had one message to give him, a punch in the face for ruining a girl's life, for insulting him publicly and for his goddam all-around arrogance. He went back to his truck and waited, hoping Cocheta would leave first, which she did. He waited for what seemed like ages until Daniel Perrault slowly advanced onto Prattle Hollow with his headlights off. Swiggert gunned his pickup and sideswiped Daniel's, sending him sideways into a shallow ditch. Momentarily dazed, Daniel pushed and pulled himself with difficulty out of the driver's seat, cursing.

"What's the idea here? Where'd you come from and why'd you run me off the road?" he bellowed.

Swiggert aimed a blow to the right side of his face. Daniel staggered backward and stared at his assailant through hazy, watery eyes.

"Why, you! I know you! What are you doing here? *Qu'est que tu veux*?" He lunged at Swiggert tearing, at his shirt but Swiggert hit him again on the jaw and Daniel lost his footing, falling backward into the ditch. Then he lay still.

• • •

"It was an accident, Sheriff, I swear I only wanted to let him know I'd seen him with Cocheta, knew about his cheating, and I panicked when he seemed so lifeless. I tried shaking him and pulling him to a sitting position. He was bleeding bad from the back of his head." Swiggert was sweating, beads accumulating on his forehead and wet rings at his underarms.

"Why in the name of God didn't you call an ambulance?" Sheriff Stryker asked through gritted teeth.

"You know there's no cell service up there. I thought maybe he was just unconscious, and I didn't want to leave him there to go home and call. I moved my truck into the driveway and behind the cabin, then righted his pickup. I worked fast, out of panic someone might see me, even though I knew that was unlikely. I ripped his T-shirt off of him and tried to staunch the blood from whatever he hit his head on. He'd tossed the sleeping bag they'd used in his pickup bed, so I wrapped him in it, stuck the wallet I found on the dashboard into the lining, and zipped it up as best I could. I wanted to leave him somewhere he'd be found right away and identified. By then, I was crying and scared. I was afraid he might be dead. You know the rest." Swiggert ran his hands over his close-cropped hair, tears glistening in his eyes.

"After I laid him down by the highway, I knew he was dead. He wasn't breathing anymore."

"Why, Ronnie, why that way?"

"It was an accident, I didn't think it was my fault! I just wanted his body found as fast as possible."

"Where the hell is his pickup?"

"I can show you."

Spike Stryker was in a state of complete emotional turmoil and shock as he followed Ronnie out the back door into the woods behind the house. His bowels churned. They walked single file along a bramble-covered path, proceeding cautiously, thorny vines occasionally catching at their shoes. His own deputy was responsible for the death of Daniel Perrault, accident or not! What was Ronnie thinking while the whole force was out interviewing and trying to pull evidence together to solve this bizarre death? As sheriff, he'd be the laughing stock of law enforcement. How was he supposed to handle this? What would he tell the widow? Jesus, he wouldn't wish this on his worst enemy.

"I drove it along an old fire road a hundred yards further down the hollow and took it as deep into the woods as I could. It's covered with a tarp. It's got the missing flip-flop I picked up when Bodie and I came up here to search; his bloody shirt and his cellphone minus the battery are in it too."

"Let's see it."

Ronnie pulled part of the tarp back revealing the side where he'd sideswiped Daniel, a blue streak from his pickup clearly visible on the driver's side door. He reached for a dark green garbage bag and opened it.

"You kept these things? Kept this from all of us? Knowingly obstructed an ongoing investigation of the death of Daniel Perrault? I'm having a hard time believing this." Spike stood, arms akimbo, shaking his head in disbelief. "Can't believe you'd stalk the man like that, wait to ambush him, then cover up what you'd done. Ronnie, I gotta take you in."

Ronnie's face collapsed in a panic. "Aw, c'mon, Sheriff. You're not gonna hang me out to dry on this, are ya?" he pled. "We stand together, the force. The guy was screwing an innocent seventeen-year-old girl and him an old guy, a married man! He stiffed half the county, not paying 'em for their products or work. Basically spat in my eye when I was only trying to enforce our laws. Threw his so-called fancy-schmancy ideas around with no consideration for the locals. He ain't a big loss for us, is he, Sheriff?"

Spike weighed his options, none good. His deputy responsible for someone's death and cover-up? A kid he'd had so much faith in? A hard worker he'd held up as an example to other deputies? The department would never recover. They'd look like fools, running around interviewing "suspects." They were the Wayne County Sheriff's Department! He couldn't let it fall apart on his watch. His deputies were a close bunch, some even related.

He thought again of Daniel's widow. What would be the least painful for her to hear? Would it help her to know her husband was the victim of a stupid, jealous assault that went awry? That if Daniel Perrault hadn't been drunk, all he'd have suffered was a black eye? He didn't think so.

"You figure out how to get rid of this pickup, Ronnie. I don't want it found, ever. I don't want to see you at the station for the rest of the month. You're under the weather again, okay?"

Sargent Stryker had never felt as sick to his stomach as he did getting into his patrol car on Prattle Hollow after learning about Ronnie's repulsive obsession with Daniel and the girl, and worse, the cover-up. He wanted to go home and cry like a baby in Pearl's arms, but he couldn't even breathe a word of this to her; something like this wouldn't stay between the two of them for five minutes. Ronnie had a point, though it aggrieved him no end to accept it — country people here stand together, loyal to a fault to kin and friends, a clan mentality, us against them. Sometimes that meant Wayne County was a dark place for outsiders. It's just the way the wheels turn around places like this.

Ronnie'd be acquitted anyway, if it came to that. His remorse was genuine even if his actions were perverted and cowardly. For Beth to go through that was unthinkable. Spike would make sure that boy never got promoted as long as he was sheriff. Better yet, he'd figure out a way to get him fired from the force. He'd never be able to look at Swiggert without the horrible memory of this mess bubbling up in his gut, making him sick.

He drove to the Perrault house to provide an update on the investigation, get it over with. He wouldn't, couldn't, lie. Just hedge without falsifying facts. Explain Daniel Perrault rubbed a lot of folks out here the wrong way, but he couldn't find a shred of evidence of *anyone* wanting him dead. The investigation would continue, regardless, until they got to the bottom of it.

Beth left Wayne County for good the following week. She and her mother accompanied Daniel's parents, and his ashes, to Périgord. She thought she might remain there until she had Daniel's child and then decide her future.

One by one, Sheriff Stryker told those he'd investigated they were no longer suspects and could get on with their lives.

As time passed, the case would fade, people would lose interest and eventually forget about it. The evidence box with Daniel Perrault's wallet, including the little lock of ribbon-tied hair, one yellow flip-flop, gray sweatpants and the sleeping bag would be taped closed and filed away as a cold case.

Sheriff Stryker dismissed Ronnie Swiggert for dereliction of duty two weeks after his confession, using his continued absence as the reason. Spike became gloomier and more melancholic as time passed. He mulled over the sequence of events often, sometimes even thinking of revealing the whole cover-up, though it would surely mean prison time for him. One morning his heart palpitations were so profound that he drove himself to Bristow Hospital. His dilemma over the Perrault case had twisted his core into a painful knot he couldn't loosen, day or night. *How could he carry out his duties?* He couldn't even look at himself in the mirror.

Pearl worried that his inability to solve the case was making him ill and hiding the truth from her was almost unbearable for Spike. Finally, just before Christmas, he resigned as sheriff, citing his heart issues. He and Pearl discussed moving from the county, and Spike pushed for a decision by spring. He knew leaving wouldn't solve his anguish, but at least he'd never have to look at anything connected with the crime ever again.

He'd seen the darkest underside of Wayne County, and of himself. For Daniel Perrault, it had been fatal. For Sheriff Spike Stryker, it was a nightmare he would shoulder for the rest of his life.

ACKNOWLEDGEMENTS

Thank you to my readers: Monira Rifaat, Connie Novak, Sandra Schiffman, Joyce Wenger and editor Melody Culver. A big thank you to graphic designer Magdalene Carson. And special love and thanks to my incredibly supportive husband, Doug.

ABOUT THE AUTHOR

Between a Rock and a Dark Place is Suzanne Schiffman's second novel. Her first work of fiction is *One Fine Day*. She lives in rural Virginia and on Amelia Island Florida.

www. suzanneschiffman.com

CANAMBOOKS